For Jeremy

ACKNOWLEDGEMENTS

To my agent Serafina Clarke for all her enthusiasm for this book, as well as for her help and support in everything else – a warm, grateful thank you

Chapter One

'*La Piccola Valle della Tristezza*? What an odd name for a house.'

Henrietta, bouncing the baby on her lap, looked up at her sister Isabel. 'It's not just the name of the house, it's the name for the whole cluster of houses, three or four if I remember correctly. It's a tiny hamlet, a compound.'

'A *villaggio*,' Isabel said. 'The Italian word for a small cluster of houses. Not quite a village, but—'

'Yes, yes,' Henrietta interrupted impatiently. 'As I was saying, the place was probably one large farm once. It has since been converted into several houses.' She gave the baby another bounce and her soft white skirt flounced wispily as she did so, almost engulfing the infant who looked, at this moment, rather like a plump bright olive on a mound of goat's cheese.

'"The Little Valley of Sadness". Is that really our sort of place, Henrietta? A fifty-two-year-old drop-out and an unwed mother of forty.'

'Less of the forty – in my heart I'm a mere twenty,' Henrietta said. 'But you're right. When I heard the name, it seemed perfect for us. So lyrical.'

'I wish you understood irony,' Isabel muttered, but her

sister was lyrically continuing: 'When I heard the name, *La Piccola Valle della Tristezza*, I saw centuries of Italian art, music, painting, born of the struggles of the soul, of life's interminable sadness ... I saw struggling peasants eking a living from the olive groves ... I was bowled over by the poetry and the paradox. I knew we *had* to live there.' She smiled beatifically at the baby, who took no notice and began to cry.

Isabel said prosaically, 'So it wasn't, then, that Umbria is so much cheaper than Tuscany, that you decided to buy there?'

Henrietta chose not to hear this crass remark and cooed lovingly at the infant in her lap who cried louder.

'I think she's hungry,' Isabel told her.

Henrietta stood up, the baby perched precariously on her shoulder, the child's thick black hair stark as a charcoal drawing against the white cotton of her dress. 'I never knew babies got so hungry. When we get to *La Piccola Valle*, I shall have time to feed her day and night, whenever she likes.'

'Like centuries of Italian peasant women,' Isabel smirked.

'Exactly.' Henrietta was quite serious. 'I can't wait. I feel the name is an omen. All that sadness rolled into one small valley. How Dante-esque! How intense! I'm sure the whole place will be pulsing with melancholic fortitude, empathy, the warmth created by generations of heroic stands against adversity . . .'

The baby shrieked in protest. Perhaps she knew better.

'*La Piccola Valle della Tristezza*? But whatever does it mean, darling?'

Carl, robust, his newly washed hair clinging tenaciously to his scalp, took out his Italian-English dictionary. 'Something about sadness in the little valley. Good heavens, I thought all that was in the past. I hope we haven't bitten off more than we can chew.' He smiled to show he did not mean this.

Hugo, naked on the sofa, put up his hand, kneaded his

forehead with long thin fingers, and looked as if he had bathed in *angst*. This suited his pale wintry face, angelic lambswool hair, and deep green eyes glinting like emeralds in the snow. "Little Valley of Sadness". God, I love it. The music of the sound, the grandeur of its philosophy, the humbleness and beauty of humanity. Giotto and all that. We must live there.'

Carl nodded with radiant satisfaction. 'Dear boy, we are. I've already put down the deposit.'

'*La Piccola Valle della Tristezza*! Bernie, we've made it, we've arrived, we're here!'

Bernard was too busy extricating his youngest son from the bowels of the Ford Estate to pay much attention to his wife Mary. The boy was finally found, fast asleep and sullen at being awakened, amidst the old quilts, feather pillows, leaking flasks and broken crayons that accompany a long family expedition.

'Bernie, it's beautiful! Needs decorating, of course, but *still*!' Mary, plain and virginal as her namesake despite the evidence of the three lusty sons she had borne, beamed joy like a nuclear power station at her husband, ignoring the plaintive demands for water and toilets from her boys.

Bernard said nothing. He was a taciturn man, probably because of his height. For years his words, uttered at an altitude of six feet six inches, were lost in sudden gusts of wind, or faded away before they reached the ears of lesser, shorter mortals.

Silence never deterred Mary. She repeated, in appallingly mispronounced Italian, '*La Piccola Valle della Tristezza*. What *can* it mean?'

Bernard thought about this and decided he wasn't much interested. Language, including his own, was not his strong point.

Mary went on, '*Piccola* is little, I looked that up before the Italian dictionary got lost. Bernie, we'll have to send to

England for another one,' she fretted as her husband fitted the large clunky key into the rusty lock.

'And *valle* can only mean "vale", like a vale of tears or something. Now *tristezza* . . . that sounds like it comes from trees . . .'

Bernard turned the key. It jammed.

'That's it! "The Vale of Trees" – how wonderful.' Mary flung her thin arms happily, if somewhat vaguely, open, indicating all manner of joyous things to come.

Bernard rattled the door, trying to unstick the lock. The boys had gathered with their parents on the steps, weaving in and out of Bernard's long sturdy legs like ribbons around a maypole.

Mary, oblivious, beamed brightly at her husband who was now pushing, in the phlegmatic manner which was his way of expressing temper, against the stuck door. '"The Vale of Trees" – what a nice place to raise the children. Much cheerier than a Vale of Tears, what?' she shouted up at him, trying to be heard against the strong breeze that was beginning to whip across the fields. 'It makes me think of sturdy green oaks, of family picnics on sunny afternoons . . .'

She said no more. The door suddenly opened, and all five members of the family stumbled rather ingloriously into their new home.

Several months later, a solid no-nonsense Volvo Estate drove around the narrow roads skirting Lake Tresimino, narrowly missing a local bus coming in the opposite direction.

'In Umbria, as in the rest of Italy, you drive on the right,' Isabel said through gritted teeth when they had got over their fright.

'I know, I forgot.' Henrietta took a deep breath. The baby was howling in the back seat. 'Now what's the matter with *her*?' Henrietta said, somewhat crossly for a new mother.

'She's probably a bit nervous,' Isabel explained mildly. 'We did almost get wiped out, you know.'

'Nonsense! That's why I bought this Volvo, they can survive anything. I can't take any chances with the baby.'

Isabel said nothing, thinking wistfully of her sister's vintage MG, traded in for this solid steel symbol of security. I don't remember motherhood changing *me*, she thought with some perplexity. Maybe it was because she was almost twenty years younger than her sister when it was thrust upon her, by fate or whatever, like a bouquet of flowers foisted upon an unsuspecting celebrity at a public function. First there is effusive gratitude, then the dawning realization that, whatever the pleasure the flowers give you, you are still lumbered with the sweet though cloying blooms until the event is over.

They drove on for a bit in relative silence, the baby giving up and confining her protests to the odd hiccup or two. The lake on one side looked peaceful, at ease, having belched up its rich intake of summer tourists, now slumbering tranquilly, digestion at rest, in the soothing September sunlight. Henrietta, sobered by her slight lapse, concentrated on the road.

As they left the lake and drove deeper into the countryside, the baby, having drifted into an uncertain sleep, woke up with a sudden total certainty that she was being starved to death, and shrieked so raucously that Henrietta stopped the car at once. Behind her the driver of an ancient blue van leaned out the window and shouted, '*Ma è pazza? Guida come una novantenne!*'

'What is he saying?' Henrietta asked, the car still stationary in the middle of the road.

Isabel sighed. Sometimes travelling with her sister was a strain. 'I believe he is asking you if you are crazy, and accusing you of driving like a ninety-year-old woman.'

'How sexist! What about a ninety-year-old *man*? I think I'll tell him.' She opened the car door.

'You don't speak Italian. Perhaps it would be better to pull over to the side of the road. Look, we're in a village. Should we go into that little bar, and you can feed the baby there?'

The two women walked into the bar, which was inhabited by old men drinking grappa. On the few tables, covered with oilskin cloths, there were jam jars filled with blue and yellow plastic flowers. Isabel found this endearing. In her fluent Italian, she ordered two cappuccinos from the proprietor, a tiny grizzled man whose face and scalp looked identical, each sprouting what seemed to be a two-day stubble of hair.

'*Che bel bambino,*' he rhapsodized as he brought the coffee. Obviously a grandpapa himself, he chucked the baby under the chin.

Isabel explained that the *bambino* was a *bambina*, while Henrietta took the compliment serenely, accepting it as the truth. '*Lei è inglese?*' The proprietor pulled up a rickety wooden chair and settled down at their table.

Isabel, gratified that the question did not sound like an insult, explained that they had bought a home in Umbria and were moving here permanently. Before long the other four men had joined the conversation, not all of which Isabel could understand because there was so much dialect.

'They seem to be concerned about the identity of the father,' she said at one point.

Henrietta, kissing the fed and contented infant's fat cheeks, said, 'Tell them that the father was a Calcutta anarchist shot in a squalid battle over ancient and unimportant borders.'

Isabel said, 'I can't translate that.'

'Well, it's true.'

'I know, but I don't feel up to it. Think of the questions they'll bombard me with after that.'

The proprietor had gone out into the kitchen, bringing his wife and a basketful of warm *cornetti*. The wife and the croissants, which Isabel accepted politely, looked uncannily alike, both round and puffy and of a pale golden complexion.

'You must have one too,' she hissed at her sister. 'They'll be insulted if you don't. They have offered the pastries because of the baby. Italians love babies.'

Henrietta looked greedily at the pastry. 'I can't,' she wailed. 'My waistline. I haven't lost the weight I gained with the baby.'

Isabel stared at her. She carefully put down the pastry which was halfway to her mouth and said, 'Henrietta, are you mad? The baby's adopted. How could you put on weight?'

Henrietta had the grace to look disconcerted, which she covered up by taking a croissant and thanking the proprietor and his wife in such mindblowingly dreadful Italian that Isabel blushed. Henrietta, mouth full, said, 'I was such a serious bag of nerves right up to the time I went to India to collect the baby that I gained half a stone.'

Isabel, reassured, dimly remembered the ups and downs and strange quirks and mood changes of becoming a mother, and concluded that it wasn't all entirely due to hormonal changes in the body but also to some radical emotional changes in the brain. She smiled kindly at her sister and ordered more coffee for them both. Henrietta, slim and stunning in a long white tunic and trousers none the worse for the long car journey, smiled back, but her eyes were watery. For the first time since the adoption she was assailed by doubts, which was totally out of character. To hide the tears she clutched her new daughter harder, looking down with a tiny but sharp arrow of insecurity on the thick black hair and dear little olive face, wondering if she were worthy.

The baby, whom Henrietta had named Krishna in a somewhat confused attempt to honour the gods of the *Bhagavad Gita* and thus to preserve the child's heritage and culture, deflected the arrow and smiled. She outdid herself cooing and gurgling and doing all the tiresome things necessary to procure the love of adults. She intuited that it was a good sign, this barb of insecurity in her adoptive parent, for when was love, *real* love, arrogant and smugly sure of itself? That was for other emotions, infatuation and romantic longings and fantasies. Krissy, as she was called by all who knew her, wanted the real thing, as all babies do.

'Look, Isabel! Oh, look at her smile. Oh, Isabel, isn't she beautiful?' Henrietta, Madonna-like in white, long golden hair streaming like angel's wings down her back, blew kisses to her daughter who was busily tying love knots that would last forever in her new mother's heart. The baby gurgled, the proprietor's wife crooned, the men clucked, and even Isabel remembered, down the tunnel of the years, a faint light of maternal glow that had once been fierce and blazing.

The baby yawned, having made her point, and promptly fell asleep.

It was dark when they finally got to *La Piccola Valle della Tristezza*. The bold headlights of the Volvo picked up the grass growing in the middle of the road, the cypress trees lining its edges, as Henrietta drove slowly from the nearest village, Modena, two kilometres back. 'Is this it?' Isabel was eagerly squinting into the night, not having seen the house which Henrietta, despite her lack of Italian, had managed to purchase on her own.

Henrietta turned sharply left, juddering the car up a dirt track filled with potholes and some overripe peaches and apricots which had fallen off trees alongside the track. 'Nobody seems to have harvested any of this fruit. What a waste. Next year I want to make preserves.'

This remark was so out of character that Isabel decided to ignore it. First the country house in Umbria, then the Volvo, now peach preserves? She shuddered and tried to be patient. Her sister would get over it. Sudden motherhood had rushed straight to her brain, causing it to become unhinged for a time. It happened to them all, and was probably necessary. Something to do with the survival of the species.

The car stopped in the middle of what appeared to be a farmyard. The headlights picked out a small barn full of straw, a stone farmhouse with a tiled roof, a deranged dog barking dementedly at the tyres of the car. 'Is that the house?' Isabel asked with some trepidation, because the roof seemed to be scattering its slates around the ground like children shedding clothes in summer.

'No, that's the main farmhouse. Look, you can see the farmer and his wife peeking out from behind their lace curtains. Isn't that sweet? Look how they're trying to be unobtrusive, not wanting to offend but naturally wanting to see their new neighbours. I'm sure they've never even met an English person. How glad I am we chose unspoiled Umbria, rather than Chianti-Shire.'

Henrietta said this with such smugness that Isabel wanted to remind her again that Tuscany had been her first choice, but economics had ruled this out. Instead, she said, 'Which one is ours? Or rather, yours?'

Henrietta said graciously, 'It's your home, too, even though it's mine on the deed.'

'Your money too, but thank you anyway, Henrietta. Now which one is it?'

'Here, behind the car. And see, there's another old barn opposite that has been converted into a delightful house, probably by the farmer who lives in the big farmhouse. Most likely his mother and father are living there. The Italians are very family-oriented. The whole clan probably live here or nearby.'

As they unloaded the baby and other necessities from the Volvo, Isabel wondered fleetingly how Henrietta could claim to be an expert on Italy, having been here only the once. But she was fond of her sister, and so decided not to be annoyed. Besides, all minor irritations were promptly forgotten as Henrietta produced the key and they walked into the house. It obviously had been a farm cottage, but it had been modernized with taste and simplicity. ''Etta, it's lovely,' she cried when Henrietta turned on the lights. The walls were bare gleaming stone, and a plain wooden staircase led elegantly to the first floor. The ceiling was white and low, and an immense fireplace, ready for use, took up one side of the room.

'Isn't it a great find?' Henrietta enthused. 'What sold me was the fact that it's so cosy as well as elegant. The Italian home is a study in line and symmetry, but often lacks that lived in, homey feel which I wanted for my baby.'

Isabel was too taken with the house to admonish her sister for quoting back to her the literature she had given her on Italy. Isabel had a great deal of printed information on the country both in English and in Italian, for two years earlier, at the age of fifty, she had obtained a degree in the language. But all she said, as she embraced her sister fondly, was, 'It's beautiful, 'Etta. Thank you for sharing it with me.'

Krissy, squashed between her mother and her aunt as they hugged, decided she was being treated badly and indulged herself in a loud squawl.

'My darling precious baby, my little Hare Krishna, my little Italian cornetto,' Henrietta sang as she danced around the room humming snatches of Indian chants mixed with the chorus of the more popular operas of Verdi. Krissy, confused, was placated by the sight of Isabel, her sensible aunt, rushing around unpacking jars of baby food. Her squawling faded into a mild whimper.

'I do hope this baby isn't going to grow up with an identity crisis,' Henrietta said suddenly. 'She'll have to learn some Indian dialect. It's part of her heritage. And, of course Italian, if we're to live here for a few years, possibly longer. Not to mention English.'

'She'll be fine,' Isabel said, leaving a jar of Heinz Lamb Stockpot to heat in the modernized kitchen and returning to the living room to admire the furniture, which her sister had bought hurriedly but with her usual good taste on that one visit to Italy. Henrietta, sitting on a fat sturdy armchair, the gold of her hair blending with the deeper gold of its upholstery, white tunic billowing like clouds across a fragile dawn, looked like a Virgin in a Renaissance painting.

'Oh, shit,' said the Virgin look-alike, wrinkling her rather puggish nose, the only imperfection in an otherwise flawless face. 'The baby shat.'

Krissy, having evacuated her bowels with that heady intensity which is lost in adults, smiled at her parent, oblivious of the smudgy stain seeping out of her Babygro and on to the white trousers, and from there the dark gold of the armchair. Having made her territorial stance, she settled into her new home, clamorously demanding food and a clean nappy. Both were hastily provided.

'Well, little one, do you think you're going to like growing up in Italy?' Henrietta asked rhetorically some time later. Krissy, half asleep on her mother's now slightly less than impeccable white lap, belched in reply.

Isabel, having fended off the black dog outside which broke off its baying at the moon to bark hysterically every time the door was opened, fetched some suitcases from the car and said, 'Our neighbours are at the window again.'

'Oh, lovely, what a sense of community. How different from London where no one gives a toss about your comings or goings. Should we invite them over for a Campari and soda? I bought some at the duty-free. Italians don't go to bed early. Perhaps they'd appreciate a nightcap.'

'Henrietta, it's after eleven. Let's wait until tomorrow.'

'I suppose you're right, but I'm longing to meet them. I bet they don't speak English. You'll have to translate for me until I get the hang of it.'

'That's what I'm here for.' Isabel neglected to add that Krissy would be translating Italian for Henrietta long before she herself got the hang of it. 'Look, can you hold this door open? I'll bring in the last of the luggage.'

'Right, I'll pop the baby on the sofa here. There, I've got the door. Oh, Isabel, look, those Italian peasants are at the window again. They must have children, look at the swings set up in the front garden and the toy tractors on the lawn. How nice for Krissy, having Italian friends to play with. They're *still* at the window . . . should I wave at them?'

'I don't think so,' Isabel said, struggling with the heavy cases as her sister peered at the house opposite. 'I believe they're trying to be inconspicuous.'

'*Buongiorno!* Oh, shit, I mean *bon noche* or *bueno sera* or is it – oh, hell, what *do* I mean? Never mind, they'll know I'm trying to establish contact.' And Henrietta waved frantically, her pearly hand glinting in the moonlight. The lace curtains immediately shut, the light went out, the room plunged into darkness.

'There, they'll know we're friendly now. I wonder if there's a baby? Wouldn't that be delightful, a proper Italian *bambino* for Krissy to grow up with? Oh, Isabel, I shall stay here forever, I can feel it now, I know it in my bones.'

The dog, seeing Henrietta wave her arms about, gave an encouraging yelp, hoping this was a game he would be asked to participate in. Isabel pulled her sister inside and shut the door. The dog, deprived of its amusement, slunk back into the hay barn. It was the most excitement he had seen since the arrival of the other inhabitants of the rather isolated hamlet, who were now whispering to each other in the house opposite.

Mary, shutting off the light quickly, said to Bernard, 'There, they've seen us. How embarrassing. They'll think we were snooping.'

Bernard did not find it at all embarrassing. He had joined his wife at the window purely from an insane sense of joy at seeing an English licence plate in front of the house, and the reassuring solidity of a sensible Volvo instead of the stream of old Fiats and Vespas in the village, the Alfa Romeos and

Mercedes and Moto Guzzi motorbikes in the towns. He had missed the comforting familiarity of Fords and Land Rovers on the neighbouring farms Back Home, the reassuring bulk of the West Devon Bridgeman & Son Farm Suppliers lorries pulling up at the gates of his old farm. So the unknown Volvo with its GB sticker parked in the middle of the yard of *La Piccola Valle* touched him as, many years ago, the memories of chaffinches sitting on orchard boughs had touched his fellow expatriate, Robert Browning.

The lace curtains closed, Bernard and Mary groped their way in the dark into the kitchen at the back of the house, where she made them a cup of Horlicks. She had brought jars of it with her for the children, but they had quickly assimilated into their new home and were now demanding milky coffee or rich chocolate drinks, much to Mary's horror. That left four and a half large jars of Horlicks for her and Bernard to consume.

Doing his bit, Bernard silently drank a second cup while Mary discussed their new neighbours.

'How odd,' she said, stirring a teaspoon of Golden Syrup into her cup. The children had abandoned that as well, saying it was far too sickly to be mixed in with coffee or their evening chocolate. Mary wondered uneasily if they were becoming European, but looking at her husband reassured her. It was hard to imagine any sons of Bernard achieving cosmopolitan status.

'How odd,' she said again. 'Two women, a baby, no man.'

Bernard thought about this. 'A Volvo like that is a man's car,' he finally said, chauvinistically. 'Perhaps the father is arriving later.'

'That's rather strange. Why aren't they travelling together?'

'Perhaps there *is* no father. Perhaps she's an unwed mother.'

The phrase sounded strange coming from Bernard's taciturn lips, through which never a word of gossip passed. It sounded oddly exciting, even risqué. Back on their farm in Devon,

Mary would have been surprised to hear her husband talk of such things, but here, in this glamorous country, it seemed almost natural. Perhaps he too was becoming European? It was all rather disconcerting.

'I suppose it's possible,' she mused. 'I mean, if I were a single mother I would want to run away from home. I know times have changed and all that,' she struggled on, trying to achieve Bernard's level of newly acquired sophistication, 'but still, narrow-minded people do gossip, especially in small towns. Perhaps the mother couldn't face her family.' She thought of her own mother and shuddered.

Bernard considered this for a while. 'Could be,' he said enigmatically.

'And what about the other woman? Who's she? She's older, but not old enough to be a mother. A sister? They don't look at all alike, and frankly she looks too old to be the other one's sister.'

Bernard pondered this while Mary washed out the mugs and dried them carefully on her National Trust bluebell tea-towel. 'Couldn't see them clearly,' he said at last.

Mary could. She had been at the window longer than he had and so had noticed many things by the moonlight and car lights. She thought the woman with the baby looked about twenty, all that long blonde hair and slim figure, but she also knew that night was kind to women of a certain age. Mary had a sly – what she called feminine – intuition that in the cold light of day the slim blonde would look older than she'd first appeared by moonlight.

The other one was harder to place: she was older, and plumper, but her plumpness was round like apples in her well-filled jeans, not droopy like pears; and a bright patterned jumper covered breasts that did not seem at all matronly but rather free and uninhibited as the woman jiggled about removing bags and boxes from the car and bringing them in. Mary thought she could like this woman, with her short cropped light brown hair, probably tinged with grey or white: you couldn't be sure by the car lights. She wasn't so certain she would get on with the other woman, though, the one dressed all in white like a ghost. Her hair surely was not entirely natural, all that golden ripe sunflower colour. Mary thought about that hair with distaste, and not a little envy.

Bernard switched off the kitchen lights as Mary checked the sleeping boys. When they had undressed and were in bed, Bernard drifting off into a dreamless sleep beside her, a thought so horrible crossed Mary's mind that she sat up suddenly, her pale-blue Victorian-style nightgown gleaming in the moonlight coming through a crack in the shutters. 'Bernard,' she whispered, wondering whether she dared say it aloud. 'Bernard, those two women ... they couldn't be ... you don't think they're ... ?'

'Lesbians?' he said sleepily, not bothering even to open his eyes.

Mary did not know which shocked her the most: the fact that the women might be two of *those* – or the revelation that her husband not only knew the word but could utter it in such an insouciant manner.

Knowing she would not sleep tonight, she sidled back under the covers, deciding both thoughts were equally unsettling.

Chapter Two

Isabel woke the next morning to the sound of the shutters on her bedroom window banging rhythmically, blown by a bracing wind from the north. Opening them, a gusty drizzle hit her face and she gratefully shut the window and went back to bed. She could hear Krissy grizzling next door, and Henrietta getting out of bed and going to her. Isabel, looking at her watch, smiled in silent amusement at the thought of her sister, always a night person, rising every day at this hour with such saintly fortitude.

'Bloody hell, child, do you know what time it is?' Henrietta snapped as she picked up the infant.

Outside the dog was barking at a tractor hurtling across the yard. 'What is all this activity?' Henrietta demanded of no one in particular. 'The bloody middle of the night and the whole world seems up and about.'

Isabel heard her sister's bare feet padding down the polished wooden stairs and smiled again, picking up the book on the bedside table that she had been too tired to read the night before. It was the latest novel by Umberto Eco, in Italian, not translation, and Isabel was enjoying the luxury of reading in the language purely for pleasure after years of study. Cuddling down into the eiderdown, cushioned against the twin blows of very early morning and a nasty wet day, she opened her book, reflecting that there was a good deal to be said for having one's babies relatively early: one could shed both them and their father in the mellow years and take on sweeter things, like literature and art and music.

This thought, delicately seeded, sprouted greenly when, half an hour later, Henrietta appeared with a cup of tea. 'I heard you going to the window,' she said, settling herself and a contented belching baby on Isabel's bed. 'I can't believe you're awake at this ungodly hour when you don't have to be.' She played with Krissy for a few moments, then smiled serenely in Isabel's general direction. 'I saw the farmer,' Henrietta stated grandly, as if she were announcing the visitation of no less a person than the Pope himself. 'He was doing something with the straw next door, loading it on to the wagon and taking it somewhere on the tractor. The dog was going beserk beside him.'

Isabel put on her interested look, the one she had used many times in tedious lectures at university. It wasn't that she didn't enjoy talking to her sister, it was just that she was lost in a world of Italian intellectuals and was loath to let go of it for Umbrian farmers. Besides, the Lapsang in one of Henrietta's collection of exquisite China cups was soothing, a welcome contrast to her usual morning drink of Nescafé in a chunky Oxfam Third World mug, and she wanted to savour it silently. She thought, rather guiltily, that she was going to enjoy living with her sister.

'I went out to the car to unload some of Krissy's toys and things and there he was, staring at me.'

Isabel regretfully said goodbye to Umberto Eco, closed her book, and said, 'The dog was staring at you?'

'Don't be silly. The Italian – the farmer.'

'Oh. What was the dog doing?'

Henrietta stamped her bare foot prettily on the polished wooden floor on the bedroom. 'Never mind about the dog, he was just running about yapping. Why are you so interested in the dog?'

'I just think he might be a bit of a pain, all that howling day and night.'

'Forget the bloody dog! There I was at the car and there was this dishy Italian farmer – one of your true peasant types, Isabel, as rooted and grounded in this valley as the olive trees themselves – anyway, there he was, staring at me.'

Henrietta laughed, a tinkling porcelain sound, and Isabel thought rather crossly that maybe it was a good thing she was out of London and away from the fashion crowd, the designers and models and hangers-on she'd worked with. Much as one loved one's sister, a tinkling porcelain laugh was rather a lot to be asked to live with. The baby, who had been spluttering merrily on the bed, broke wind with gusto, as if to agree.

'He looked bewildered, poor man,' Henrietta was tinkling on. 'I can't blame him, he's probably never seen an English woman before.'

'Don't be daft. This may not be Tuscany, but Umbria gets its fair share of Brits too.'

'But not here, Isabel. We're so isolated! He was certainly staring at me as if I was completely foreign to him.'

Isabel thought: He's probably never seen an apparition like *you* before, of any nationality. She looked at her sister's long flowing white lacy nightgown, with a dressing gown of the same fabric thrown lightly over her shoulders. All that voluptuousness barely concealed underneath, plus golden hair delectably ruffled in sleep, and pearly bare feet as well, for Henrietta didn't own anything as mundane as a pair of slippers. No wonder the poor farmer stared.

Isabel sighed, able to enjoy Henrietta's beauty with detachment, as she would a painting. She had long got over the jealousy inspired by the birth of a plump, cherubic sister when she herself was twelve years old, a gawky skinny adolescent with dull pale hair, thick glasses, and a tendency to blush a choleric red when anyone other than immediate family and her one and only friend spoke to her directly. Her parents, delighted that after all the years of trying they had at last produced a sibling for their awkward only child, expected Isabel to love her new sister. She didn't, of course. But only at the beginning.

As the years went on Henrietta grew, to no one's surprise, more beautiful with each sunblessed day. She also, which *did* rather surprise them, grow in character, to her sister's delight and her parents' chagrin, for this manifested itself in a steely will. Ignoring her stunning looks, which to her credit never meant that much to her, she proceeded towards her goal in life, mainly to get as much fun out of it as she could. From their rather strict, but now bewildered, parents, Henrietta gained concessions to attend parties, rock concerts, to have friends of both sexes, all of which filled the once sombre house with life and delighted Isabel no end. Unfortunately by this time she was out of the house and married, but even from a distance her sister's antics made her exceedingly pleased Henrietta had been born. Rather to her surprise, she found she did indeed love her sister, as her parents had urged her to do from the beginning.

By then too Isabel had realized she had married in haste. She had heard too many comments, earlier on, from well-meaning friends of her parents about how Henrietta was of course the beautiful one, but Isabel, though plain, had the brains. This had had the effect of encouraging her to marry the first eighteen-year-old who told her she was prettier than her sister, despite her having obtained the highest exam results possible. It could only have been a lie, she realized later, but the deed was done and university a distant dream by them. The marriage hadn't stood a chance.

Isabel came groggily back to the present, surprised to find Henrietta was still droning on about the farmer.

'He's so dishy, Isabel. I mean, to die for. Tall, but not

skinny; on the contrary, I could see his muscles rippling under his shirt. And he's got the best of those Italian good looks – God, you can tell a mile away what his nationality is. Dark hair, very straight but very thick, flopping over his face as he tosses the hay or whatever it is into the tractor. And deep brown eyes—'

Isabel interrupted her waspishly. 'Rippling muscles? Deep brown eyes? Sounds more Barbara Cartland than Italian.'

Henrietta took no notice. 'He's wearing really old jeans, faded, but not the Calvin Klein designer ones that everyone in London wears. These are just old working jeans – but the way they fit his body! I nearly had an orgasm just looking at him. And then he's got this amazing black jumper on, but what a cut! It wouldn't be out of place on a catwalk in Milan though it was most likely knitted by his old mother. There's a hole in one elbow too,' she finished admiringly. 'The look's so authentic – I know people in London who would kill for it. And here we have the living breathing model.'

'Christ, Henrietta, stop sounding like a psuedo-trendy fashion designer.'

'I can't, I *am* one. Oh, how I'd like to capture that quintessential Italian look in a design.'

'You can't,' Isabel said perversely, for this was all getting a bit much and she felt she deserved another cup of tea. 'And you are *not*. A fashion designer, that is. Not anymore. You are a *mother*.'

Henrietta did not take this for the provocation it was intended to be. 'I know!' she shouted joyfully, picking up the now sleeping Krissy and putting her into the cot in the next bedroom. 'Oh, Isabel, aren't I lucky? Dear little Krishna . . . my very own Hare Krishna. Dear baby. Lucky, lucky me!'

Isabel turned her attention back to Umberto Eco, wondering why both he and she were so cynical. Though Henrietta's sincerity was both real and radiant, it made Isabel feel faintly nauseous. She wished her sister would come back into the real world. Yet what indeed was the real world? Certainly not her sister's other life, with her slick international friends from the fashion industry. Maybe after all Henrietta *had* found a real world, at least her own version of reality, and what in the end does any of us have but that?

Umberto Eco was making Isabel philosophical. The shutter banged again, the tractor outside roared across the yard like a prehistoric dragon, snorting pollution into the wet humid air. The dog howled in a frenzy of delight as an ominous drum-roll of thunder crashed over *La Piccola Valle della Tristezza*, followed by a crescendo of rain playing fortissimo on the rooftops.

Morning had broken – with a vengeance.

It rained and rained. All day it rained, hard metallic drops pounding on the slate roofs of the tucked-away hamlet and on the rich dark earth of the farmyard, turning it to sludge. It fell on the black dog who howled with excitement at every crash of thunder. The wind came up, making everyone fretful. Krissy muttered baby curses and refused an afternoon nap; Isabel fretted because she was longing to go out and explore the area; Henrietta grizzled because she was aching to meet the Italian neighbours, and even *she* didn't have the effrontery to bundle herself up against the driving wind and rain to brazenly knock on their front door.

What she had in mind, actually, was a casual encounter. She had envisioned lounging in the front garden with the baby gurgling at her side like a warm brook in summer, and the Italian farmer walking past with a cow or whatever in tow. Then, seeing Henrietta, he would stop and say something meaningful in low, mellifluous Italian. Since she was wearing a pair of immaculate white jeans at the moment, and the garden looked like a cesspit of murky mud and all sorts of unspeakable sludgy things, this was of course totally impracti-cal, as was the fact that even if it happened, even if he *did* speak, she would not understand his Italian. Feeling somewhat defeated, Henrietta resigned herself to staring out of the window, and waving at the tractor every time it passed.

'I wonder if I could teach him English?' she mused.

Isabel, curled up on a low, comfortable yet elegant sofa, looked up from her book to see if this required an answer. She was just in time to see her sister bestow a breathtaking smile through the window pane, fogging it up with her hot eager breath. She turned to Isabel in triumph. 'He stopped and waved to me! He was just going into his house and turned to look this way and saw me. I smiled and he waved!'

Isabel studied her sister suspiciously. 'Isabel, you're not starting to fancy that farmer, are you?'

'He's rather tasty, you have to admit. And I've always had a soft spot for Italians. In Milan—'

'But you're a mother,' Isabel said rather lamely.

'So are you. Have *you* given up sex?'

'Yes. Lately.'

'Only because you're wary after that affair with your lecturer.'

'Cautious.'

'Anyway, just because I have a baby doesn't mean I can't have a relationship with a man.'

Isabel closed her book with a bang, hoping this would adequately express her disapproval, but all it did was wake up Krissy who had at last grizzled herself to sleep in her baby chair. Henrietta picked up her shrieking daughter to cuddle and comfort her, which she did to soothing effect.

Isabel decided not to be placated by this show of maternal devotion. 'The man's married, Henrietta. *Married*. You do not have affairs with married men.'

Henrietta had the grace to agree. She broke off the lullaby she was crooning to Krissy and said, 'You're right, I don't, I never have. But of course the Italians are different. The farmer's wife most likely expects him to have an affair, so long as he's discreet. Italian men don't go confessing things like Englishmen do to salve their consciences, and so making it worse for everyone. Although the Italian wife may know she pretends she doesn't, and although the Italian man does, and knows she knows, he pretends he doesn't. And so everyone's happy.'

Isabel, stunned by this convoluted glibness, shook her head. 'He's a neighbour, 'Etta,' she said seriously. 'For God's sake, don't get involved. It would be a frightful mess.'

Henrietta, worryingly, didn't reply to this, but instead put on her beatific Madonna look, which Isabel knew well. It was the look she used when she was deadly determined to get her own way; it was the implacable look seen so often before on her: when their parents had tried to discourage her from joining the fashion world; when friends had advised her against a beautiful but dangerous new man; and, not very long ago, when friends and family tried to stop her from adopting an orphan child from India shortly before her fortieth birthday.

'You're mad,' her father had said. 'To give up everything you've worked for. Your successful career, your life-style . . .'

Henrietta had adjusted her expression to The Look, smiled serenely, and didn't remind him how bitterly he had opposed her beginning that career in the first place.

Ex-lovers tried to persuade her against it, most likely because she remained friends with them and they were used to taking advantage of her generosity in the way of occasional loans, a bed for the night, a good meal and plenty of booze in her house in Islington. But whenever Henrietta mentioned such words as *baby* or *commitment* or *family*, they mysteriously faded away. Her maternal hormones were beginning to pump insistent messages through her skin, and former and potential new lovers dropped away like flies at the first squirt of insecticide.

So Henrietta, as she had done all her life, took matters into her own hands. She did her homework, found out where a single mother might, just might, adopt an orphan child, and knowing through the cosmopolitan world in which she lived all the right people in all the right places, came home after months of fighting Indian bureaucracy with Krissy. The old house in Islington was sold at an inflated price, the new house in Umbria bought, and here they were.

Isabel sighed for the third or fourth time that day. Where did she fit into all this? she sometimes wondered. It had seemed such a good idea at the time, the two sisters living together in Italy. Isabel was between jobs, knew Italian, would supply companionship, translating skills and occasional baby-sitting while Henrietta would supply the cash, of which there was still a healthy amount left after she had settled her accounts in England.

But this? Isabel thought. It was one thing supplying ballast for a rather floaty sister, but to reprimand her for flirting with a neighbouring farmer? It was ridiculous. Henrietta was too old to have a nanny, and Isabel too tired to act as one. 'I am not my sister's keeper,' she said aloud.

'Oh, good,' Henrietta said placidly, rocking her dear little raisin daughter in her soft white pudding lap. 'We shall get on brilliantly then.'

Krissy, jiggled up and down like a currant in a food processor, gurgled disbelievingly.

'I saw you, Bernard, I saw you wave. Who were you waving at? Surely not one of *them*?'

Mary whispered the word fearfully, as though the children might hear and be tainted. Since the boys were all at school this seemed rather pointless, Bernard thought.

'Which one was it?' Mary persisted. 'The young one or the older woman?'

Something tripped in Bernard's stolid brain, some warning mechanism more used to detecting footrot in his sheep than simmering emotions in his wife. But he ignored it and said truthfully, 'It was the one with the long golden hair.'

It was that *golden* that set off Mary's own early-warning system. For Bernard, the descriptive phrase was unnaturally poetic. Words spurted from her as from a cut artery and bled over her husband. 'She looks like a tart. I saw her coming out of the house this morning half naked – prancing about all in white like that, with her hair not even combed and her breasts showing under the nightdress.'

This latter was not strictly true, but Mary in her excitement had become over-imaginative. Unfortunately, it had the effect of stirring something in Bernard, something which had lain dormant since Mary had, with the birth of her sons, become a staunch Earth Mother, more interested in making bread than making her husband.

He said, to cover both his embarrassment and the strange primitive thing happening under his trousers, 'Do you think I can have some of your delicious scones?'

This deflected Mary, as he knew it would. Though she worked long hours trying to provide Bernard with the food he had grown up on – rich Devonshire cream teas, Cornish pasties, fried English breakfasts – it was sometimes a thankless task in this country. It never occurred to him to give unsolicited praise for something so basic as food, which had never interested him anyway except to provide fuel to keep the great furnace of his body supplied with the energy he needed for work. Therefore it was with joy that Mary leaped up now and with alacrity placed four halves of perfectly baked scone, laden with clotted cream she had made herself, on his plate. Nearly breathless with excitement, she added the strawberry jam from Sainsbury's which she had carted all the way from England.

'Are they good?' she asked as Bernard picked one up and was about to pop it in his mouth. 'Are they tasty?'

Bernard, who was imagining that the snowy mound of

cream was his new neighbour's white breast and the jam the redness of her nipple, dropped his scone in horror as he realized his wife was reading his thoughts.

'Oh, look, Bernie, you've made a mess of your Marks and Spencer's jumper.' She fussed over him, wiping off the cream and jam. 'That jumper's getting tatty, look at the hole in the elbow. The next time Mum comes over, I'll have her bring over another. I need some Marks and Sparks knickers too.'

Bernard, relieved, submitted to being wiped. He sensed that Mary would have liked to run the cloth over his mouth, like she did with their youngest son, but she restrained herself. He thought of knickers, and decided that his new neighbour most likely did *not* buy hers at Marks and Spencer's. It was the most erotic thought he had had in years, and for the second time that afternoon there was a fitful stirring under his trousers, luckily hidden under the table.

Mary, having cleaned her husband's jumper, knew with wifely intuition that it was time to clean up his mind. 'Anyway,' she purred, 'I'm sure those two women are . . . you know. What we were saying last night.' She played her trump card. 'They don't like men.'

The beast below the table, dealt a mortal blow, stopped rearing and went back to sleep. 'I'd forgotten that,' he said weakly, adding with uncharacteristic lack of deliberation, 'What a waste.'

'It makes sense,' Mary rambled on, 'because I've read that those sort of couples . . . you know, ones who are, uh . . . well, anyway, they're allowed to adopt children. Not in England, of course,' she hastily reassured Bernard, who had totally lost interest in the conversation and wasn't listening anyway.

'Uh?'

'You've got a bit of jam on your chin. There, that's better. Yes, I don't know where I read it, probably in the *Telegraph* back home, but it's a worry. They live right next door, for goodness' sake. I mean, how can we keep it from the boys? Oh, dear, how upsetting it all is.'

Bernard took another mouthful of scone. 'Are they good, Bernie? Better than the last batch? . . . Bernie, what should we do about the new neighbours? Such bad luck. Of all the farms to buy, we buy one next to *them*. I knew we shouldn't have come to Italy . . . I know you wanted to buy more land for your sheep, and build up your herd of prize cattle, but I'm sure it's not healthy for the boys, having *them* so close. Oh, dear, we'd never have had this problem in England.'

Bernard, his mouth full, said, 'I like the wallpaper you put up in here.' And so, for the second time within the hour, paid his wife an unsolicited compliment. He had learned, subconsciously, to cover devious thoughts by deflecting them in the mirror of his wife's vanity over her domestic skills. What an extraordinary afternoon!

For the next twenty minutes Mary forgot everything else as she enthused about wallpaper. She even forgot *them* as she overdosed her husband with long-suppressed enthusiasm. Perhaps, she thought, as he sat stuffing his face with scones, apparently listening to every word she said – perhaps after all Europe wasn't such a bad thing. Two compliments and twenty minutes of attention was more than she had had from him in years.

Poor Mary. She is not yet aware of just how European her husband will indeed become. She does not know that in a few short hours he will meet *them*.

Chapter Three

The dog instigated the first meeting between neighbours. The rain had at last stopped, and the Italian moon was boldly undulating through the still damp air when Bernard, driving the tractor back through the yard for the last time that evening, accidentally ran over the poor bedraggled creature.

The dog lay in the road howling in distress. Bernard stopped the tractor and ran to him. Mary joined him, as did all the boys in their British Home Stores pyjamas. Isabel and Henrietta flew out of their house – Isabel to see if she could help, and Henrietta at last spotting the chance to meet her Italian farmer. Krissy, on her mother's hip, watched the scene with wide-eyed fascination.

'*Muoviti*! You must call the vet!' Isabel cried in her impeccable Italian.

Mary and Bernard, of course, did not understand a word. 'Goodness,' Mary cried. 'Bernie, they're not English at all, they're Italian! That explains everything. Oh, I *knew* they couldn't possibly be British.'

'Oh, shit!' Henrietta cried, staring at Bernard with wide disbelieving eyes. 'You're English?'

'So are you,' he replied inanely.

The dog, sensing no more attention was going to be paid to him that evening, stopped howling, for he had not been hurt, merely stunned. He jumped up and began wagging his tail, yapping merrily to show what a jolly joke it all was. Isabel expressed some relief at his miraculous recovery, but the others were too busy staring at each other to notice.

Mary, remembering her manners, introduced herself and the boys, and added as an afterthought, 'And this is my husband Bernard.'

Everyone looked up as if to the moon, which Bernard's face was obscuring. Isabel and Henrietta saw an ordinary benign man with an ordinary benign expression on his face staring down at them from a great height. Henrietta turned away first, and sighed, and contemplated the shattering of illusions.

'I'm Isabel Norland, and this is my sister Henrietta and her baby Krissy.'

Sister? Bernard looked at Henrietta's profile, the darling flat nose, the endearing firm chin, the brush of gold on that smooth cheek, and felt love rush into the emptiness inside him which he had previously filled with Mary's meals. Her *sister*? She was all right then, she was *normal*, and the look she had given him when she'd stood there by the car that morning, nipples straining against the white fabric of her nightdress . . . He broke off, and mentally corrected himself. That was just Mary's imaginings. There'd been no nipples visible under the nightdress, he was sure of it.

But there *was* that look: that hadn't been in his imagination. Bernard had seen that look sometimes on the faces of foreign women on late-night television, before Mary shut it off just as things were getting interesting. He didn't know English women could look like that – like they wanted to get inside you, like they wanted to suck you right up, like they wanted to – oh, dear, it was happening again! Hiding himself behind the tractor in embarrassment, Bernard took deep steadying breaths. Stumbling in his confusion, he trooped behind the women and baby and his noisy sons towards his house, for Mary had invited everyone inside for a cup of Horlicks.

Once there, the boys were dispatched to bed and the door was shut in the dog's face as he was ordered to the hay barn. 'Did you bring him from England or find him here?' Isabel asked politely.

Mary said, 'Oh, no, we were married in England,' before realizing that Isabel wasn't talking about Bernard but the dog. 'I mean,' she chattered on, trying to cover her error, 'we didn't have a dog in England. Well, a sheep dog, but he was old anyway, and Bernard hasn't got around to getting one here in Italy. No, we haven't got a dog.'

Howling at the back door protested against this statement. 'Him?' Mary burbled, as her two new neighbours looked at her. 'I don't know who that dog belongs to, he seems to just live here. No one in the village has claimed him. I feed him, but he's a bit too motheaten to bring inside. The boys, you know.' She nodded sagely if somewhat mysteriously.

Henrietta, eyes already glazed with boredom and hardly noticing Bernard who was staring at her greedily, as if she were clotted cream, hissed to Isabel, 'Can we go home now? We've done the neighbourly bit.'

She hissed back that they certainly could not.

Mary, rather enjoying being the perfect hostess – they had not had proper visitors in the house since they'd moved to Italy – gushed, 'Do you like added sugar in your Horlicks? Or can I offer you Golden Syrup? I brought tons of it from England for the boys, but—'

'Could I have tea?' Henrietta interrupted petulantly. Isabel kicked her. Even Krissy gave her a cross look.

'Would you like Earl Grey or plain PG Tips? We have both, of course.'

Mary bustled, Bernard sat and stared, Henrietta sulked, and Isabel tried to make small talk. 'And you'll have some scones,' Mary cried, having found some equilibrium in her life for the first time since the new neighbours had moved in. Normality had been restored at last, or at least as normal as it was possible to be in Italy. It seemed the women were not what she had feared; most likely a husband for Henrietta, her baby's father, was on his way to Umbria right at this moment. How good for her own boys (and in this she included Bernard) that this was so; what a relief that they'd be spared having to adjust to an unnatural complication.

It was lucky she was busy getting the hot drinks for she missed the expression on Bernard's face as he watched Henrietta hum quietly to her baby.

Ah, Mary, whispers the moon, hums the damp air scented with washed green fields. *Ah, Mary, perhaps not all of your boys will be spared. Look over at your husband's face and see that perhaps there is one who is already lost.*

But Mary, oblivious, did not look. She was engrossed in telling the new neighbours how she tracked down English supplies in the unsophisticated villages around them, and where they could actually find custard powder if they were prepared to travel further afield to a larger town.

The baby yawned, and fell asleep. Henrietta did too, until a pinch administered by Isabel woke her.

In a spare spacious flat in London, Carl Gilbert, civil servant, is also almost asleep as his lover of many years, Hugo Westlake, dresses and prepares to go home.

'I don't see why I have to go,' he says petulantly, as he has done a hundred times before.

'Scandal, dear boy,' Carl soothes him, as he has soothed a hundred times. 'I work for the government in an important position. I've managed to keep you secret so far.'

'In the closet, you mean. Isn't it time you came out, Carl?'

He shakes his head gently. 'I want nothing to spoil my early retirement in a fortnight's time. You know that. Just be patient, dear boy.'

The dear boy, who is in his mid-forties but, like Cliff Richard, remains forever adolescent, shakes his lambswool hair, which looks as if it should be wisped around a Christmas tree, and grumbles a bit, but finishes getting dressed.

'Be patient,' Carl repeats soothingly. 'We shall be in Italy soon. Everything's in order: the flat sold, the removal van ordered, our new home waiting. In Italy we can live together openly and honestly. In Italy people are more tolerant.'

Hugo, ready to leave, brightens at this, emerald eyes glittering like fairy lights. 'I shall write some of my best poetry there. I need to feel the earth under my feet, the solid companionship of people who have lived in one place for centuries. London is too transient, Carl. I need roots, I need to find my true self. I have a premonition it will all happen for me in Italy.'

Carl, who knows Hugo but loves him anyway, says absent-mindedly, 'Of course it will, dear boy.'

Hugo, as a matter of fact, has never had a poem published. He earns a bit of cash writing verse for greetings cards, and satisfies his soul by penning convoluted stories in rhyme which he publishes, with Carl's money, himself. Hugo takes Carl's subsidies for granted, believing that the arts should be thus endowed. That the arts and he, Hugo, are two entirely different things, he cannot grasp, nor does Carl wish to disillusion him.

'*The little valley of sadness* . . . ah, Carl, I can't wait to get there. What power, what imagery it invokes. I shall come alive there, I can feel it.'

'I'm sure you will,' Carl murmurs kindly, thinking that Hugo is alive enough right now, thank you very much.

Hugo, dressed, walks out into the night, feeling poetry and life, those twin sirens, calling to him from across the Channel. Each, he feels, is tugging at his soul, pulling him, ensnaring him. He will write a poem about it.

Hugo is almost right. Life is indeed about to ensnare him. Poetry hasn't got a chance.

'Oh, Mum, it's a huge lorry. Come and look!'

'Do look out of the window, Mum.'

'Look, it's from England.'

The three boys, John, Richard and David, in unison like a Greek chorus, ran out of the house without even putting on their coats though it was the middle of November. Mary thought crossly, as she ran out after them, that they were becoming irresponsible, living in Italy.

It had been Bernard's idea to go abroad, start farming afresh without huge debts and an impossible overdraft. A sheep farmer originally, he had always kept a few head of cattle, and hoped that in Umbria he would be able to expand his herd of prized and cherished cows, while he made a living with his flock of sheep. Land was still cheaper in Umbria than in Devon or Cornwall, Bernard had learned from the *Farmers' Weekly*, and so, after long deliberation, he'd made the big decision to relocate his family.

Mary had, to start with, gone along with this, seeing herself as next in a long line of British women who had stood by their men as they explored and inhabited and conquered foreign fields – not to mention killing off the natives, which she didn't like to think about. Now, however, her sense of adventure was paling, like the colour from pressed flowers. She was missing things like Sainsbury's in Exeter, the coach trips with the WI to London once a year for pre-Christmas shopping or to see the latest musical. She missed the gentle rhythm of her Friday morning keep-fit classes in the Community Centre, and market day on a Tuesday where Bernard bought or sold sheep or one of his beloved calves, and where Mary met her female friends over stalls selling farm eggs and local cheeses.

In fact, she decided as she buttoned and zipped David, the

five-year-old, into his bright green anorak, it was her women friends she missed the most: the endless discussions during coffee mornings of recipes, children, husbands . . . and, yes, because they were not backwater bumpkins but knowledgable modern farmers' wives, of more worldly topics, such as whether ecologically sound, green detergents really did clean as well as other, more politically incorrect brands. These things mattered to Mary: she prided herself on not being a frivolous woman.

Henrietta, who *was*, and proud of it for she thought the world too full of people who took themselves seriously, also saw the removal van arrive from England that morning. It had stopped at the converted barn, the one empty dwelling left in the *villaggio*. Since the November day was mild, with a pale but encouraging sun sifting through grey but flimsy clouds, she did not put on her jacket but went out in her white canvas trouser suit. Mary, dressed in assorted shades of brown and a green waxed jacket and Wellington boots, thought malevolently that it was about time Henrietta gave up this affectation of always wearing white. Henrietta, on the other hand, thought it about time Mary stopped trying to look so *To the Manor Born*. All that green rubber and wax gave her the creeps.

The two women had not become friends.

Isabel, driving into the farmyard, noticed her sister and their neighbour eyeing each other suspiciously, like two cats wondering who will get the warmest spot in front of the fire. She parked the car, took Krissy out of the baby seat, plonked her in a pushchair and wheeled her over to Henrietta and Mary, now ignoring each other pointedly as they watched the removal men opening the back of the lorry.

'Ah, there you are, Isabel, and there's my dear sweetie darling lovely baby. Coo-ee, Krissy darling. How was the shopping trip?' Henrietta lifted her daughter from the chair, tickling her tum and playfully nibbling the baby's red running nose as she wiped it clean with a tissue. Krissy, wildly in love with her bizarre English mother, laughed and cooed at these indignities. Richard, David and John stopped buzzing about the removal lorry and began talking to Krissy as well, imitating her mother's coos and kisses. The farmyard sounded like a pen of demented pigeons.

Mary, annoyed, thought it grossly unfair that a woman such as Henrietta should inspire such maternal devotion, since she was clearly doing everything wrong. There was definitely no father, to start with. And Henrietta hated cooking; when it was her turn to prepare the evening meal, she went to the village and bought olives, artichokes, prosciutto, pasta, tomatoes, and mixed everything up in about five minutes. Or so she bragged. 'Is that any way to bring up a baby?' Mary cried righteously to Bernard. 'On virgin olive oil and *antipasti*?'

Bernard, who had become rather fond of little Krissy – lustfully imagining, in the deepest hours of his darkest nights, that he was her father, conceiving her upon the magnificent body of Henrietta on a hot summer's night in the lush paddock where his finest cattle grazed – refrained from answering. The past two weeks or so had been unsettling for him, his love (for he was sure that was what it was) for Henrietta growing round and secretive like the plump peppers that had been prolific in the back garden in the summer. He was sure she loved him back, although there had been no repetition of that smouldering look she had given him when she'd first arrived, before they'd met. Bernard assumed that this was because she was shy and demure; after all, look at the way she always wore virginal white. Clearly it was because she was so self-effacing, so loath to draw attention to herself.

He wondered if perhaps she was indeed still a virgin, and had adopted a baby because she had as yet found no man worthy of sharing her bed. Lush fantasies of how he would be that man plagued his hours on the tractor, tormented his time tending the sheep. How the fulfilment of this fantasy would affect Mary, he did not stop to wonder. Where she fitted into all this, he did not trouble himself to consider. Since Bernard had not actually thought about Mary for years, this wasn't such as aberration.

Now, bumping about on the tractor on the field next to the farmyard, Bernard saw the removal lorry arrive, then Isabel driving up, and the inhabitants of the two houses swarming about the van. Several minutes later, a very old and beautiful Jaguar pulled to a stop beside the removal van. Intrigued both by the car and by a flash of white in that sea of winter brown that was his wife and sons, Bernard decided he had done enough for the morning and turned his tractor towards the house.

The door of the Jaguar opened and the driver stepped out. He was a short powerful man with a face as gnarled as a tree root, which was not, oddly, unattractive. His hair was a mixture of black and white vying for dominance; worn slightly long, it was coarse and vibrant-looking.

'*Buongiorno*,' he said politely to the assortment of women and children standing around unashamedly gaping. How very Italian, he thought, the way the neighbours all come out to greet the newcomers. The English would have stayed hidden behind net curtains, their interest interred in the cells of their houses, not coming forth to make acquaintance until far too late for any kind of involvement.

How different the Italians were! '*Buongiorno*,' Carl said again, louder this time, embracing them all with a broad friendly smile.

Everyone spoke at once. Confused, he heard voices babbling, giving their names, pointing at houses, asking questions and making introductions. They bombarded him so with words that it took him a few minutes to realize that they were all speaking English.

Poor Carl, whisper the linden trees, rattling their moribund leaves in either sympathy or the cold wind beginning to blow over the farmyard. When he had bought the Umbrian house a year ago, there was no one living in the hamlet but an ancient Umbrian peasant, and some lone female relative in the house those two Englishwomen appear to share now. Carl does not dislike the English; he is after all one of them, but being one of them, he knows what they are like and wants to be away from them for a time. He has no illusions that the Italians are any different, but he *had* hoped that he would be spared finding out too much about them due to his poor Italian. All Carl wants, in these twilight years, is to live with Hugo in a bit of peace, openly and freely.

Peace. The poplars on the horizon catch the whispered word from the linden trees and the wind blows it around and around in their skeletal branches. How they all long for it, this assortment of pilgrims milling around the sleepy farmyard in the little valley of sadness. Peace and the Good Life, whatever that may be.

For Henrietta, that vision in white, the Good Life is motherhood; for her sister Isabel, the space to shed her responsibilities to husband and family and be herself.

Mary, her clean face gleaming in the tolerant winter sun, sees the Good Life as raising her four darling boys, the three so little, the fourth so big, on wholesome nourishing food and clean ironed clothes. It is unfortunate that this has to be done in Italy, with overdraft rates being what they are Back Home, but there you are.

Bernard, halting his tractor beside the lorry, the dog racing hysterically beside the wheel, wants the Good Life also, which to him is to be left alone to dream dark dreams of mysterious white ladies while he is cooing to his beloved cows or ministering to his substantial flock of ewes.

And Hugo? He wants peace more than any of them right now, for he is in the passenger seat of the Jaguar, fast asleep, having been sick in the car throughout most of the journey.

See, the wind chatters to the trees, *how his fine lambswool hair fluffs out on the car's dark upholstery, see the paleness of his cheeks, the dark circles under those emerald eyes.*

And see how he jumps, terrified, as the dog, having joyfully spotted new prey, leaps into the farmyard, howling a greeting, and presses his muddy paws on the lovingly preserved car.

'Down, you filthy animal!' Mary cried, trying to pull him away.

'It's all right,' Carl said grimly, while inwardly gnashing his teeth.

'I wish you'd control your dog properly,' Henrietta snapped at Mary.

'*My* dog? I told you it wasn't ours.'

'You feed it. It must be yours. There isn't another house until the village.'

The dog, knowing it was being discussed, yapped jauntily and licked Krissy's face. John, Richard and David hooted with laughter and tried to get it to lick theirs.

'It probably belonged to the old man who lived here before us. He died, and his mother moved away.'

'Mother?' Carl asked in confusion. 'But he looked eighty himself.'

'They live a long time around here, I suppose. All that olive oil.'

'Or they did until the English came,' Isabel muttered to the dog. She gave the poor homeless mongrel a pat, which sent him into such spasms of ecstasy that he tried to mount Henrietta's canvas-trousered leg, thinking it was a white poodle.

Hugo, head pounding, stepped out of the car. The dog, pulled off Henrietta's leg by several pairs of hands, greeted him raucously. Hugo, dazed, tried to get his bearings. He had never seen so many children and infants and women and animals gathered together since his last school outing, and he had been sick then as well.

Trying to sort out who was who, and why they were all shouting so, and in English when they were supposed to be Italian, he was aware of a roaring in his head which gathered to a crescendo, causing him to fear the onset of a migraine. The noise stopped as quickly as it had begun, and Hugo realized with deep relief that it was only the tractor which the farmer had moved out of the way of the removal lorry. Hugo looked up to see the farmer get off the old, rickety, and dangerous-looking machine, and walk towards the group.

Bernard saw the lean man with all the fine frizzy blond hair staring at him and, remembering to be English and hospitable, smiled back.

Hugo, stunned, watched the man walk towards him, saw the smile that seemed to be drawn from the dark depths of his troubled soul, saw it lift and lighten and beautify that sombre intense face, those dark enigmatic eyes. Hugo saw it all and was smitten, stricken and sickened by love, not unlike the effects of the salmonella poisoning he had suffered some years ago.

Bernard, seeing Henrietta in her radiant white clothes, albeit somewhat dog-tarnished, looked at her with the same expression as the dog wore on its face earlier when straddling her white poodle-like leg.

Yes, thought Hugo. *Yes, yes, yes!* He fancies me too. It never ocurred to him that the look he had intercepted was aimed at Henrietta, not himself.

Damnation, thought Carl. *Not again. Please God, not again.*

Henrietta's delicate brow crinkled, seeing how Bernard stared at her, thinking what a bore it all was, that bovine farmer with the sex appeal of a *zucchino* lusting after her like a goat on heat.

Well, I never, thought Bernard. She looked at me, and she seemed troubled. She's worried that I'm married, poor maid.

Oh, dear, Mary mused to herself. *I wonder if I have enough of that Victoria sponge left for everyone if I ask them all over for morning coffee.* She rather liked the idea of being the gracious hostess in this God-forsaken place. The others were odd perhaps but at least they were English. It was, after all, something for which to be thankful.

Aloud, Isabel said, 'I'm sure you'd like tea or coffee before starting to unload all that?' The removal men, who were sitting in the cab of the lorry waiting for someone to get on with it and unlock the door, perked up.

'All of you come in, please. I've just been to the village and stocked up on *amaretto* biscuits, and we've got some choco-latey things as well. You too,' she added with a smile to the boys, who like the dog were never sure whether they were welcome or not.

They all trooped into Henrietta's house, Mary cross because Isabel had beaten her to the neighbourly gesture. Isabel, noticing her sudden animosity, said, 'Do you have any of your homemade scones? I'm sure they'd be much more welcome than my store-bought biscuits.'

Mary, transformed, ran back to her house to fetch the Victoria sponge. She had liked Isabel from the start, she decided, though the older woman kept herself at a distance. Mary thought that must be because of the flightiness of her sister. She was sure that if Henrietta were not around, she and Isabel would have lovely long chats together.

It's time I asserted myself, Mary thought forcefully, gather-ing sponge cake, scones and some leftover clotted cream from the fridge. She would make friends with the older woman, sister or no sister, for it was just what she needed, a good English chum from Back Home to whom to pour out her homesick heart. A surrogate mother perhaps, though Isabel was hardly that old.

Poor Isabel. The morning heats up with indignation on her behalf, the sun sizzles in protest. She has just turned her back on the impossible demands of three adult children whom she loves but has grown impatient with, needing a break from the outpourings of post-adolescent hearts. Little does she know that she is just about to acquire a new confidante, and not even an Italian one at that. Are there to be no consolations?

In Henrietta's homey yet elegant Italian country house it looks as if an English tea party is taking place. Isabel has even placed a tea cosy on the pot.

Chapter Four

'Oh, wasn't he charming, that older man? And the other one – Hugo – how refined.'

'Uh?'

'What's the matter, Bernie? Why aren't you eating your steak-and-kidney pie? Isn't it tasty? The boys all had seconds, but they gulped their food quickly so they could go outside and watch the removal men. Their manners have deteriorated dreadfully.'

'The removal men's?'

'The *boys'*, Bernie. Just think. Carl, the older man, is a retired civil servant. Mother will be *so* impressed.'

'Mmm.'

'Such good manners he has! They'll be wonderful neighbours, such a good influence on the boys. So well-bred, Bernie, so knowledgeable about how to treat women. Do you know, he thought my scones were far tastier than his own mother's?'

'Mmm.'

'Oh, Bernie, is that all you can say? Don't *you* think my scones are tasty?'

'Mmm-hmm. Yes, dear. Delicious.'

'I have to confess, I didn't take to the other one, the

younger man, Hugo. He wouldn't eat a thing, said he was ill.'

'Mmm?'

'I must say, he seemed rather dozy.'

'Mmm.'

'I saw him look at that Henrietta, though. Couldn't keep his eyes off her.'

'What? Are you sure? When was that? What did she do? Did she notice him? Was she looking back at him?'

Bernard, aware as soon as he had spoken that he shouldn't have, began hurriedly eating steak and kidney along with limp watery cabbage. Mary eyed him suspiciously. 'Delicious,' he cried ecstatically, to deflect her gaze. 'This pie is delicious!' He filled his mouth so full he choked, and Mary had to thump him on the back for several minutes before he was himself again.

Later, after eating two pieces of apple pie to shield himself against further suspicion, Bernard dared bring up the subject a second time. 'You think then that, uh, that Hugo, uh, that he, you know, that he . . . ?'

Mary, lulled by the sight of her special pastry disappearing down her husband's gullet, said innocently, 'Oh, yes, fancies her like anything. It's quite obvious. You were sitting next to her on the sofa, drinking your tea, remember?'

How could Bernard ever forget the way Henrietta's white canvas trousers, sullied somewhat by the erotic ecstasies of the dog, had rubbed against his Marks and Spencer's navy ones on the soft lush sofa.

'Uh, no, don't remember.'

'Of course you do, Bernie, it was only an hour ago. I was helping Isabel pass around the scones, Carl was sitting on one of those gold armchairs and Hugo on another, looking quite pale and ill. You and Henrietta were sitting opposite him on the sofa.'

'Oh. Now I remember.' Bernard strove to look innocent.

'Is your irritable bowel syndrome returning, Bernie? You look strange. Have some more tea. I've mixed PG Tips and Earl Grey because the Earl Grey won't last till Christmas if we're not careful. And don't tell me, Bernie, that you can buy Earl Grey in Italy. Have you seen what they charge?' Mary shook her head at the audacity of foreigners.

Bernard looked outraged as well, but only because he had a sudden, peculiar urge to throttle his wife. Instead, he said, 'Uh, about Hugo . . .'

'Well, I'm surprised you didn't notice. He didn't stop staring at the sofa where you and Henrietta were sitting. I had to ask him three times if he wanted a slice of saffron cake.' Mary spilled the tea she was pouring into Bernard's cup, so affronted was she by the memory. 'He fancies her, all right,' she said darkly. 'I can always tell.' She pressed her lips grimly together.

Bernard drank his third cup of tea quickly, feeling this conversation was getting out of hand. But he couldn't resist asking, as he got up from the table and went to find his boots, 'And, uh, Henrietta? Does she fancy him too, d'you think?'

'Not a bit of it,' Mary said firmly. 'That woman fancies only one person. It's so obvious, I'm surprised even you haven't noticed.'

Bernard's heart lurched with terror. He wasn't sure whether the coming pronouncement would fill him with joy or dread. But it wasn't at all what he'd expected. 'She fancies herself,' Mary said flatly. 'There isn't room for anyone else in that ice-white heart of hers.'

At that moment, the ice-white heart, buried deep within Henrietta's voluptuous body, was warm and melting as she sang lullabies to her baby. For in this respect Mary was wrong. Henrietta *was* in love: passionately, devotedly. She was in love with her baby Krishna, her wonderful plump black-eyed Indian daughter.

'Krissie-bye baby, on the tree-top,' Henrietta crooned as she kissed and cuddled her baby. She had wanted this daughter for years, despite appearances to the contrary. When she and Isabel were children, it was Isabel who had seemed destined for greatness, for a superlative career in whatever field she chose. For Isabel excelled, in those days, at just about everything.

Henrietta, on the other hand, had wanted, simply, marriage and babies, in that good old-fashioned order. And there were, of course, platoons of young men marching to the heady tunes of love and lust ready to make her dream come true. But somehow things always went wrong. Henrietta, to everyone's surprise, including her own, revealed a rather picky, not to say prickly, streak inside all that golden suntanned exterior, and as the years rolled by, she discarded most of her admirers as unworthy. Those whom she didn't discard, discarded her, after tearing their flesh messily in the barbed wire that throughout the years had wrapped itself treacherously around her heart as man after man proved unworthy.

An artistic talent, a love of clothes, a genius for design and colour, propelled Henrietta first to art college, then into the heady world of fashion. Here her star shone; it wasn't long before she was working for one of the top London houses. And here she stayed, highly paid, acclaimed by her colleagues, resisting the urging of friends to start her own label, her own business. Henrietta was totally lacking in commercial sense; she just loved designing clothes. She was successful not because she strove to be, or made cunning but brilliant contacts, but simply because, as so seldom happens these days, she was bloody good.

And so, when the baby came along, it was not hard for her to give up her job, for she loved Krissy much more even than she had loved making clothes. She could, of course, have afforded a full-time nanny, kept her job as so many of her colleagues did. But what was the point? Henrietta knew herself well, knew she would begin to envy the nanny, knew she would be craving to spend more time with her new daughter. She had waited forty years for Krissy's arrival and wasn't about to put her in anyone's care other than her own.

'Bye, Krishna bunting, momma's gone a-hunting,' Henrietta sang in a lilting voice, trying on an Italian accent since here she was in her sweet new Italian home.

The house was actually Isabel's brain-child.

'I'm going to raise my baby in the country,' Henrietta had announced one day when her sister was visiting her in London.

'You mean, sell this house?'

'Yes, of course,' Henrietta had retorted. Patience wasn't her strongest virtue. 'How else could I afford a place in Dorset or Devon or Somerset, or wherever the countryside is these days? I wouldn't dream of raising my child in a city. They always turn out so pasty.'

'Mine didn't,' Isabel said indignantly. 'My children are exceedingly robust.'

'Oh, I forgot about your children. Well, yes, they're all right,' Henrietta conceded, somewhat grudgingly. 'But, anyway, I've been looking at houses in the south-west. They're all frightfully expensive.'

'You'll have to go north.'

'I wouldn't mind, but it's so cold. You know I like sunshine, warmth. And my baby, of course, will be from India. The problem is, I shall need money to live on for the next few years, until the child's in school and I can go back to work.'

Isabel pondered this. She had just returned from Perugia, where she had spent nearly a year teaching English to Italians. She had loved Umbria, but detested teaching. Now, at a loose end, undecided what to do next, she was back in London, fretting and missing Italy.

'Henrietta,' she said slowly, 'have you ever considered

living in Italy? There are still reasonable properties to be had, if you avoid the popular areas like Tuscany.'

And so the deed was done. Henrietta, delighted, had shrieked, 'Will you come with me, Isabel? Be my assistant, my translator? Live with us, until you decide what you want to do with yourself?'

This suited her and the deal was made. Impetuously, Henrietta had flown to Milan, cornered a colleague who had a villa on the Umbrian/Tuscan border, and coerced him with her usual charm not only to help her buy the house, but to supervise the building work and modernization necessary before she and her new baby moved in.

A couple of months later, on Isabel's birthday, Henrietta presented her with glossy photographs of their new home, as a birthday surprise. 'And you can't even speak Italian,' Isabel had said, stunned. She'd looked at her sister with new respect, her own heart singing with sudden joy for she loved Italy with the same passion as Henrietta was about to bestow on her new adopted baby.

'Henrietta, stop crooning to that child for a minute and come and talk to me,' Isabel said now. All the neigbours had gone after the impromptu late-morning tea-party. Outside in the yard the dog was happily barking at the removal men unloading the lorry, blocking their movements with jaunty leaps and pirouettes. One of the men, who had eaten too much of Mary's Victoria sponge and felt ill and bad-tempered, tried to kick him but missed and fell over. The dog sympathetically licked his face.

'What do you think of our new neighbours?' Isabel asked.

Henrietta reluctantly took Krissy, who had fallen asleep in her arms, upstairs to her cot. Sometimes she wished she were a kangaroo, so that she could carry her baby close to her at all times, awake or asleep.

'Hugo and Carl?' Henrietta said when she returned to the living room. 'They seem quite pleasant. Gay, of course.'

'I thought so. I liked Carl, he seemed to have a sense of humour. It's hard to tell about Hugo, he was terribly droopy, but I suppose that was because he was ill.'

'I'm relieved they're gay. Heterosexuals can be so demanding sometimes.' Henrietta sounded impossibly world-weary as she said this. Since she had discovered that Bernard was not Italian, she had given up on man/woman love forever. Luckily she was not finding this difficult, with Krissy growing and gurgling and bewitching her way into her mother's affections.

'Many of my dearest friends are gay,' Henrietta went on. 'They don't hassle and stalk you like male heterosexuals.'

Isabel, who had never in her life been stalked, or for that matter even unduly hassled, by any man, either gay or homosexual, pondered this. Perhaps there were advantages to having one's assets hidden away in the head instead of blatantly exposed, the way Henrietta's were. Isabel studied her sister, the way she often did, as one studies a breathtakingly beautiful work of art. But something was different today. Was there perhaps a slight second chin beginning to emerge beneath the delicate lines of the first one? Isabel looked harder. The elegant white trouser suit, muddied by the dog, looked less than impeccable; moreover, it was definitely slightly tighter around those perfect little buttocks.

'Henrietta!' Isabel shrieked. 'You're gaining weight.'

'New mothers often do,' she replied serenely. 'Especially if they're not breast feeding. Hormones, you understand.'

Isabel was about to tell her not to be so bloody silly, that adoption did not wreak the physical chaos in a woman's body that pregnancy does, when she remembered there was something more important for which to reprimand her sister. 'Henrietta, you must do something about poor Bernard. I can't bear to see him mooning around you the way he does.'

Henrietta shook her head impatiently. 'I know, he's deeply embarrassing. I thought he'd have an orgasm sitting here rubbing his thigh against my leg on this very sofa.'

'He didn't?'

'Well, not really,' Henrietta conceded. 'It was more accidental than that. We were squashed rather close so our legs couldn't help rubbing together. I could see beads of perspiration standing out on his forehead, he was getting so aroused.'

Isabel, annoyed at the complacency in her tone, snapped, 'I told you not to stoke the woodburner so high this morning, it's far too hot in here. I was sweating too, and I assure you I most certainly was not aroused by any of today's company.'

Henrietta smiled serenely. 'I can't help it if he fancies me, Isabel. Most men do.'

She said it in such an off-hand manner, without a shred of vanity, that Isabel couldn't reasonably be cross. 'Well, don't encourage him,' she said crossly.

'I don't, I go out of my way to be appalling to him, but he doesn't seem to take any notice of my body language. See what I mean about heterosexual men, what a hassle they are? Give me the Carls and Hugos of this world any day.'

Isabel saw her point. But wasn't quite sure she agreed.

'Pity they're not gay,' Carl said to Hugo as they sat drinking coffee in the kitchen, on top of a packing case. 'One can be quite good friends with homosexual females, they don't hassle you the way heterosexuals do.'

Hugo, downing soluble Aspirin with mineral water, felt in too much of a turmoil to answer.

'They were pleasant enough, though,' Carl mused. 'The blonde seems besotted by her baby, hard to get her to concentrate on anything else, but her sister's interesting. Imagine leaving a husband and three children at the age of forty-seven and going to university to get a degree.'

'Her children were quite grown-up when she left them,' Hugo murmured, trying to keep up his part of the conversation to prevent Carl from noticing that his mind was elsewhere.

'True. But it must still be a big step, leaving your husband of twenty-nine years.'

'Hmm, I suppose so. Especially for passions intellectual rather than physical.'

This mention of passion stirred the unease slumbering in Carl's subconscious and brought it bounding back into his memory like a young Labrador. 'Hugo,' he began gently, 'I do think, dear boy, you should leave our new neighbour alone.'

Hugo chose to misunderstand him. 'Henrietta? Oh, Carl, she's delectable. A painting, a poem, a song. A perfect example of glorious, voluptuous womanhood. But you know that my few skirmishes with heterosexuality were dismal failures. Not for me, darling. No need to worry.'

One of the removal men, appearing at that moment in the kitchen to ask a question about a walnut desk, glared at him with open disapproval. Hugo flashed his emerald eyes, somewhat shadowed by the dark circles underneath, and smiled seductively. The removal man, speechless at this effrontery, backed out of the room.

Carl, not to be side-tracked, said, 'I don't mean Henrietta, darling boy. You know very well whom I mean. I mean that straight young farmer next door with the very nice little wife and three young children.'

'Ah, Bernard. Yes. Do you think he's *that* young? He must be in his early-thirties at least.'

'Only just, Hugo, only just. And thirty *is* young these days from where we stand, don't you think?'

Hugo, who was quite attached to Carl in his own way, refrained from saying that where Carl stood was about fifteen years further away from thirty than Hugo himself.

Carl went on, 'You know I've always turned a blind eye to your little passions, dear thing, but this is rather different. This is right next door, and it's not London. The man's also a straight arrow heterosexual. I'm sure he doesn't even realize we're not.'

Hugo, having seen Bernard's look of passion flared in his direction in the farmyard, disagreed but tactfully kept quiet. After all, he had been with Carl for twelve years now and knew how to handle him. If he were discreet he could have his cake and consume it with gusto.

Carl, seeing Hugo acquiesce, knew the matter was far from closed, but kept quiet. He had loved Hugo for twelve years and knew how to handle him. He knew his lover wanted to have cake and stuff himself with it too, just like a child. It was up to Carl to see he didn't sicken from it.

Outside Mary walked by to the hen house to collect her eggs. She couldn't resist peeking in at the uncurtained window and saw Carl standing over Hugo, the older man's hand on the other's shoulder. How nice, she thought as she went on her way. Two friends, so fond and caring of each other. Two bachelors, sharing a cottage: how sensible. The thought that they might be more than friends was not allowed to perch even fleetingly in the twiggy nest of Mary's brain, nor in Bernard's either. Having been made to feel foolish over their precipitate conclusions about Isabel and Henrietta, they were certainly not about to do the same thing again with these new neighbours.

The hens, clucking and scolding, reminded Mary of her mother, who was arriving next month for the Christmas holidays. A widow for some years now, Claudia was far too attractive and assertive for a woman of her age, or such was the opinion of her daughter. Claudia was in her late-fifties, and should by now be more content to take a back seat in life instead of grabbing the steering wheel whenever she could.

Mary gathered the eggs and wondered. The cypress trees punctuated the dirt track as strange thoughts circled like buzzards in her head and she gazed ahead, unseeing. She saw her mother, so brazenly independent since Father had died, so unseemly in her enjoyment of her widowhood. Staring at her new neighbour's house, Mary saw Carl at the window, saw him spot her and wave. As she waved back she thought excitedly: Yes, this will do just fine. Carl was more or less her mother's age, perhaps a few years older. Hugo must surely be more like a son to him than a companion. The younger man had said he was a poet. Carl must be some sort of patron of the arts, offering shelter and peace to Hugo as he struggled with his muse.

The thought filled Mary with awe. How noble and self-sacrificing! But Carl must be lonely, surely, for the company of a woman? A woman his own age . . .

Becoming agitated by her own thoughts, Mary dropped an egg, and, flustered, nearly dropped a second. She had just had a wonderful idea: she would have all the neighbours around for a proper, traditional English Christmas dinner. She would stuff them all with proper British cooking at its finest, show them how neighbourly she and Bernard could be, and best of all, introduce Claudia to their distinguished new neighbour.

Waving frantically to Carl once again as she bobbed back up the lane to her own house, Mary hummed to herself as lists of Things to Do for the Coming Festivities danced gaily in her head.

'Ah. Oh . . . Signor Manetti. *Buongiorno, io sono*, . . . no, shit. I mean, *io ho* a problem, or *problema*, or whatever it is.'

'Ah, Henrietta Bayliss, of course I remember you. We handled the purchase of your property. Have you settled in now?'

'Oh, I forgot you spoke English.'

'But I have not forgotten you. Here, step into my office, we can speak more privately there. I shall tell my secretary not to disturb us. And this is . . . ?'

'Oh, sorry, I forgot you don't know Isabel. This is my sister, Isabel Norland.'

'I am happy to meet you. I am Fabrizio Manetti, Miss Bayliss's *avvocato*, her lawyer.'

'Yes, yes, I told her all that. And this is my daughter, Krishna.'

'Krishna? An unusual name for a female child, no?'

'I call her Krissy,' Henrietta replied serenely. 'Blending the tradition of her Indian roots with contemporary informality.'

Fabrizio blinked with incomprehension. Looking at the sleeping infant in the pushchair, he did some mental arithmetic. How could he not have noticed that this beautiful woman was pregnant the last time he'd seen her? To cover his confusion he said, 'Such a sweet *bambina*. Such thick black hair. She does not look like you, I see. Perhaps she takes after her father?'

'I suppose she might. He was an anarchist, killed in a border dispute in one of the lesser provinces of India.'

Fabrizio looked shocked, probably because Henrietta delivered this bombshell with what appeared to be a complete lack of emotion. Isabel glared at her, smiled at the lawyer, and felt obliged to say, 'My sister never met the child's father, nor her birth mother. Henrietta went to Calcutta to adopt the baby several months ago. Her own mother abandoned her after the father was killed.'

'Ah,' Fabrizio said. 'I see.' Though of course he didn't. He sat behind his solid polished mahogany desk and motioned the women to sit too. 'Now what can I do for you today?'

Isabel listened peacefully while Henrietta talked. As they drove to Perugia, Isabel had stopped badgering her sister to abandon this ridiculous mission and begun to enjoy the drive. The November day was cool but sunny, and the sublime Umbrian light of late-autumn highlighted the wooded valleys, the groves of olive trees, the vineyards. She looked forward to a leisurely lunch with her sister, perhaps at the Cafe del Cambio in the Corso Vannucci, or any of the other restuarants on that broad popular street. Coming back to Perugia was like coming home again.

Fabrizio was listening attentively to Henrietta's story, studying her face closely as she talked. Isabel, watching the Italian, decided she liked the way he was actually listening to what her sister was saying rather than admiring the delectable lips that were saying it, the way men – and not just Italian men, such was Henrietta's charm – tended to do. Isabel also liked the way the *avvocato* seemed to be taking Henrietta seriously, though Isabel knew the matter to be fairly trivial, involving a dispute between Henrietta and their neighbour, Mary, over a boundary. Although the dispute remained, on the surface, friendly, with both Bernard and Isabel advising the women to stop being so bloody silly (though he conveyed this more laconically than Isabel), the two opponents seethed like a cauldron of boiling beetroot, red with both indignation and antipathy.

'So you see,' Henrietta was saying now, 'I'm sure that line of crab-apple trees belongs to me, though that sad, sad woman claims they're hers. Look, the deeds are very clear.'

'Ah, so,' Fabrizio said cautiously. 'Yes, I see the boundary on the deeds, but there is no mention of any crab-apple trees or indeed any trees at all.'

Isabel smiled to herself, and Fabrizio turned at that moment, caught the twinkle in her eye, and asked, 'Is there anything you would like to add, *signora*, to clarify this for me?'

Isabel, ignoring her sister's withering glance, said, 'I think it's a storm in a teacup.'

'Pardon? I am afraid my English—'

'Your English is fine,' she said, and then proceeded to tell him in impeccable Italian what she meant by 'storm in a teacup'.

'How exquisite your Italian is!' Fabrizio cried admiringly, and the two embarked on a long and lively discussion of how Isabel had learned Italian, and Fabrizio English, until

Henrietta, thoroughly bored, demanded, 'What about my crab-apple trees?'

Fabrizio said he would do what he could. He took down the name of Mary's lawyer who was also in Perugia and said smoothly that between the two of them, they were sure to work something out. Then he invited the women to lunch.

'Well, that was a pleasant surprise,' Henrietta said to her sister a couple of hours later, after they had thanked Fabrizio and said a fulsome *arrivederci*. They were walking slowly down the Via dei Priori in the old medieval city, taking advantage of the autumn sunshine, warmer now than it had been this morning. 'What a delicious meal. And Fabrizio certainly knows how to pick his wines.'

Krissy, almost asleep in her pushchair, belched a few times in agreement, having sampled everything from the pasta to the *gelato*.

'I like him,' Isabel said.

'Attractive, too. How old would you say he was? Early forties?'

'Hmm, I suppose. More or less,' she replied casually, looking around her appreciatively at the ancient buildings and churches as they walked down the sloping street.

Henrietta said, 'He's got one of those gaunt faces that are so interesting. And those dark, brooding, deep-set eyes.'

'Did you think they were brooding? I thought they were mischievous and full of fun.'

Krissy burped again, rolled her eyes, and fell fast asleep. Henrietta said, 'He's just the right height. Not too short, not too tall. I don't like men who are too tall. All that lankiness puts me right off.'

'He's got lovely hair,' Isabel mused. 'Dead straight, but thick and dark.'

'Yes,' Henrietta agreed. 'But he'll probably lose it in a few years' time.'

The two women looked at each other and laughed,

dismissing Fabrizio as women can so disarmingly do. Arm in arm they wandered through the old city, ending up in Piazza Danti, Krissy still peacefully asleep, the afternoon perfect and golden.

Fabrizio, walking back to his office after lunch with the two Englishwomen, whistled jauntily in the November sunlight. The younger one, he thought, the blonde, was spectacular; as an Italian, he could appreciate her exquisite face and form, her sense of style.

But the other one, Isabel, intrigued him more. She gave off such a heady aroma of sex appeal, all the stronger for seeming completely oblivious to it, that Fabrizio had felt himself in a state of near out-of-control arousal throughout the excellent lunch. Henrietta was the perfectly formed flower: a white daffodil or tulip perhaps, stunning to the eye but somehow scentless. Isabel was a wild violet, her charms hidden in long grasses, exuding heady perfumes that lingered long in the memory.

Thinking these poetic, if slightly over-the-top thoughts, he returned to his office, glancing surreptitiously into the taste-fully framed mirror in the reception area to make sure he had not been more than emotionally ruffled by his lunch. Francesca, his secretary, found him staring at the ceiling above his desk, and said conspiratorially, 'You're in for it now. Your wife is on the telephone, furious with you for forgetting to meet her for lunch.'

Fabrizio swore and picked up his phone. As his wife ranted on about his usual misdemeanours, he seemed to smell the intoxicating scent of wild violets in the room. Closing his eyes, he saw himself lying in a bed of the voluptuous flowers, hotly naked, with that sensual Englishwoman plucking at him as one would handle the sweetest of flowers. He thought of her features: those wonderful cheekbones that age would never ruin, those overlarge brown eyes with flecks of gold that shone with humour and good-will and intelligence, that spiky short-cropped hair that curled around her neck like the first tenuous vines of summer creeping up a garden wall.

At about the time in his fantasy that Isabel was draping violets around his tree trunk of an erection, his wife suddenly shrieked, 'I've had enough, do you hear? I'm leaving you, this time for good. Don't try to plead and beg with me, I've made up my mind and nothing you can say or do will change it.'

To her great surprise, and, it has to be said, annoyance, Fabrizio said breezily, '*Benissimo*. Great, fine. Okay. No problem.' He then proceded to agree with all her outrageous terms and demands, including custody of the cat who was eighteen years and much beloved.

He would miss the cat, but there would be compensations. He thought of Isabel again and smiled.

Chapter Five

'Excuse me. I'm looking for Henrietta Bayliss?'

You would be, thought Mary sourly, having been admiring through the window the sleek Ferrari, and the even sleeker Italian who had stepped out of it and was now standing at her door.

'She lives in that house over there.'

'I know. As a matter of fact I handled the sale of her house – I am Fabrizio Manetti. But she is not there now, no one is.'

'Oh, you're her lawyer. I've been wanting to speak to you about some crab-apple trees. How lucky you speak English. You wouldn't believe how many Italians don't.' Mary frowned as she said this, pondering the wilfulness of foreigners. Then she brightened as she contemplated Fabrizio's amiable face, the accommodating twinkle in his eyes. 'Won't you come in? They've just gone to the village, I believe, and should be back shortly. Come in and have a cup of tea and some scones.'

Fabrizio, who would rather have had an espresso, richly strong and with plenty of sugar, decided he was too eager to see Isabel to quibble. He followed Mary through to the kitchen and watched her make a pot of tea. 'I'm having to mix

Earl Grey with PG Tips until my mother arrives in a week's time with fresh supplies,' she explained as she poured the tea.

'Excuse me?'

Luckily Bernard entered the kitchen by the back door and caused a diversion. Mary buttered scones and loaded them liberally with strawberry jam and a dollop of clotted cream she had made only yesterday from some fresh milk she had bought from a woman in the village who kept a house cow.

'Is it good?' she asked as Fabrizio's scone was about to enter his mouth. He assured her charmingly that it was, and she again thought it a pity that this man was looking for Henrietta.

That reminded Mary of the crab-apple trees, and she went on to regale Fabrizio with her version of the dispute. Bernard, embarrassed, tried to get away, especially when he heard Henrietta's Volvo drive into the yard. He hoped for a passionate exchange of glances before he went to move his sheep from one field to another.

Fabrizio heard the Volvo and also got up. In his haste to get away he stuck his elbow in the bowl of clotted cream on the table.

'Here, I'll clean it up,' Mary cried. She was mopping him up and wiping him down like a lavatory wall when Henrietta and Isabel walked in, with Krissy perched on her mother's white-skirted hip like a sassy black button.

'Fabrizio!' cried Henrietta, as one who has been mortally wounded. 'I didn't expect to see you here.' With the enemy, was the obvious implication, for Mary, sponging the *avvocato*, was obviously claiming possession.

'He loves my scones,' she said triumphantly.

'You're here, of course, to see the boundary and the crab-apple trees for yourself,' Henrietta said coldly. 'I can tell you've been side-tracked.'

Fabrizio, who didn't give a fig about any crab-apple trees but merely wanted to see Isabel, had, of course, forgotten all about the boundary dispute. Being a decent lawyer, he had made a quick phone call to Mary and Bernard's *avvocato*, an old friend and colleague of his, and after a bracing chat on the peculiarities of foreigners, they'd made a date for lunch the following week. Fabrizio was at *La Piccola Valle della Tristezza* purely on a social call, having driven all these kilometres from Perugia to drop in casually on the sisters, intending to say he happened to be passing through on his way to Lake Tresimeno. Since the tiny *villaggio* was completely out of the way not just for Lake Tresimeno but for absolutely anywhere the story was thin, but Fabrizio, after the turmoil of the past fortnight, could not think clearly. It had been harder than he had anticipated, giving up the cat.

'Well, shall we go?' Henrietta demanded. 'The boundary in question is just outside the door, in that small patch separating my house from Bernard's.'

This mention of his name by his beloved so gratified Bernard that he threw caution to the wind and stared long and meaningfully at Henrietta. She was wearing a short white leather skirt with luminous white tights, a high-necked jumper, and a white raincoat casually thrown over her shoulders. Her hair, damp from the December drizzle, curled gloriously over her shoulders.

'It's my house too,' Mary said petulantly. 'Not just his.'

They all trooped out of the back door and into the field in question. Fabrizio tried to walk near Isabel but with Mary on one side of him and Henrietta on the other, he didn't have a chance.

The dog, slumbering in the hay barn which was now also a cow shed, Bernard having moved his half dozen prize head of cattle there for the winter, discovered them when they reached the crab-apple trees and tore frenetically around and around the little party, barking merrily. Krissy, who usually loved the dog, decided this time to take offence and started howling. Henrietta, out of character, concerned more with her trees than her daughter at this moment, unceremoniously handed the child over to Bernard, who had sidled his way next to his adored one. Krissy, recognizing a friend, immediately stopped crying.

'Why, look at her, she likes you,' Henrietta said with some surprise. She herself neither liked nor disliked Bernard; she was merely indifferent to him.

Hugo, having seen all this activity from his own kitchen window, was consumed by curiosity and said to Carl, busy perfecting his Italian with the help of tapes and books, 'Look, they're all going out into the field. How strange. And the Italian who drove up in that rather gorgeous Ferrari is with them. I'm going outside. Coming?'

Carl reluctantly agreed and he and Hugo joined the group. Isabel, seeing him, explained what was happening.

'That row of crab-apple trees is the boundary between our property and Bernard and Mary's. The trouble started a couple of months ago, when the trees were laden with apples ready to be harvested. Both Henrietta and Mary decided simultaneously to make crab-apple jelly, of all things. Well, you know how competitive those two have become lately, or perhaps you haven't noticed. They nearly came to serious blows over that scrawny walnut tree between the two houses, each trying to outdo the other in gathering more of the wretched nuts to pickle for Christmas. Can you imagine such silliness? Anyhow, each has decided the apple trees belong solely to her. They've now gone completely OTT and involved their lawyers in the dispute.'

Hugo, who had been listening to this little tale with glee, being a firm believer that a spot of neighbourly acrimony was a great reliever of tedium, suddenly spotted Bernard on the other side of the trees and rushed off after him, leaving Carl to cluck sympathetically as Isabel continued, 'It's ridiculous, and I've told Henrietta, but she seems as stubborn as that other foolish woman over it all.'

Bernard hardly noticed Hugo at his side, for he was too busy cooing at the baby in rapture, feeling he was holding a bit of Henrietta in his arms as he cradled her precious black-haired Indian daughter.

'Oh, what a lovely baby! Lovely, lovely baby,' cried Hugo, his angel hair frizzing in the rain, which was now coming down harder. He detested babies, but rather liked the idea of getting closer to Bernard, maybe getting in some eye contact as they crooned over the dribbling infant. In the few weeks they had been living at *La Piccola Valle*, Hugo had been frustrated by his inability to get near Bernard, who always seemed to be doing dynamic, macho things with his tractor. When Bernard wasn't working, and actually in his house, that silly wife of his was always around, fussing over him, trying to mother him and feed him up with Cornish pasties and sponge cakes. As Hugo began popping over on some pretext or other, Mary tried to mother him as well. The trouble was, he had to eat her frighteningly awful food; if he tried to refuse, a definite coldness descended upon the Aga-roasted kitchen. And if he were denied access to Mary's kitchen, he'd hardly ever have a chance to talk to her husband.

Bernard, watching Hugo babbling inanities to the baby, was so indignant he almost dropped her. He was sure Hugo was doing this to snake his way into Henrietta's heart, knowing how she doted on the little bundle. That he was doing the very same thing himself never entered his mind. Fixing a stern look upon Hugo, he tucked Krissy protectively under his jacket, as the rain was becoming tediously persistent.

Meanwhile, at the boundary, a row had broken out.

'What do you mean, the trees belong to both of us?' Henrietta was saying to a disconcerted and by now rather wet Fabrizio.

Mary cried, 'You're just saying that because you work for Henrietta. Wait until I telephone *my* lawyer.'

'*Signora*, I have already talked to him. We have discussed your property and consulted the maps. The trees are right on the boundary line; to be precise, the line runs right down between the trees.'

Henrietta said coldly, 'I thought you were supposed to represent me?'

'*Signora*,' Fabrizio said formally, granting her the respect of the title because of the baby though he knew she was unmarried, and standing there in the rain, cheeks red with indignation, she looked no older than twenty. '*Signora*,' he repeated, somewhat pompously, 'I represent justice and truth.'

Isabel, having had enough of this silly wrangling between the two women, cheered. 'Well said, Fabrizio.'

He looked at her. Her hair, also wet, was plastered against her scalp, emphasizing her high cheekbones and wide eyes. Interesting, Fabrizio thought, how well these Englishwomen look in the rain, as if it is their natural habitat. Which he supposed it was. Then he glanced at Mary and decided that it was always a mistake to generalize.

'Let's all go to our place for coffee or a drink – or both, why not?' Hugo cried gaily.

'What a good idea,' Isabel agreed. 'We can celebrate the end of this ridiculous dispute.'

'Thank you. It is a most gracious invitation,' Fabrizio said gratefully, thinking he had met a sensible Englishman at last. He took Isabel's arm, and she smiled sweetly at him. He decided with satisfaction that she was well worth giving up the cat for.

Henrietta sulkily refused, but Bernard had not relinquished the baby and was trotting with the others into the house so she had no choice but to follow. The dog, feeling included for once, tried to go in too but had the door slammed in his face. He barked for a bit then gave up and curled up in the back porch of Henrietta's house, where Isabel had made a bed for him out of an old crate and some ancient feather pillows.

Hugo went to the kitchen to grind the coffee, stopping first to chuck the baby under the chin because it gave him an excuse to brush against Bernard's arm. Bernard, outraged at these tactics which he assumed were for Hugo to manoeuvre himself into Henrietta's good graces, glared at him for the second time that afternoon. Hugo, misinterpreting contempt for love, was rapturous.

Carl graciously offered his visitors an *aperitivo*, and very soon both clothes and tempers were put right in the warmth and beauty of the house, which Carl had lovingly furnished with a combination of his own collection of antiques from home and elegant modern furniture in the best of Italian taste. The combination worked amazingly well and Fabrizio thoroughly approved. He talked with Carl at great length on the strategic placement of overhead lighting and lamps to read by, and of interior design in general. He approved of Carl, whom he thought had a certain sense of style. For an Englishman at any rate. A bottle of Campari was generously produced, and several bottles of soda, all of which went down surprisingly quickly.

While the others talked, Bernard clung tenaciously to the baby, knowing instinctively that this would draw Henrietta to him. Hugo loitered around Bernard, who thought he was hovering around Henrietta, who of course did not budge from her baby's side. As the redness of the Campari disappeared, to reappear as pink flushes on the faces of all present, Bernard began imagining what it would have been like to have conceived Krissy, and forbidden scenes scurried into his mind of naked limbs and long golden hair and bare ripe breasts and suchlike. Hugo, catching the lascivious look on his face, was content, thinking it only a matter of time before he would have the farmer in his bed.

Mary meanwhile was confiding in Isabel. Her Campari and soda had softened her like a meringue gone wrong; she felt all gooey on the inside.

'Don't get me wrong, Bernie is wonderful, wonderful, but he just doesn't talk to me . . . well, he does, but it's about silage wrap and drenching the sheep. And the Italians, well, you know what they're like. They speak Italian, don't they, so how can you talk to them? I mean, when I try to speak to Bernie about important things, like the boys' schooling or whether we should listen to our English dentist, who said John didn't need braces on his teeth, or to our Italian one in Perugia, who says he does – when I try to discuss these things, Bernard hardly answers, just gets stuck into his *Farmers' Weekly* which he has sent out from England, and grunts.'

Isabel, who had heard a similar monologue only the night before from her eldest daughter, who had married a computer freak at a very early age and was now saddled with four obstreperous children and a husband who read computer magazines during intercourse to prevent premature ejaculation, suddenly felt weary. She had let her daughter, who was really quite happily married but needed a moan more often than most, ramble on across the telephone wires through the Channel and across Europe; she had listened with motherly patience, but somehow felt disinclined to hear it all again from Mary.

'Won't your mother be coming over shortly?' she said hopefully when her neighbour took a breath between whines. 'I'm sure you'll be able to talk to her about these things.'

It was the right thing to say: Mary suddenly went silent. 'Oh, Mother,' she finally said after a few moments. 'Yes, well, she and I have been very close since my father died four years ago.' She sounded doleful about this, but Isabel couldn't decide whether it was because of her father's death or because of the new-found closeness to her mother. She rather suspected the latter.

Carl came around again with the Campari. Isabel accepted another drink gratefully; Mary, after protesting for a full three minutes that she couldn't possibly drink another thing and that she had to go home and start supper because the boys were due home from school any minute now, did the same.

'You're much more sympathetic than my mother,' she said

after she had gulped a little of her drink, making a noise not unlike the dog slurping Krissy's leftover milk which Henrietta always put outside for him. 'Mother always tells me to pull myself together.'

'Yes, well,' murmured Isabel.

Fabrizio, also on his second Campari and soda, came up to the two women who were sitting on a red velvet Victorian settee and said smoothly, 'May I sit at the feet of you lovely ladies?' then promptly fell over Isabel's foot and landed on her ankle, twisting it at a terrifying angle behind her and causing total confusion not to mention the end of the party.

Later, much later, coming home from the hospital, Fabrizio apologized profusely, both in English and in Italian. '*Che peccato, che sfortuna! Che casino. Chissà che spavento!*'

'Yes, yes, Fabrizio, you've already said all this. Really it's not so dreadful as all that.'

'*Mi dispiace tanto. Non ho parole . . .*'

'That's not strictly true, Fabrizio. You're not speechless, far from it.'

'Isabel, I am so sorry to have done this to you. I have the two left legs –'

'Left feet.'

'Left feet. I am awkward and gosh.'

'I think you mean gauche,' she said mildly.

'*Per favore*, how can I make amends? What can I do?'

Isabel, wincing a bit as he overtook a Honda on the brow of a hill while looking mournfully at her, said, 'Well, you could start by keeping your eyes on the road. And maybe slowing down a bit.'

'I must take you to dinner. Yes, I must, at once. You must be ravished.'

'Ravenous.'

'Yes. Near here there is a small restaurant with a superb menu. We will stop.'

Isabel, suddenly hungry after the hours spent at the hospital, having her ankle, which was rather badly sprained, X-rayed and bandaged, decided, why not? It was Henrietta's turn to cook that night, and the meal would be comprised of wondrous treats from the local shops. Pleasant enough on ordinary days but tonight Isabel felt like being spoiled. And besides, Mary had said she would call in on their return from the hospital, bringing some homemade bacon flans. Isabel was afraid she would be too much of a captive audience in her present condition.

'All right,' she said, 'but I must phone Henrietta first.'

Fabrizio wanted to carry Isabel into the restaurant, but she told him not to be so silly; she was quite able to hobble on his arm, with the help of the crutch the hospital had lent her. They were in a tiny village on the edge of Lake Tresimeno, seated at a table overlooking the water. It was dark by now, but the lake sparkled with the reflection of a skyful of stars and a gaudy full moon. The restaurant was empty except for an Italian couple in the corner, holding hands and smouldering at each other in a way that should have made the fire blaze with envy. Isabel wondered if the couple had been planted there solely for the benefit of English tourists, they were so quintessentially Italian, all those well-groomed good looks. It made her feel slightly frumpy, and she wished she had run a brush through her hair before leaving the hospital.

The staff, which comprised the owner and his wife at this late time of the year, clucked and cackled over Isabel's foot and brought a footstool for it to rest upon. The owner/chef, who looked uncannily like a cadaver with prominent bones, cheeks that seemed suspiciously red as if dabbed with blusher and unnaturally slicked black hair, served them *spaghetti alla marinara*, spaghetti with mussels, garlic, olive oil and parsley, which was so delicious that Isabel, after a few mouthfuls, forgot that she had compared his face to a death mask and pronounced him a cherub.

'You are having some colour returning to your face now,' Fabrizio said after the first course was cleared away. 'You were looking very pallid.' He reached for her hand across the table and knocked over the candle.

The owner's wife, called upon to clear up the breakage as the candle holder, made of glass, shattered into a thousand pieces on the stone floor, grew chatty when her task was finished and she had lit another candle. She wanted to know all about Isabel's sprained ankle, and told them about her own broken elbow of three years previously. By the time she left the second course had arrived: *l'abbacchio*, roast suckling lamb.

They ate and ate, and between them drank a bottle of a very good Tresimeno wine, then finished with coffee and a *limoncello*, a refreshing bitter-sweet beverage which cleansed the palate and muddied the head simultaneously. The *limoncello* came with the compliments of the owner, and they drank fulsomely to him and to his wife.

'This is complete degeneracy,' Isabel said happily. 'One way or another we've been drinking all day. Well, I have,' she added, remembering to be sensible. 'You're driving, I hope you've not had too much?'

'Trust me,' Fabrizio said, and smiled benignly at her.

They stared fondly at one other, Isabel thinking how like her son he seemed. Only older, of course. The son had just split up with his live-in lover of five years, a nice young woman of whom Isabel had been fond. He had phoned his mother last week to tell her all about it and analyze what went wrong.

Fabrizio was doing something like that now, telling her about the wife who had just left him.

'You don't seem terribly upset by it,' Isabel said, somewhat waspishly. She wondered why everyone confided in her, and thought in distress that perhaps she was becoming matronly, a grandmother type. Therefore she was genuinely bewildered when Fabrizio said, passionately, as befits an Italian in his prime who has just had a splendid dinner, 'I'm not upset, Isabel. In fact I'm relieved, now that I've met you.'

She wouldn't have understood what he was implying except that he managed to grab her hand across the table without knocking anything over.

'Oh, no,' she said, realization dawning. Then giggled.

Fabrizio was, as any Italian, or even Englishman, would be in those circumstances, crushed.

'You're laughing at me,' he said petulantly.

'No, of course I'm not, Fabrizio,' Isabel said, laughing even more. 'Well, maybe I am, but—'

'I have told you I love you and you are laughing at me,' he said darkly.

Isabel thought they were beginning to look rather like the Italian couple in the corner, who were still burning hotly at each other. The thought didn't displease her: anyone who would leave her husband at the age of forty-seven, and then in the next five years go back to university, travel to India to help her sister adopt a baby, and live in Italy on her own, was bound to have a touch of the romantic about her.

But she had a practical streak as well.

'Fabrizio, you haven't said you love me. And you couldn't possibly, anyway. You hardly know me. Besides, I'm old enough to be your mother.' This was of course an exaggeration, but she was feeling frowzy and ancient suddenly, and Fabrizio looked no older than thirty in the candlelight. These days Isabel was feeling like everybody's mother. Nonetheless she hoped Fabrizio would deny it.

He did more than that; he was outraged. Dropping her hand and summoning the owner's wife imperiously to order another coffee, he said grandly, 'I am forty-three. And you are only fifty-two.' He beamed at her, with the smug look of a man who is once again proved right.

'How did you know that?' she asked curiously.

'I was there, remember, at the hospital with you, when you

were filling in the forms. So don't give me any of this age shit.'
And Fabrizio looked smug again. He was rather proud of his
command of what he considered vernacular English.

Isabel, what with her children and Mary and Henrietta and
just about everyone else lately treating her like some wise old
woman, short of teeth but crammed with motherly wisdom,
rather liked hearing that fifty-two was young. She listened
attentively as he said he loved her cheekbones and the way she
spoke Italian with that ever so slight English accent; he said he
loved her bouncy breasts under the fuzzy red angora jumper
she was wearing; that he loved the way her black wool skirt
curled under the firm warm curves of her buttocks. Isabel, not
having made love with a man for quite some time now, was
starting to feel quite raunchy until he started on about violets.
Then she got sleepy and yawned.

'I'm sorry, Fabrizio, but I need to go home now. My ankle's
starting to hurt a bit and I'm tired. It's been an eventful day.'
She looked regretfully at him, thinking she quite liked him,
that he was certainly attractive, but thinking also how complicated man/woman relationships were when all she wanted
now was a simple life. At least until her ankle stopped hurting
her so much.

The simple life had, until now, eluded her. At university, in
her last year, she had become involved with one of her
lecturers who had just left his wife; with him she'd discovered
the blessings of sexual and mental stimulation, neither of
which she had enjoyed in her marriage.

Her husband, on the contrary, had had both. The mental
stimulation he'd said he derived from the many Adult
Education courses he took during the course of their marriage.
Over the years he became expert in the mysteries of both
dowsing and car repairing; learned Tai Chi and the basics of
Russian; studied philosophy and ballroom dancing with equal
enthusiasm. He was a gregarious man and relished the
camaraderie of the classroom, which was also a rich source of

dissatisfied housewives ready to fall in love or, better, into sex.

He'd been shocked when Isabel left him.

'But we've been so happy!' he cried wildly. 'I need you.'

'I've not been particularly happy,' she said bluntly. 'I have a dull job which I dislike but I'm not qualified to do anything else. I'm bored with cooking and cleaning and sitting home every night while you go to your classes. I have things I want to do with my life.'

'But the children, Isabel. Think of the children.'

She snorted. 'The children are twenty-seven, twenty-five and twenty-four,' she said as patiently as she could. 'If some of them still choose to live at home, that's their problem.'

With that she left. She had taken twenty-eight years to make up her mind.

Back in Fabrizio's comfortable car she leaned against the plush fabric of the seat, feeling sensual in spite of herself.

'*Sei bella al lume di candela*,' he murmured, putting his hand on her knee as he pulled into the road, narrowly missing a car pulling into the restaurant.

Isabel said, with a nervous laugh, 'We're not in the candle-light now, Fabrizio, so how can I look beautiful in it?'

'I am remembering you in candlelight. And seeing that you are even more beautiful here in the car with me, close to me . . . oh, so close!' He rubbed her knee gently.

'I think you'd better remember that you're driving.' Isabel forced herself to be practical, but was not unmoved by his hand slowly caressing her thigh just above the knee.

Her lecturer at university had touched her that way too, and she had thought she loved him. But the week before her finals he decided to return to his wife, and even though she got a decent second, she never forgave him for his timing. She should have had a first.

She had decided then, coldly and calculatingly, that it just wasn't worth it. You invested too much of yourself: a bit of body, a lot of soul, most of your heart, for returns which were minimal: a bit of sexual gratification, some brief emotional coupling, and then the pain and the loss, sneaking up behind you like some hungry animal ready to sink its teeth into your fat smugness. And the plumper and glossier you were with love and sated lust and emotional contentment, the more you tempted the beast, and left yourself vulnerable and open.

With these rather heavy thoughts, Isabel sighed to herself, regretfully removing Fabrizio's hand which was wandering like a lost soul in purgatory over her thigh. She felt stirrings in the pit of her pelvis and almost took the hand back, but at that moment he overtook a lorry and only narrowly escaped being struck by an oncoming car as he manoeuvred back into the right lane.

'It is good I had my two hands on the wheel,' he said jocularly.

Isabel, still scared out of her wits by the near miss, agreed. She took it as an omen.

Chapter Six

Christmas Eve. In the village of Modena, not far from Lake Tresimeno, peace reigns, and the tiny stone church in the village square is jammed with revellers merrily singing hymns with considerable energy, fuelled by the goodies they have consumed at their traditional Christmas Eve feast. The air inside the church is tepid, smelling of pine and incense and damp stone mixed with alcoholic fumes reminiscent of a crowded wine bar.

Fabrizio is amongst them, but his singing is weak, unenthusiastic. He is already beginning to regret the impulse that has brought him here, to this tiny village miles from his home. His Christmas has fallen apart; his wife is with her mother, whose loathing for her son-in-law is matched in intensity by his loathing for her; his own family, his mother and father, are travelling in Spain; his twin sons, twenty-one in January (how could they possibly have got that old?) are both in Paris. Fabrizio's own friends are many and welcoming, but he knows Christmas is for families. Besides, his heart is here, in this ordinary village extraordinarily lit by Christmas candles in windows, a cold moon shining through the frosty air, and starlight.

In the church Fabrizio sings, but half-heartedly. He is here because he thought, at home in the house vacated forever by his wife (though she is, of course, claiming her share of it, which is far more than it is worth), that if he went to Midnight Mass in Modena, this village only a couple of kilometres from the *villaggio* where all those strange English people lived, he could legitimately say to Isabel, 'Ah, *buonasera*, I happened to be just passing through . . .'

It sounded like a stroke of genius at the time, but here, in this church filled with families all replete with their festive Christmas Eve supper, he is not so sure. Doubts rain over him, like the needles of the tree on the altar, sprinkling the polished wooden floor.

Mass is over; he walks out of the church, a lone solitary figure amongst laughing jolly families. The air outside is cold, the stars glint malevolently. Or so it seems to Fabrizio. He will go home to Perugia; he will not trouble Isabel and her sister Henrietta. He is a proud and sensitive man and he knows Christmas is for families. He is not one to intrude.

Squaring his shoulders, taking a deep breath, he walks to his car, parked at the far end of the village by the local trattoria. He is lonely, but the decision has been made. Better a solitary Christmas than the pitying hospitality of strangers.

'Why, Fabrizio, whatever are you doing here at this hour? And on Christmas Eve?' Henrietta, in a splendid white wool kaftan, opened the door of her house.

'Ah . . . um . . . *buona sera*. I . . . uh . . . just happened to be passing by after Midnight Mass. I saw all the lights on, and thought I would wish you a happy Christmas. I don't want to disturb you but as it is the jolly season, I thought perhaps I would call in and wish you jolliness. Ha, ha. As you English say.'

Henrietta let him ramble on in this vein for several minutes until luckily Isabel, still dressed in a pair of jeans and a black turtle-necked jumper, rescued him and brought him inside. The dog, recognizing him, barked happily and jumped up frenziedly at him, snagging his exquisite burgundy lambswool jumper and clawing his new perfectly tailored trousers.

'Dog, sit down,' Isabel shouted.

'I told you we shouldn't have brought him inside,' Henrietta said.

'It's Christmas, the poor unwanted animal is desperate for company. No one else will have him. Fabrizio, would you like some coffee or wine?'

'Ah, you are kind. I have happened to bring a bottle of champagne, perhaps I should get it from the car?'

The sisters thought this a fine idea. They had only just finished decorating the house for Christmas; it gleamed and glittered and shone with sparkle and lights and baubles and mistletoe.

'Aren't we being slightly extravagant?' Isabel had remarked casually after they had strung the fourth set of lights on the enormous Christmas tree which took up most of the living room.

'It's Krissy's first Christmas. I want it to be memorable.'

'She's barely five months old.'

Henrietta didn't care; she was euphoric. It was her daughter's first Christmas and she was determined it was going to be special.

They had just finished decorating the house and were about to settle down with a bottle of wine when Fabrizio's desultory knock was heard on the door. Isabel, already fed up with Christmas, having had phone calls all evening from her children complaining of her absence along with the inadequacies of their current partner/best friend/own father, was pleased to see the visitor. Her children had rattled her; they had seemed to accuse her of abandoning them (though they were all spending the holiday with her ex-husband); yet when she had suggested they come to her in Italy, even offering to pay their fares, they were loath to leave their many and assorted friends. She had been incredibly relieved somehow, and wondered if she was an unnatural mother.

Next door the lights were on in Mary and Bernard's house; Mary was making Horlicks for Bernard and for herself, and pouring a Scotch for her mother Claudia. She had only arrived that afternoon and claimed to be suffering from jet lag, though she had only flown from London to Pisa. She thought perhaps a large Scotch would relieve it.

Bernard, hearing the dog barking, went to the window and saw Fabrizio go to his car, chased by the dog who was yapping in a staccato manner at Fabrizio's soft leather shoes, thinking it all great fun. Bernard saw the Italian open the car, get the champagne, and kick the dog gently as he returned to the house.

There was a moon that night, and by its light Bernard could see the sensual expectation in Fabrizio's face as he raced up the path, bottle in hand, dog at his heels. He saw the door open and Henrietta, resplendent in her white kaftan, greet Fabrizio merrily, take the bottle from his hands and usher him in.

The door shut, on Fabrizio and Henrietta, and on Bernard's hopes. He could cope with Hugo: those emerald eyes glinting at Henrietta, that handsome face burning with passion for his beloved. But only because Hugo was, well, normal for heaven's sake, he was British, one felt one knew where one stood with him. But an Italian? They weren't on, they weren't cricket. Bernard, aware of his own inadequacies, knew he had met his match.

Sadly, he shut the curtains and returned to the kitchen to join Mary and Claudia.

'Your hot drink will be ready in a minute, Bernie,' his wife sang out.

Bernard took his place at the kitchen table. 'I think, since it's Christmas and all that, I'll join your mother in a whisky.'

The two women looked at him. Mary, about to protest that

he always had a Horlicks before bed, decided that maybe Bernard was right; after all it was Christmas and maybe she, too, should celebrate with something just a wee bit stronger.

Claudia, watching her daughter pour herself a Campari and soda, for which Mary had acquired a taste during that strange afternoon six weeks ago at Carl's house, and her stolid son-in-law gulping Scotch as if it were his first taste of water in a desert, raised her glass in a toast to the two young people. Maybe after all Italy was influencing them in a positive manner. The thought slightly dissipated some of the gloom she was feeling about spending Christmas in her daughter's household.

'Who is the father of that woman's child?' Claudia said to Mary in a loud whisper. Christmas dinner, cooked in the traditional English way with plenty of sprouts, thick Bisto gravy, and the martyrdom of the cook slaving away while everyone else drank sherry and made merry, was in full swing in the dining room of Mary and Bernard's farmhouse. The Laura Ashley curtains, matching the Laura Ashley napkins and the Laura Ashley tablecloth, were open to the farmyard and the dog howling miserably, wanting to get in.

'Please, let him in, let him in!' cried Richard, John and David, who were seriously hyper with all the excitement.

'He's quite house trained,' Isabel said.

'He's become quite fat,' Carl remarked.

'That's because we all feed him,' Hugo said. 'He has three homes now.'

'Whose dog is it?' asked Fabrizio.

'No one's. It was here when we moved.'

'Abandoned?' Claudia said indignantly. A true English-woman, she loved animals, and was far more concerned for their welfare than she was for human beings'.

The dog was let in, and locked in the kitchen after trying

to leap up on the table to investigate the turkey. He was given a laden plate and told by Mary to behave himself.

'You were asking about the father of my child,' Henrietta said sweetly when all the fuss had died down. 'He was a revolutionary activist, some would say anarchist, in India before he was gunned down.'

Mary, dispensing crackers, regretted she had not had time to fill her mother in on all the vagaries of the residents of the Little Valley of Sorrow before they arrived for Christmas dinner. She had almost, before hitting the Harvey's Bristol Cream in the kitchen, regretted inviting all the expatriates for this important meal, but now, seeing her mother seated next to Carl, pulling a cracker with him, she felt it was all worth it.

Fabrizio, in some confusion over the crackers, the sweet sherry he had been forced to drink, and the strange suet stuffing nestling beside the mound of roast potatoes on his plate, smiled in bewilderment at Henrietta who promptly put a paper hat on his head. Bernard, watching, poured himself more wine. He had been devasted when she, ravishing in a white wool dress with pearl buttons down the front, had rushed into their house a few hours ago and asked if Fabrizio could join them for Christmas dinner.

'He's lonely, he's just split up from his wife. We couldn't send him away last night to an empty flat so he stayed on our sofa. I haven't the heart to tell him to go home now, on Christmas Day.'

Mary, in the middle of doing important things to the Christmas pudding, said fine, fine. Bernard said not a word, but his heart was smitten. Claudia, eyeing Henrietta with her long golden hair and the top button working loose on the low-cut wool dress, poured herself another whisky.

Now, not only had the top button come totally undone, the second and third were also sliding precariously out of their moorings. Bernard, sitting opposite, watched, fascinated. The dinner was almost over; the remains of the Christmas pud lay washed up on the table like seaweed on a beach.

'Shall we go into the other room?' Mary said gaily, cheeks flushed with success. Everyone, even Henrietta, had said what a delicious meal it was. Mary, luckily, hadn't noticed Isabel delicately pinching her sister's elbow when the compliments were being dispersed.

The company left the table and reassembled in the sitting room, prettily furnished with plump country armchairs in floral covers. Carl gallantly let himself be steered by Mary next to her mother on the blue sofa with its swirls of daisies and other flowers. He felt mellow this Christmas Day; it was after all the first time he had celebrated the occasion openly, in straight company, with Hugo. He felt a rush of warmth towards Mary who had invited them over just like any other normal couple, and this good will spilled over on to her mother. Determined to be charming and make the widowed mother's Christmas as happy as his own, he turned to Claudia with a charming smile.

She was a little woman and he had to look down on her, even from a seated position. Her feet, trimly shod in black patent high heels and sheer nylons, hardly reached the floor, but what she lacked in height she made up for in width. It was not that she was an obese woman; she had, in fact, quite slim legs and hips, but her shoulders and chest were massive, like the figurehead of a ship. When she walked, teetering on the black high heels, she looked like a Bantam hen: small, chirpy, and top-heavy. Her face was not dissimilar either; her mouth was sharp and pointy like a beak and her eyes small and beady. Her hair, dyed now for many years, was a farmyard shade of brown and auburn and stood up in the front rather like a cock's comb. Despite all this she was not unattractive; her teeth were good and her chin firm and unlined.

'How long are you staying in Italy?' he asked.

'Oh, about a month. Poor Mary could do with some help with the children – they seem to be becoming quite unruly. Then I must return. Business, you know. My late husband had his fingers in so many pies,' she added mysteriously.

The conversation, stilted after so much wine and food, dwindled throughout the flowery sitting room until someone suggested a walk. This was seized on by all as a brilliant idea to fill in the gap between dinner and returning back to their respective houses at a polite civil time.

The day was clear, windless, perfect. Claudia was kitted out with a pair of Mary's wellies, and Henrietta, much to Bernard's sorrow, covered up the flimsy lace on her partially exposed white bra with a thick heavy white jumper. Fabrizio too was lent boots, because it was decided the party would go off the road and into the woods at the bottom of one of the fields. Henrietta fetched her backpack for Krissy which Bernard insisted on wearing, knowing it would force her to walk by his side.

They started off jauntily enough, walking first down the dirt track with the tall cypresses. Then they branched off across a grassy field, the dog racing around and around them in a great all-embracing circle.

'How's your foot?' Fabrizio asked Isabel solicitously.

'Oh, just about better now, thank you.'

'It was all my fault. Such clumsiness – how can I ever forgive myself?'

Isabel, having heard this countless times in the last few weeks, didn't think it required an answer. Fabrizio had been a frequent, if uninvited, visitor at the house, bringing her flowers, books, compact discs and chocolates to wile away her time as an invalid. He insisted on taking her on little day trips while her foot was healing. They went to Citta di Castello and to Gubbio, Isabel hobbling on her stick through narrow cobbled streets, Fabrizio insisting they rest often in sweet little restaurants where he treated her to lavish lunches.

He took her to his house in Perugia, cooking her seafood pasta in his modest but tasteful home behind the old city walls.

'Why won't you?' he had said, after they had finished the meal and a bottle of wine and were sitting on his long, low, black leather sofa. His hand was under her grey cardigan which she had worn buttoned up to the neck; it was now partially unbuttoned, revealing a sensible cotton bra, not a scrap of lace in sight.

'I love you,' he had whispered, insinuating his hand under the bra and gently massaging the large pink-beige nipples.

'But I don't love you, Fabrizio,' Isabel murmured, enjoying it all immensely.

'That's all right. I can cope. You'll love me soon enough.'

The bra somehow came off and then Fabrizio's tongue was wrapping itself sensuously around her left nipple while his hand was doing something excruciatingly delightful under her skirt.

'May I?' he whispered humbly into her ear.

She suddenly didn't see why in the world not, but before she could say so, she was assaulted by a torrent of words in Italian. Confused, because it was a woman's voice, Isabel sat up quickly.

'Oh, shit,' Fabrizio said in English. 'It's my wife.'

'Whatever did you say to her?' Henrietta asked later, laughing her head off at the story.

'I didn't say anything, she did all the talking. She claims she's going to have Fabrizio for adultery now, and so get the whole house or more money or something. Italian law defeats me, I couldn't understand the legal wrangling.'

'And will she?'

'Fabrizio thinks not. She's been having a romp herself here and there and doesn't really want the house. She apparently has money and a flat of her own. But there'll be a messy legal battle.'

Henrietta laughed and laughed. 'The Italians love battling over love and sex and intrigues,' she said smugly, glad she was a mother and no longer interested in such sordid things.

Fabrizio, at Isabel's side now as they walked through the woods, had not had another chance to get her into his bed, mainly because she'd made sure such chances never arose. Much as she would have enjoyed the sex, she had acquired, along with her degree, the knowledge that sex, whatever anyone said, was often laced with emotion, which caused loss of tranquillity. She saw Fabrizio, but kept him at bay.

'You were so cruel to me last night, making me sleep on the sofa,' he complained. 'I lay awake all night imagining myself in your bed.'

'That's not true. I went downstairs to get a drink of water at four and you were sound asleep. I put the blanket back over you, it had fallen off.'

Fabrizio was both touched by this evidence of her affection, and annoyed with himself at being asleep and so once again missing his chance. Before he could say anything, however, they had joined the others at the edge of the woods looking out over some scrubby neglected fields.

'This is all for sale,' Bernard was saying, 'the woods and all those fields. I wanted to rent them, but our lawyer, who's been making inquiries for us, said the owner is holding out for a sale. It's terribly overpriced; the land isn't that great, but I could drain the fields and grass them over. Seems a waste, somehow.'

This was such a long speech for him that the others were quite overwhelmed and didn't know what to say. Finally Claudia asked, 'Why are they so expensive?'

'I don't know.'

'The owner's probably wishing for a developer to buy,' Fabrizio said. 'With all the English coming over, they'll want amenities.'

'God forbid!' Henrietta exclaimed. 'This is the countryside. We don't want golf courses on every hillside and sports complexes on every other field. We could have stayed in England for that.'

Everyone agreed except Claudia, who said rather scathingly, 'I should say a golf course would be the best thing ever to happen to this village. There certainly seems nothing else to do. And those fields look pretty useless to me.'

Bernard, horrified, tried to protest. He had been coveting the fields since he had moved to Umbria, dreaming, when he wasn't dreaming of his beautiful neighbour, of how he would convert them to grassy meadows which would feed the cows he longed to buy. There was no way he could expand his prize herd without more land.

'I wish I could afford to buy them,' he sighed. 'They're perfect for what I want.'

Claudia looked up at him, which hurt her neck because, in her borrowed wellingtons, she barely came up to his navel.

'You have no sense of vision,' she said scornfully.

Bernard, who spent his days and nights envisaging those fields at the edge of the woods grassed and cultivated and boundaried by wild flowers, and he and Henrietta making love in then all day while his precious cows grazed companionably alongside, thought this rather unfair, but felt he couldn't say anything. Luckily Krissy, who had been asleep in the backpack, suddenly awoke and began to cry raucously. Everyone spoke at once about how quickly the afternoon had gone and now suddenly it was beginning to get dark and they must get back.

Bernard, the last to leave the damp overgrown field, looked at it wistfully, as at something he desired but would never have. In much the same way as he often looked at Henrietta.

'What a lovely Christmas!'
'Thank you so much, Mary.'

'Nice to have met you, Claudia.'

'Delicious meal, Mary.'

'Super day.'

'Mary, Bernard, many thanks, a splendid Christmas.'

'*Molte grazie*, Mary. *Arrivederci*.'

'Oh, I've never had my hand kissed before!'

The neighbours took their leave of Bernard and Mary and Claudia and wandered back to their respective houses. The air was full of cheer and good will and bonhomie as everyone kissed each other and swore it was the best Christmas they had had in years.

'God, Isabel, why did we stay so long? Oh, how Mary irritates me. She stuffs Bernard like a goose and tries to do the same to everyone else.'

'Now don't bitch, Henrietta.'

'Why not?'

'Because it's Christmas. And they're neighbours. And you've just eaten a huge dinner.'

'I shall have indigestion for hours.'

Fabrizio, listening to all this, said, 'You do not like each other? But you are all English.'

This made everyone laugh, and Henrietta stopped bitching except to say darkly, 'If Bernard looks at me with that mooning look in his eyes one more time, I shall have to take matters in hand.'

Bernard's eyes were currently fixed vacantly on the ceiling. His sons had finally collapsed into bed and his mother-in-law was sitting delivering a monologue on something or other in the chair next to him. Bernard was sick at heart from seeing his beautiful Henrietta surrounded by lusty admirers: an angelic-looking poet and a dark Italian. What hope did he, a poor (so to speak) English farmer, have? He sighed.

'And the dress that woman was wearing . . . the

outrageously sexy little white wool number, pretending to be so simple. That was a Max Mara if ever I saw one, and we all know what *that* costs.'

Claudia's words jolted Bernard to attention. 'Oh, you mean Henrietta?'

Claudia nodded. 'Your dear departed father-in-law had some money in fashion once, and I learned a thing or two about it. That dress was a designer item for sure.'

Mary entered the room, carrying the Horlicks. She felt slightly headachey and had decided everyone had had enough dissipation for one day.

'She used to be a dress designer, apparently,' Mary said as she handed around the white milky drinks.

Both Claudia and Bernard looked at their flowery mugs with loathing, but were too worn out to make a stand.

'She always wears white,' Mary went on, sipping her drink contentedly, feeling herself back in focus again after the blur of the afternoon. She wondered if her standards were beginning to slip under this Mediterranean influence, and felt vaguely troubled.

'Always wears white? Here in this god-forsaken place? Why?'

'An affectation, obviously,' Mary said uncharitably. 'She thinks a lot of herself, I'm sure. I can't see how her sister puts up with her.'

Mary thought fondly of Isabel, unwittingly comparing her with her own mother who had, in the twenty-four hours she had been in Italy, managed to find fault with everything. Mary thought of the six weeks ahead with gloom, until she remembered Carl.

'What did you think of Carl, Mummy?' she asked brightly. Mary, despite the sherry haze she had been in most of the day, had been aware of him talking busily to her mother.

'The civil servant?' Claudia frowned and her daughter held her breath. 'Seems a decent sort of chap. And I like a man who wears a suit to a luncheon party. There are so few about nowadays.'

Bernard wondered if his mother-in-law meant there were few suits, or few luncheon parties, but didn't think it interesting enough to ask. He lapsed back into his reverie, dreaming of Henrietta lying in the straw, nuzzled gently by his cherished calves who mooed in approval as he manfully pushed them aside and put his calloused fingers gently inside that lacy bra he had briefly glimpsed.

Mary closed her eyes and dreamed about her mother being taken off her hands for the next few weeks by a devoted Carl, who was obviously in need of a woman's company.

And Claudia? What does Claudia, eyes closed also, dream about in this dream house in Italy, in the Little Valley of Sorrow?

Claudia dreams too. She dreams she is drinking Scotch instead of this vile mucousy venom her wispy daughter has thrust upon her.

Claudia's dream, at least, will be realized. She is older; she knows dreaming accomplishes nothing unless accompanied by action.

She opens her eyes, gets up, and reaches for the whisky bottle.

Chapter Seven

'What? She wants me to *what*?'

'Take her mother, Claudia, out for the day. Bernard's too busy staring at his sheep or whatever he does and Mary says she's still a bit nervous on the Italian roads.'

'But why me? Why not Isabel or Henrietta?'

'Isabel's just started work for Fabrizio, Carl, remember? At his office in Perugia. And Henrietta has her hands full with the baby. Besides,' and here Hugo couldn't help smirking, 'Mary says her mother thinks you're a perfect gentleman. It's because you wear suits all the time.'

At this, Hugo guffawed. He had questioned Carl's decision to bring his many and varied suits from his civil service days in London; but Carl, not exactly parsimonious but anxious not to squander money unnecessarily, had insisted, saying it would be a shame for them to go to waste: he would wear them until they were completely worn out. Besides, he rather liked suits; unike most men, he found them comfortable. He also derived a certain pleasure from the contradiction of his staid outward persona (for his suits were never less than sombre) with the gay (in every sense of the word) man lurking inside.

'Well,' he said irritably, 'tell her I can't go. Tell her I'm ill or get vertigo on winding Umbrian roads. Tell her anything,

I don't care.' He looked at Hugo, suddenly suspicious. 'Why are you and Mary setting this up? Come clean, now.'

Hugo, who was setting it up to get Claudia and Mary out of the house so that he could catch Bernard on his own, said innocently, 'Mary, as you know, has taken to telling me her troubles occasionally, and her biggest headache right now is her mother. She needs a break.'

Carl, who was not stupid, said craftily, 'All right, dear boy, I shall take the dragon out once, just once, on a day trip. But only if you come along too.'

Hugo was prepared for this. 'Oh, Carl, I'd love an outing, but I thought it would be the perfect time to start on my new musical, the one I told you about. I've got such good idea, sort of Dante put to music. I'll do the libretto, of course, and it will be magnificently operatic, the book and lyrics sheer poetry—'

Carl was unimpressed, and interrupted this rapture to say gruffly, 'Well, one day isn't going to make much of a difference.'

'Yes, it will. You know how hard it is for me to get started on something and you do distract me, darling, I need to be completely alone for a day just to get going. I'll make it up to you when you come back, dearest.'

Hugo pursed his rather full lips and widened his glinting emerald eyes at Carl, who knew when he was defeated. 'All right, tell Mary I'll take her and her mother out tomorrow, to Perugia if she likes. Show her the old city and the cathedral. We can have lunch somewhere. Mary did have us over for Christmas dinner after all.'

Hugo, victorious, scampered across the yard and was rewarded by finding not only Mary and Claudia but Bernard in the kitchen, drinking tea and eating sponge cake.

'I've just been talking to Carl,' he said, accepting tea which was weak and tepid but which he drank manfully, so to speak. 'He suggested that perhaps you two lovely ladies would like a day trip tomorrow? Visit the sights of Perugia and have a spot of lunch at one of the local restaurants.'

Claudia, smoking a cigarette which she had taken up again, thinking she couldn't last the next few weeks without something to distract her, considered the suggestion. The thought of a day in a city sounded quite appealing; she had been here ten days and so far had seen the village, which seemed to consist of nothing more than the church, a few little shops which looked like houses, and a great many Italian country people. She had also seen quite a few fields and a nearby town which had even more Italian provincials. She was not exactly having a stimulating holiday.

'Tell Carl it sounds a good idea.'

'What fun!' Mary said. She felt she needed a day out, and was becoming rather fond of Hugo, who gossiped with her almost every day now in her kitchen about this and that and the neighbours next door and how plump Henrietta was becoming with all that rich Italian food she bought and how bossy she was as well. They speculated about which of the two sisters Fabrizio was going to bed with, Mary trying to look shocked when Hugo said both, probably. They nattered about how Krissy should be raised and how Henrietta wasn't doing it properly, and whether a chocolate sponge made with golden syrup rather than sugar was truly better, because it was more moist, or merely sickly. It was the kind of thing she used to talk about to her women friends back home, the kind of thing she had hoped to talk to Isabel about, but somehow it was Hugo who seemed to fill the cracks of loneliness with his Polyfilla prattle. Mary, having found a soulmate at last, didn't care who it was: Hugo talked English and, more importantly, understood it, letting her unleash the words that had been trapped inside her during these long months in Italy.

'You're going, of course, aren't you, Hugo?' she asked.

'No, I'm afraid not. Perhaps another time. I've just started a piece of writing, want to get on with it.'

Mary, though deeply disappointed, could not protest. Everyone knew a poet's art was sacred.

The next day, luckily, was clear and dry, and not very cold at all considering it was January. Hugo had got up early, wished Carl a pleasant day, and walked down to Modena, ostensibly to purchase goodies for the evening meal but really because he hoped to waylay Bernard, already out in the bottom field, on the way back.

In the village everyone was frisky because the winter's day was fine, the sun was out and, presumably, Hugo thought, because they were Italian and not prone to the sullen intro-spection of the English. Daniella, in the café which was also a bakery and cake shop, helped him choose pastries and flirted with him outrageously, even though she was well over sixty and enormous. She saw no reason why men should stop finding her attrac-tive, and indeed they didn't. The shop was always full of men who came to buy bread and stayed for an innuendo or two. It kept them all young, and merrier than they might have been otherwise when the winter days were gloomy with fog or rain.

Alberto the postman greeted Hugo heartily. 'Ah, you have some Christmas cards from England, and so do your neighbours. Take them now and pass them around.'

Alberto not only spoke in Italian but in the dialect of the area, and Hugo could not make it out. Daniella repeated it in loud slow Italian, and still Hugo, no linguist, was perplexed. Great hilarity ensued as Daniella and Alberto mimed the whole thing as if it were all a game of charades, and between the two of them managed to make him understand. He took the letters for *La Piccolo Valle della Tristezza*, not sure whether it was quite right and proper for Alberto to dispense with his duties in this lighthearted manner.

'The English, they are late with their Christmas cards,' he said disapprovingly, never even considering it could be the fault of the Italian postal system.

Hugo did a great deal of serious head nodding and smiling, to show he understood, which of course he did not, and amongst many cries of *arrivederci*, began walking up the road to the hamlet.

The day is sweet, the winter sun shines approvingly on Hugo. As he passes their houses, the villagers greet him enthusiastically, waving and nodding like erratic wild flowers lining the tiny lanes. Soon the buildings thin, leaving rolling fields dotted with woodland, vineyards and olive groves, the odd stone farmhouse around a corner, placid sheep munching in the crisp but warming air which is becoming decidedly spring-like.

And then, oh, joy, there is Bernard at the side of the road, muttering obscenities, kicking his tractor for all he is worth, the dog at his side nipping and snarling at a wheel in loyal solidarity.

'Bernard, what's wrong? Can I help?' Hugo, wildly solicitous, runs to his side, aware of the heaving muscles under the Marks and Spencer's jumper, the heavy breathing, the dark alluring perfume of sweat and cow dung. He is about to put his hand in a comradely manner on Bernard's shoulder but the dog, over-zealous as usual, is jumping up in greeting and manages to spoil the moment.

Bernard has been out on his tractor bringing in some early lambs from the field to the shed, for the warm sun is deceptive; there will be a heavy frost tonight. And now there is a fault in the motor. Bernard, demonstrating, does something right and the tractor springs to life. Overjoyed, he is about to leap on to it and go his way but Hugo, thinking quickly, says, or rather shouts over the roar of the tractor, 'I have some post for you. I'll bring it over at lunchtime.'

Bernard shrugs, uninterested, and says, politely, yes, thank you, and bounces off across the field, his mind on more important things. It never occurs to him to wonder why Hugo has to wait to drop in the post, nor for that matter why he doesn't hand it over then and there. Hugo, jubilant, his moment come at last, sings and skips all the way back to the valley. The dog, sensing something a bit livelier than following a tractor round and round, abandons Bernard to follow Hugo, only to find the door slammed in his face when they get to the house.

Poor dog, *his* moment has not come. He slinks back down the field to find Bernard.

The morning dragged slowly for Hugo. After ten minutes he abandoned all efforts to start his Dante-esque musical and decided to write a poem instead, about Bernard's broad shoulders and the erotic scent of cow-shit, but got so horny he had to stop. Instead he would play music, he decided, something Baroque. He put on Pachabel's 'Canon', lay back on the black leather sofa and thought about Bernard. He was sure the farmer, despite his marriage, had deeper, more sensitive leanings, and would be open to propositions. Hugo had noticed how Bernard sulked and frowned and brooded, how often he didn't hear what was being said to him, how his dark eyes clouded over at frequent intervals with lust and passion. Hugo knew the signs; he felt them himself frequently. He had high hopes for his lunchtime meeting.

At one o'clock, having showered and changed into his tightest Levis and the jade wool jumper that matched the colour of his eyes, Hugo walked across the yard, snarling at the dog who threatened to leap up at him and muddy his stonewashed denim. He was carrying an iced bottle of champagne and a box of Swiss chocolates. At precisely one minute past one he knocked on the door of Bernard's house, using the brass door knocker that came from England. At precisely two minutes past one the door opened, and Mary stood in front of him.

'Hugo, what a surprise! But I thought you were locking

yourself up in your study, working all day? Come in, Bernard's in the kitchen eating lunch. Would you like some?'

'Mary? Oh, God – Mary! I thought you were in Perugia with Carl and your mother?'

'I decided not to go. Three's a crowd, and I've never liked being a gooseberry.' She giggled girlishly. Hugo hadn't a clue what she was talking about. 'Come in, come in,' she trilled. 'Join us for shepherd's pie. There's plenty, if that's why you're hesitating.' She smiled coyly at him.

'Uh, thanks. Pie, yes. Shepherd's. Yes, I see.' Hugo stood looking at her, unable to move. He was aware he was holding a bottle of champagne and a box of chocolates.

Mary thought Hugo looked rather strange, pale somehow and shaken, not his usual sophisticated self. He seemed uncertain, which was very unlike Hugo.

'What is it you have there?' she said, to make him feel at ease.

'Oh. Ah. A present. Yes, a present. For *you*,' he fumbled on. 'Champagne, and these chocolates.'

'Ohhhh, Hugo, you darling! What a wonderful gesture. But whatever for?'

'Because – well. Because, that's all.' He shifted his feet and looked uncomfortable, for all the world like a recalcitrant teenager.

And suddenly Mary twigged, light dawning in her innocent heart like a door opening at last. Hugo had fallen in love with her.

Carl, escorting Claudia around Perugia, found to his astonishment that he was enjoying the day out. Appalled, at first, that Mary had changed her mind about going, he soon realized that without her daughter around, Claudia became less negative, though it could also have been the fact that they had left behind the joys of the countryside for the rather less muddy pleasures of the city. Whatever it was, Claudia, though not exactly enjoying herself, at least didn't find fault. And she had her own ideas for the day, saving Carl the wearisome task of seeking out her likes and dislikes and in general playing the genial tour guide.

'No, I'm not that keen on churches,' she said brusquely. 'If you've seen one you've seen the lot.'

'Oh,' said Carl, rather put out because he had quite looked forward to exploring some of the finer ecclesiastical buildings of the city.

'Should we go to the Etruscan tombs, then?' he said to his companion. 'Most interesting, pre-dating Roman times.'

'What I'd like, actually, is to look in estate agents.'

'What?'

'You know, get the feel of the market. My late husband dabbled in property. I myself find it soothing.'

'I see. Are you thinking of buying something in Italy?'

'You never know. It would depend entirely on the market. My late husband knew a great deal about property.' Claudia nodded enigmatically, her little twinkling bantam eyes displaying real warmth for the first time since her arrival in Italy.

'So what I suggest we do,' she went on, 'is to go our separate ways for a few hours. Shall we meet at that restaurant opposite at one o'clock? I've looked it up in my Michelin guide and it's supposed to be good. I think we'll be ready for a decent meal by then. And we shall each pay our own share, by the way. I'm longing for some gourmet treats after nearly a fortnight of Mary's stodge and I intend to lunch well.'

Carl, astounded, agreed, and spent a pleasant morning returning to his favourite haunts in the city.

The restaurant Claudia had chosen was dark and sultry after the winter sunlight, which was making a serious attempt to lull people into a spring-like daze. It was quite full, but they managed to get a table in the corner. Bronze lamps gleamed everywhere, and the tablecloths were white. The waiters wore trim black trousers over their tight little buttocks, which both Claudia and Carl surreptitiously noticed and appreciated.

The food was exquisite. They had rocket salad with avocado and asparagus, and a plate of spaghetti with a sauce of tomatoes, basil and mushrooms. They ate crispy duck on a mound of rice, washed down with Valpolicella, and finished with ice cream smothered in a raspberry sauce. With coffee, Claudia confessed a weakness for amaretto, so they each had one, and then both lit a cigarette and smoked their heads off, though Carl, like Claudia, had given up the habit years before.

'Ah, bliss,' he said, inhaling deeply, then coughing bronchially. They had taken two hours over their lunch.

'Well,' said Claudia after they had smoked in comfortable silence for a while, 'shall we do the same this afternoon? I expect, being English, you want to take a gentle walk after this huge repast, and I need to see a lawyer. Business, you understand. My late husband maintained that business can be done at any time, even after lunch.' She blew an enigmatic smoke ring in his face. 'Shall we meet again at five?'

'You haven't bought your *palazzo* yet, then?' Carl said, teasing her.

'Oh, I really have no intention of buying. I like to nose about, that's all, see what's going on. My late husband, you know, such a dear man, he dabbled in everything,' she said vaguely. 'One does become addicted to it.'

He was content to humour her. She was quite right; he did feel a little stroll around the town would be just the thing. But, being a gentleman, he asked politely one last time, 'You're sure you don't want to do a spot of sightseeing?'

'My late husband once dabbled in tour coaches, so I have had enough of sightseeing. He would have been immensely successful in the venture, had it not been for the *carabiniere*.'

Claudia refused to expand further, and they parted amicably for the next couple of hours.

★

'Did you have a good day out? Where did you go? What did you see?' Mary cried when her mother returned in the dark of the early evening.

'We saw Perugia,' Claudia replied shortly.

'And Carl? How did you get on with him? Do you like him ... do you think ...' She trailed off, not wanting to be too obvious. But she had seen Carl kissing her mother on the cheek, on both cheeks actually, when they'd returned and headed for their separate houses, and she had high hopes. Besides, love was in the air, for hadn't Hugo, albeit inadvertently, declared himself to her today? Mary was still flushed with delight after the revelation. Until today Bernard was the only man who had ever loved her, and as he appeared to love his cows in much the same manner, there didn't somehow seem to be much magic in it.

'Carl is most sympathetic. A gentleman. We're going out again next week, possibly to Siena.'

Mary, never having heard her mother say anything positive about anybody, was overjoyed. She was sure her matchmaking was a roaring success. Now all she had to do was to find a nice girl for poor Hugo, because when her mother moved in with Carl, Hugo might feel a bit of a gooseberry. The trouble was, Hugo was in love with *her*, Mary, which complicated it all terribly. Thinking about it, she wasn't even so sure she'd like to find a nice girl for Hugo. She'd rather like him all to herself, in a corner somewhere, in the attic perhaps, always waiting for her, always loving her, always ready to be taken down and dusted off whenever she needed a bit of dewy-eyed devotion.

She sighed, happily troubled. Carl and Claudia, how perfect. How clever she was to have brought off such a successful piece of matchmaking.

How thick my daughter is, Claudia thought benignly, accepting it as one of those irritating but unimportant little facts of life, like fleas or traffic wardens or the necessity of paying a television licence back home in England. She knew

Carl was gay, had done since she'd first met him on Christmas Day, but she wasn't about to impart that to her daughter. Claudia liked secrets; had many; saw no reason to give out any information about anything to anybody. She had learned this from her husband who had found it invaluable in business, especially the somewhat shady businesses he had been prone to become involved in.

'Are you hungry?' Mary was asking her mother. 'We've had our tea, but I saved you some shepherd's pie.'

'No, thank you. Carl and I had espresso and cakes at a café on the way home. A Scotch would be pleasant.'

Mary fetched the bottle unhappily. She thought her mother was overdoing it a little; men never liked a soak. She hoped Claudia would be careful, and not blow her chances with Carl.

'Cheers,' her mother said cheerfully, not asking Mary to join her. 'Cin-cin, and all that.'

She knocked back the drink, feeling better than she had for two weeks. It had been an interesting day.

It had been an interesting day for Isabel also. Her day had been spent in Perugia too, in Fabrizio's office, familiarizing herself with all the properties on his books. The *avvocato* had recently expanded his business to extend to the buying and selling of property, and that was what Isabel had been hired to look after.

She had been delighted when Fabrizio had offered her the job, working with him showing around the many and varied English people who were interested in buying property in Umbria. There were advantages for both of them: Fabrizio genuinely needed someone to deal with this surfeit of English, and Isabel, with her mature confident appearance, her reassuring air, indeed her very Britishness, would be able to lull prospective buyers, make them feel safe and secure. They would feel they could trust her, would tell her all their problems with the Italians, complain to her about the very people in whose country they were about to live.

Isabel, on the other hand, had postponed worrying about money until after Christmas, so the job came at exactly the right moment. Although Henrietta, who had always been generous with the easy manner of one who can afford to be, was happy to pay Isabel's way in return for a bit of companionship, this was not the older woman's style. She liked to work, liked to pay her own way. When she left her husband they had been about to sell their large house in Chiswick anyway and move someplace smaller, so she took her half of that, which was not an inconsiderable sum, and invested it, used it wisely while getting her degree. She had received a grant, never having had one before, and she had worked during the summers, accompanying elderly travellers around the British Isles as a courier. She still had a tidy sum in the bank but wanted to leave that untouched, as in reality she had no home, no career, no pension plan or insurance policy, and knew that one day she might, perhaps, want to settle down. Exactly why, she couldn't for the moment think, but you never knew. She rather revelled in this rootless, carefree existence after years of responsibility, but conceded this could ultimately get wearing when one was ancient and very likely exhausted from gadding about.

So this job with Fabrizio was perfect, for she had promised her sister she would see her through the first year with the baby. It would give her an income and stop her from being bored, which she could see happening, being cooped up with Henrietta and Krissy all day.

'And so, Isabel, what do you think of my business?' Fabrizio asked that evening over a quick supper at a local trattoria. He had suggested a long leisurely meal at a somewhat posher restaurant he knew, but Isabel didn't want to get involved in that. However, she was hungry, and wanted to chat, so they compromised on the small, informal place.

'I'm finding it interesting,' she said. 'It's a wonderful way to see every corner of this part of Umbria. I just hope I can tolerate the English house buyers. Some of them aren't exactly the finest example of British man and womanhood. In fact some of them are pains in the butt, to be truthful.'

'If they're truly repulsive, Isabel, you can send them to some other estate agent. We have business coming out of our noses.'

'Repulsive isn't exactly the right word, Fabrizio, but I know what you mean. And it comes out of our ears, not our noses.'

'Ah, the English.' He smiled tolerantly. 'If they were all like you . . .'

'None of that,' she warned. 'Eat your pasta before it gets colder, Fabrizio, and remember, we're here to talk about business.'

He reluctantly turned his attention to his supper. 'Yes, the business. Well, I have something for you to tell your neighbour, Bernard, about that land he wishes to buy. It's on the books of several estate agents, and as a matter of fact it is now on mine.'

'What?'

'I felt a little sad for poor Bernard: so in love with your sister, so in love with the land, not able to possess either. So I found the owner, contacted him, tried to tell him that his price is unreasonable and that if he would only consider lowering it, I had a buyer for it at once.'

'What did he say?'

'He wouldn't move, I'm afraid. He said he wasn't in a hurry and could wait until someone paid his price. That was when he asked me to put it on my books also.'

'What a shame. Still, it was kind of you to try.'

'Poor Bernard. I too know what it's like to long for something one will never possess.'

'Poor Fabrizio. Do you think it would be vulgar if I had *tiramisu* after that huge dish of pasta? I always eat when I'm nervous, and all this talk about possessing makes me very jittery. My ex-husband talked like that.'

Fabrizio, defeated, ordered two espressos and the dessert, with a dish of *gelato* on the side. He was not the first man to turn from lust to gluttony, nor would he be the last.

Bernard, going out to the barn to check on a sick cow, saw the Ferrari drive up and deposit Isabel and Fabrizio in front of the house. Isabel was in the process of buying a second-hand Fiat to carry her to and from work; in the meantime, for just these few days, Henrietta drove her sister to Perugia and Fabrizio happily took her home, though it was a good half-hour's drive.

'Come in for a coffee?' Isabel asked. 'Henrietta would like to see you, I know.'

'Hmm. In a minute.' He pushed her gently against the bonnet of the Ferrari and began kissing her slowly, sensually.

'Hmm, Fabrizio. That's enough. We're business associates now, colleagues, you have to be more professional.' She opened her mouth wider under his lips to show just how professional she was.

'Hmm.'

'Mmm . . . Fabrizio.'

Bernard, watching this from the shadows of the barn, was so aroused it took him a full minute, during which time Fabrizio was gently manoeuvring his hand up inside Isabel's skirt, to realize it was Isabel panting and moaning on the car bonnet, not his own precious beloved Henrietta.

'Yah-hoo!' he shouted joyfully, totally forgetting himself.

His spontaneous, primitive cry, erupting from a heart seething volcanically with the fire of love and lust and all such dangerous things, caused havoc. Fabrizio and Isabel, scared witless, leaped apart; Henrietta flung open the front door; Carl, opening his bedroom window, leaned out to see what was happening. The dog, having been behind the cow shed tracking a rabbit, rushed noisily into the fray.

Bernard, oblivious, walked past them all and into the house. There was only one rival now for Henrietta's love and that was Hugo. He might be a poet, he might be tall (though not as tall as Bernard) and beautiful, and as garrulous and charming as Bernard was taciturn and awkward, but he was British, Bernard could handle him.

His moment was coming; he could feel it. He was so euphoric he even grinned at his mother-in-law, Claudia, who thought how particularly wet he looked when he smiled but declined to say so, mellowed by her second Scotch. Instead, she offered him the bottle, which to her surprise Bernard accepted with alacrity, saying he was celebrating. Luckily, she couldn't be bothered to ask why, knowing the answer would bore her.

When Mary came downstairs from reading to her children, she found her mother and her husband drinking whisky like nobody's business. After a moment's hesitation, she decided to join them. It had, after all, been a most enlightening day.

Bernard and Claudia, deep in their own thoughts, would have agreed.

Chapter Eight

'*Buongiorno*, Daniela, Alberto! Krissy, wave – *ciao ciao* – to Auntie Daniela and Uncle Alberto, there's a *bambino bellissimo* – or I suppose you're a *bambina bellissima*. Damn these feminine and masculine endings! Why can't the Italians be androgynous, like the English?'

Henrietta, dressed in her white Levis which were beginning to look rather less than pure and immaculate, thanks to the muddy feet of the dog, took Krissy's little hand and waved it gaily at the Italians while sweetly muttering, buying bread and cakes from Daniela as she did so. January had so far stayed unseasonably warm and fairly dry, and she had taken to pushing her baby down to Modena and back every morning, thinking the fresh air and the exercise would do them both good.

Alberto the postman eyed her appreciatively. He was thirty and single, and fancied himself just a little, thanks to a doting Italian mother and his own natural birthright as a full-blooded Latin. He was starting to fancy Henrietta as well, but although Italian, he was surprisingly realistic enough to know she was out of his league. So he contented himself with meeting her on these sunny winter mornings at the bakery where they sat at one of Daniela's four tables, drinking cappuccino and speaking a mixture of bad Italian and bad English to each other. Henrietta liked these meetings because she was not only learning Italian but imbibing some local colour. Alberto liked them because he was not only learning English but also gaining some prestige in the village, Henrietta being universally appreciated, by the men with lust, and by the women because she doted upon her infant exactly as they did on theirs. And baby Krissy enjoyed these morning sessions because she knew she would be fed sips of sweet frothy topping from the cappuccino, and morsels of almond pastry, and be made a fuss of by Daniela, who had raised seven children and numerous grandchildren and still had a soft spot for babies.

After a half hour or so of idle chit chat, during which a good proportion of the retired men in the village joined in, both to coo over Krissy (Italian men being proud of their ability to sentimentalize over babies) and to stare lasciviously at Henrietta, the party broke up as Alberto was reluctantly forced to continue his rounds. Henrietta ambled slowly back to *La Piccola Valle della Tristezza*. She missed Isabel now that her sister had begun work in Perugia, but not so much as she had thought she would. Krissy, becoming more and more fascinating with each day, preoccupied her fully, and Henrietta was beginning to think her true career lay in motherhood. Not only was she never bored, she felt positively stimulated with each hour in her daughter's company. And when the baby was asleep, Henrietta sat at her sewing machine, designing and creating exquisite little playsuits, dresses, bonnets and jackets for her olive-skinned daughter, who was growing strong and confident in the midst of all this adoration.

Today, walking back slowly from the village, Henrietta, like Hugo a couple of weeks ago, feels the wintry sun smiling sweetly on her and her baby, feels the good will of the villagers as they beam and call greetings to her, feels herself growing, expanding with motherhood, becoming plump and good-natured, round-faced and contented.

But Bernard, chugging around on his tractor checking his ewes in the lower field, spots her firm white buttocks in the too-tight Levis and, dazzled, forgets completely what he is doing. Abandoning the newborn lamb he was about to bring up to the shed, he races across the field to reach her side before she gets to the house. He jumps off the tractor, plants himself in front of her and tries to look casual, saying, inanely, 'Oh, Henrietta. Uh, it's you.'

Henrietta, about to retort with some caustic witticism as: Who the fuck did you think it would be? and thus destroy Bernard forever, is prevented from showing this less than genteel side of herself by the arrival of another vehicle, zooming out of the *villaggio* and heading towards the village. It pulls to a screeching halt in front of Bernard and Henrietta and out bursts Hugo. 'Bernard! It's you,' he cries, leaving Henrietta not only ignored but despairing of the level of conversation among her neighbours.

Bernard, defeated in the face of Hugo's beauty, not to mention the beauty of Carl's Jaguar which he is driving, retreats to his muddy tractor and roars away. He has forgotten all the joy he felt upon discovering that Hugo was his only rival; now, seeing Hugo, looking into those lazy emerald eyes, he feels he has no hope at all.

And so he tortures himself, racing madly round and round his field, watching Henrietta and Hugo standing in the road talking for what seems like hours. Bernard is sure they are declaring undying love for each other; worse, he is sure they are making an assignation to meet in a hot torrid bed somewhere.

The truth is, they are discussing London and discovering mutual acquaintances, not to mention a mutual old lover who years ago pleasured each of them (separately, of course) in a most satisfying manner. The rapturous look Bernard glimpses on their faces, as he speeds precariously close to them on his lumpy old tractor, is for passion remembered, no more than that.

But how is Bernard, simple Bernard, to know all this? Devon born and bred, son of a struggling small farmer, how is he to know of the naughtinesses of the city, of the wicked ways of some of its inhabitants? These stories are for the likes of Hugo and Henrietta, not for Bernard.

And so he sits, sulking, on his tractor, feeling the world spinning on without him; feeling for the first time in his life that there is a great deal going on out there that he has missed out on.

That night the sky darkened early, and January, put out by the presumptuous unseasonal warmth, rallied. It rained and rained, and then blew and blew; as if this wasn't enough, it grew decidedly cold. Henrietta and Isabel, cosy against the storm, were playing Scrabble by the wood-burner when the phone rang.

It was Libby, Isabel's daughter, phoning to say she was getting married in a few days time and wanted her mother at the register office.

'She'd like you to come as well, if you like?' Isabel told Henrietta when the ebullient Libby had finally hung up. 'But she understands you may not want to travel, with Krissy and all.'

'She means she doesn't want any babies at her wedding. Crying at all the wrong moments, and spoiling the atmosphere,' Henrietta said with no animosity.

'Probably. But I know you don't want to go any more than I do. Unfortunately I'm the mother and you're only the aunt. I suppose I'd better. I wonder if she knows what she's doing?'

Fabrizio, when told by Isabel that she needed a long weekend off to return to England, decided to come as well.

'Don't be silly, what about the office?'

'I haven't had a holiday for a year, and January's not a busy time. And my wife is giving me constant headaches – I need the break. Besides, I love London in winter. Let's go together, take more than a weekend – a week or two.'

'Fabrizio, you're my boss, and a friend I hope, but not my lover. A holiday together implies that we are.'

He came over all dignified. 'I will not trouble you in London. You may stay with your daughter, and I in a hotel, and we can meet daily for lunch or the theatre.'

Isabel saw the advantage of this. Much as she supposed she loved her daughter, and the man Libby was to marry (with whom she had been living for years), Isabel knew that she would be bored if left in their company for too long. The thought of Fabrizio's being with her in London was not at all unpleasant.

They decided to drive, as Isabel wanted to bring back numerous things: books, some favourite paintings she had left behind, other personal belongings still stored with friends. The weekend had grown to two weeks, as Fabrizio had anticipated, and they were going to take a detour to stay a night in Venice, a city Isabel had never seen.

She had insisted on booking two single rooms in the small hotel near the Rialto where they were to stay. Fabrizio was scandalized.

'We are two adults,' he said. 'We both crave each other's bodies. What is the harm?'

'The harm is that if I sleep with you, old-fashioned though it may be, love might happen.'

'So? Love has already happened for me.'

'I don't need it, Fabrizio. Love kept me in a disastrous marriage for years. Love nearly failed me all my exams. Love, so far as I see, is destructive. If we sleep together, the friendship goes, we grow demanding, start to know loss. Believe me, Fabrizio, I'm older than you and I know. Love is out for me, I'm afraid.'

But Isabel had not counted on Venice. She fell in love with the city on the Number One *vaporetto*, standing at the back of the chunky boat in a drizzling rain as it slowly steamed down the Grand Canal. Who could not fall in love with it all: the hidden canals, the rhythmical lapping of the water, the lights of the *palazzi* reflected eerily in the black water?

As if this wasn't enough, she fell in love with Fabrizio a few hours later, after they had walked hand in hand in St Mark's Square, still in a fine drizzle of rain, and drunk wine from the Veneto in a tiny restaurant he knew on the Campo Santo Stefano. In between times they had crossed over mist-shrouded canals on tiny stone bridges, watched the opaque red lights of gondolas in the dark water, kissed under the bronze and stone statues of ancient winged lions.

'Ah, Fabrizio, ah, ah . . .'

Thus spake Isabel, some hours later, in a double room of the hotel that Fabrizio, sure of Venice's powers of seduction if not, modestly, his own, had booked well in advance.

He answered in kind, with much moaning and groaning and sighing in Italian, and the night was spent very satis-factorily by both parties.

The next morning, waking up to a deluge of tiny tongue kisses all over her naked and uncovered body, Isabel, always practical, looked at the bedside clock and saw they would miss breakfast if they didn't go downstairs immediately. Having been poor a great deal of her life, and never having had the disposable income to stay in hotels even when she considered herself rich, she had been looking forward to all the sensual joys, like an opulent breakfast with lashings of strong black coffee, such an experience could bring.

But Fabrizio's tongue was darting over her nipples, then down over her belly, and then . . . oh, then! She knew she would forego breakfast forever if he would never stop doing exactly what he was doing to her at that moment.

It was then that she realized she was truly in love.

★

'You're what?' Henrietta cried in disbelief, ten days later when Isabel and Fabrizio finally arrived back in Umbria. He had dropped Isabel at *La Piccola Valle* and gone straight to his office, for there was some minor crisis he needed to sort out as soon as possible.

'It was Venice, 'Etta. That did me in.'

'Oh, Venice,' Henrietta snorted dismissively. 'Venice is always blamed, to excuse the inexcusable. Men behaving badly, like Byron. All those mistresses throwing themselves in canals after he dumped them. You be careful you don't end up in a canal, Bel,' She snorted again, crossly.

Isabel thought her sister must be joking; then, as Henrietta lay down on the floor on her stomach to coo and tickle Krissy who was sitting on a blanket, decided that she was too far gone in motherhood to remember what it was like, being wildly in love and walking through the rain in the anticipation of explosive sex in a very short time. And in Venice, too.

So she just said, mildly, 'Fabrizio didn't behave badly. On the other hand, perhaps I did.' She remembered, with no guilt whatsoever, that it had been *she* who'd insisted on staying in Venice another night, even though they were nearly late for her daughter's wedding. And that it had been she, too, whose tongue had caressed Fabrizio's most intimate places as they missed breakfast yet again a second morning.

Henrietta, clapping hands with her daughter, noticed the dreamy look on Isabel's face and said, caustically, 'I thought you told me you weren't going to get involved again, Isabel. After that lecturer.'

'I know. It was Venice that did me in,' Isabel repeated helplessly.

'Pat-a-cake, pat-a-cake − Krissy do it now! That's it, darling, aren't you a clever *bambina*? What I can't understand, Isabel,' she said, still clapping hands with Krissy, 'is how you can still be a slave to romantic love when you have children. One doesn't need any other fulfillment in life surely?'

'What a load of crap you talk sometimes, 'Etta,' Isabel said fondly.

But Henrietta didn't hear her. She was pat-a-caking away with her daughter, thus finding complete fulfillment and, incidentally, amusing Krissy no end. Isabel lapsed into a spaced-out reverie, thinking of the past week. Finally Henrietta said, 'While the earth was moving so fortuitously for you, Bel, metaphorically speaking of course, do you realize the earth was moving here too? Literally, I mean.'

Isabel started guiltily out of a daydream of tongues and rain and missed breakfasts to say, 'I heard on the news about the earth tremors in Umbria, but they were reported as only slight, no damage done. But I see that Mary and Bernard's place has lost some slates.'

'Yes, one fell off just as Hugo was going outside and hit the side of his head. No doubt it was loose anyway; there was only a very slight tremor.'

'Is he all right?'

'Yes, but he had a bit of concussion, had to go to hospital and was kept in overnight.'

'Poor Hugo.'

'Carl nearly had hysterics, would you believe? He's normally so self-contained. He saw Hugo fall to the ground and acted like a man demented. Thought he was dead, I suppose. He started shrieking at Bernard, who was outside too. Hugo was ogling him as usual when the slate came off.'

'He just won't give up on Bernard, will he. And Bernard's so obviously straight.'

'Bernard is just so *wet*. Anyway, Carl shouted at him, said it was all his fault and that Hugo was going to sue.'

'Oh, no, he won't, surely?'

'Well, Carl probably would have calmed down, but Bernard suddenly got uncharacteristically huffy and said that if anyone in *La Piccola Valle* deserved to be hit, it was Hugo. That enraged Carl, and then Mary came out and started yelling at them both, and it was some time before anyone remembered Hugo lying there unconscious and called the doctor.'

'Oh my God! And where were you during this fracas?'

'Upstairs, having a nap with Krissy. We'd both been up half the night before – she had wind or colic or whatever you call baby indigestion. I never felt a tremor, nor did Krissy. And we missed all the shouting outside.'

Isabel, marvelling over her sister's ability to sleep soundly even when the earth was moving, asked, 'So how did you find out about all this?'

'Mary came over and told me.'

'Mary?' Isabel was confused. 'But she never comes here, not when *you're* here. She loathes you as much as you loathe her.'

Henrietta smiled serenely. 'Mary had nowhere else to go when Carl and Hugo left for the hospital. Bernard went off in a huff to talk to his cows, and Claudia apparently had drunk herself into a stupor in the sitting room. The boys were at school, so Mary was stuck at home alone with her terror.'

'Terror?' Isabel was losing patience. 'Stop being so bloody mysterious – *what* terror?'

'Of earthquakes, of course.'

'But there wasn't one. You said it was an insignificant tremor.'

'Not to Mary it wasn't. She needed comfort.'

'And came to *you*? She must have been out of her head with fear.'

Henrietta threw Isabel a wounded look. 'I can be quite comforting when I choose. Anyway, she was bursting to talk as well. You know how she loves to talk.'

Isabel pondered this as Henrietta went back to playing with the baby. 'Well,' she said at last, 'I'm glad you two aren't so hostile to each other anymore.'

''Bye baby bunting,' Henrietta crooned contentedly. 'As a

matter of fact,' she said to Isabel when she stopped singing, 'Mary walked out of here in a fit of pique.' She began crooning contentedly to her baby again.

'Oh, no. Why?'

'God knows, the silly cow. Because I told her some home truths, I suppose.'

'Henrietta, no. What exactly did you say?'

'Just that. That she was a silly cow, but I said it kindly. She thinks Hugo's in love with her. All I did was put her right, told her he was gay. She should be grateful, but instead she got all sniffy and walked out.'

Isabel put her head in her hands, suddenly feeling tired from the emotional strain of falling in love, and the physical strain of a week's active fucking.

'The Little Valley of Sadness,' she said wearily. 'More like the little valley of petty misunderstandings, of sniping, back-biting, neighbourly acrimony . . . And I think I'm getting a bloody cold too.' She suddenly felt depressed, and too weary to decide if it was because she missed Fabrizio inconsolably, or was about to get over him and so have to endure the flatness of not being in love again.

'I'm going to have a whisky,' she decided. 'A good British Scotch, then an early night.'

'There's no whisky, I'm afraid. Claudia took our last bottle the day of the tremors. She said if there was going to be a major quake, she wanted to enjoy it drunk. I rather think she just wanted to be drunk, quake or no quake. Not that I blame her, holed up with those two.'

'No whisky? I never got any on the trip home. Shit! That bloody woman, that selfish sod. You'd think she'd have replaced it. Jesus, what a thoughtless bitch.'

'Little valley of sad, sad pettiness,' Henrietta said with a maddeningly superior smile.

Isabel, her flash of anger gone, was able to dredge a weak smile out of the mire of her muddy depression. 'Maybe I'll go to Mary's and borrow some Horlicks,' she said, starting to giggle.

'Oh, yes,' Henrietta cried. 'With Golden Syrup, what a treat!'

Their giggles turned to laughter, and Krissy, watching them, smiled complacently, the only one in the Little Valley of Sadness who was perfectly content with everyone around her.

At that moment, in the big farmhouse, Mary was fretting, wanting to talk to Bernard alone. She had been trying for ages, ever since the day of the tremors, but there seemed to be always children or her mother about, and Bernard always seemed to go up to bed before her, sound asleep and snoring when she entered the room. Now the boys were in bed asleep but Claudia was glued to the radio, listening to a financial programme on the BBC. Bernard, drifting into a doze on the sofa, was roused swiftly by a nudge from Mary, asking him to bring in some coal for the Aga in the kitchen, the shiny red one she had brought over at enormous expense from England.

Once Bernard was in the house, she was able to seat him at the kitchen table in order to taste the rich chocolate sponge cake she made that morning. Bernard, despondent, took a huge portion, largely to keep the peace. Mary was usually less irksome when people were eating monstrous quantities of her food. She took it very personally if they only had small helpings. Luckily she was married to tall, broad Bernard, who took constant stoking and fuelling and only seemed to grow taller and stronger, never bigger and fatter like others would. A lesser man would have gone under in a sea of flab within months of the wedding day.

'Bernie, I – is it good?'

Bernard, his mouth full, nodded, trying to convey by grimaces and rolling eyeballs that her cake was another resounding success. He knew by experience that anything less would throw her into acute depression.

Mollified, Mary tried again. 'Bernard, I, uh, I need, that is, I want – to talk to you.'

Bernard immediately panicked. Wildly he asked for more cake; wildly he praised and raved and expostulated on the succulence of the chocolate sponge melting in his mouth and trickling like nectar down his gullet. But Mary, for once, was not to be deflected.

'It's about Henrietta,' she said, then stopped.

This was it then. Poor Bernard sees his marriage pass before his eyes like a drowning man; he sees Mary gone back to her mother, his boys taken from him; sees his beloved cattle and sheep sold to pay maintenance and alimony. Mary has found out about his secret love for Henrietta.

Henrietta . . . He sees her gone from him forever, now that Mary knows. But wait, no. He sees the look on her face now that he is free, alone, a single man once again, for obviously that is why she hasn't responded to him, why she avoids him: because of Mary and the children. Why did he not realize this before? He sees her eyes glow with pleasure as Mary and Claudia and the boys fly back to England, imagines Henrietta taking a tentative step towards him, holding out her hand . . .

'Yes, Mary, yes?' Bernard says courageously, the next part of his vision already burning in his brain and groin. 'Yes, Mary, what is it you would like to talk about?'

And she, looking at her dear sweet boy, can't do it, can't disillusion him. She had been waiting for this moment to tell him of Henrietta's revelation about Hugo, but now that her time has come, she can't go on with it. Even though Carl is suing Bernard because of the loose slate on the roof, and Hugo doesn't love *her*, Mary, because he's one of *them*, thus condemning her to the dull tenor of life with Bernard devoid of any fantasy, she can't tell her husband. He's too innocent, she decides; it is not her place to corrupt him. True, he had seemed blasé when they thought Isabel and Henrietta were gay, but Mary has heard that men, while accepting this, cannot accept the same thing in their own sex. Mary prides herself on her knowledge of the world. She still has women's magazines sent over to her from England, and she listens to the BBC whenever she can: Mary *knows* these things.

No, there was no sense in troubling Bernard about Henrietta's revelation. He disliked Hugo as it was, though why was a mystery to Mary. Perhaps, she thought now, with sudden insight, it was because he thought Hugo fancied *her*? The more she thought about it, the more it seemed the answer. After all, she herself had been fooled by Hugo's constant attention, so why not Bernard, so much simpler, poor dear boy, than she herself?

Bernard was *jealous*! The thought was so pleasing that she almost stopped loathing Henrietta for a moment, for telling her the truth about Hugo and thus making her feel a total fool.

Henrietta. Mary let her thoughts dwell on the odious woman for a few moments. With satisfaction, she remembered that her neighbour was definitely putting on weight, a second chin delicately but surely beginning to emerge under the first and her waistline beginning to thicken under those stupid white clothes she wore. She was eating too much, obviously, and not looking after herself, just swanning around the house with that baby. With a bit of luck she'd get grossly fat, and all those stupid vain Italian men who came occasionally to deliver the post or help Bernard drench the sheep when necessary, would no longer gape at her like she was the Queen or something.

A slight cough from Bernard brought her back to reality, which was her dear cosy kitchen with the Aga puffing away in the corner and her dear husband Bernard looking at her enquiringly, waiting to hear what she was about to say. Mary hesitated, then made up her mind. It was not a bad thing to have Bernard feel jealous over her and Hugo; it was a new and not unpleasant feeling to have her husband feel *anything* about her. Let him think Hugo was smitten with her. Let him not know, ever, that Hugo was one of *them*.

The thrill of this deception, the thought of Bernard's passions stirring as she flirted mildly with Hugo (for surely she could flirt with a gay man? She was not sure of the etiquette of this, but never mind), brought a rosy glow to her usually pallid face.

Bernard, still looking at her, said pompously (though he thought it was bravely), 'What about our neighbour, Mary? You said you wanted to talk to me about Henrietta.'

'Oh, yes, well. What it is, you see, is that I thought – oh, dear, what was it I thought? Oh, I seem to have forgotten – I know! I was just going to say that we ought to ask her over for supper one evening, and Isabel too of course. The boys just love that little baby, and, uh, I thought . . .'

She stopped speaking, totally appalled at what she had just let herself in for.

Bernard, reprieved, his marriage saved, had only an instant of heady relief before being plunged into despair, seeing a vision of Henrietta blurring and fading before his eyes like Cinderella at the stroke of midnight.

Luckily, he wasn't required to answer, for Claudia walked into the kitchen. 'Well, I'm off to bed,' she said, yawning, her beak-like mouth opening wide like a gosling waiting to be fed. 'A busy day tomorrow. Carl is taking me to Florence. It's quite a drive, so we're leaving at seven.'

Mary stared at her in horror. She had forgotten her mother and Carl, forgotten the two or three day trips they had had together, her mother returning from each one smiling smugly to herself and once even singing a little Italian ditty in her chirpy voice. Claudia was obviously falling in love with Carl, who was one of *them*, and it was all Mary's fault.

Guilt and confusion and hopelessness and helplessness

mingled together in Mary's mind, causing terrible chaos and despair. Oh, what a dreadful place was this Tristezza, this 'Vale of Trees' place which summoned visions of lawn parties and civilized English things like cricket and walks in National Trust gardens, only to exorcise those pleasant ghosts with the stark ugly reality of its awful *foreign-ness*.

She must tell her mother about Carl, tonight, right now before she went to bed, right now before Claudia spent another whole day with him tomorrow.

'Ah, Mummy,' she began, calling her mother back from the stairs she had been about to ascend. 'Uh, can I talk to you? That is, I'd like to tell you something.' She paused, dumbstruck. Claudia stopped with one foot on the stair and waited impatiently.

Ah, Mary, can you do it? Meek little Mary, sweet English rose and mother of three wholesome boys. Can you, truly, tell your mother, who terrifies you, that the man she hopes to marry is a . . . a . . . a homosexual?

Mary shudders, then blushes; aware of both her husband and her mother watching her and waiting for her to speak, she says, first falteringly and then more and more confidently, her voice and determination gathering strength as she makes her decision: 'I . . . just wanted to tell you, that, ah, well, you see, I wanted to say – before you left tomorrow, that is – I wanted to say . . . that it's going to rain. Yes, rain tomorrow. You see, it's cleared, hasn't it, after all those storms a few days ago? But it definitely said on the television – the children heard it, their Italian is so good, you know, not like mine – they mentioned winds and showery patches throughout central Italy, and that surely means us, don't you think? So be warned. Take your unbrella.'

The silence that follows when she finally stops this waffle is stunning. Claudia and Bernard look at her as if she is mad, then Claudia shudders and rushes upstairs while Bernard, wishing he could do the same, sits stoically waiting for his Horlicks.

Mary, cloaking herself in the flimsy shawl of routine, feels a crisis has been averted and is almost happy.

Ah, Mary, whispers the wind as it encroaches upon the little valley of either sadness or trees, depending on the state of your Italian. *You wait, Mary, you wait. What is normal to you is just a gossamer web, easily dissolved by the grit of reality.*

Mary shudders, and huddles nearer the Aga. She blames what she thinks is a chill in the air on the Italians, as she does most things. The coal here is obviously inferior, the Aga not working properly. Immense relief goes through her as she finds something solid and ordinary to worry about, and she begins to discuss with Bernard the pros and cons of bringing over quality Aga fuel from England.

He drinks Horlicks and despairs.

Chapter Nine

'Bye, Claudia, *buon viaggio!*'

'Have a safe trip!'

'Love to the old country, Claudia.'

'Come back to Umbria soon.'

'*Arrivederci.*'

'*Ciao,* Claudia.'

The inhabitants of the Little Valley, petty hatreds forgotten for a few minutes while saying goodbye to one of their own kind, all clustered around Bernard's farm van as it slowly drove away down the narrow lane.

Neither he nor his mother-in-law said much during the uneventful drive to Pisa; Claudia chain smoked and Bernard, laconic as ever, was deep in thought, contemplating loss: the loss of Henrietta, on whom he had given up, unable to compete with handsome and sublime poets; and the loss of the land he coveted. Wanting to expand his flock of sheep, he had made another offer for the land below his fields, hoping, forlornly he knew, that perhaps Claudia would volunteer to contribute a loan. Encouraged by Mary, he phoned the original estate agency handling the land only to be told, devastatingly, that it had been sold.

Goodbye, dream. Goodbye, vision. There would be no

healthy cattle meandering through the strong young grass on the way to the stream; there would be no draining and fencing; there would be no wild flowers at the edge of the meadow with Henrietta lying in his arms amongst them. He knew that he was getting his fantasies a bit mixed up but what did it matter? The property was gone, Henrietta untouchable and unreachable, the February sky dull and overcast, and what did any of it mean anyway?

After they had been driving an hour or so, Claudia decided she wanted a cup of coffee.

'Mary has packed us a flask, Mother,' Bernard said. 'Earl Grey, and some scones to go with it.'

Claudia did not think this worthy of an answer. Bernard pulled off the main road and drove a couple of kilometres into the nearest town, parking in the narrow main street and meekly following Claudia, her high heels pecking on the rough pavement, into the nearest café. It was huge, with hundreds of tables, or so Bernard thought until he realized that the walls were all mirrors. Faced with the sight of a dozen Bernards towering above the same number of tiny Claudias, he hastily sat down, wondering where in the world he was going to put his legs as the tables seemed to be made for dwarves.

Placidly, in unapologetic English, Claudia ordered two cappuccinos and an assortment of cakes. They ate in matey silence for a while, a rare treat for Bernard. He had to stop himself from automatically praising the cake, the coffee, the sugar lumps, everything in sight. After a while, as Claudia smoked her second cigarette, he thought maybe he ought to make polite conversation; after all, she was his mother-in-law, and who knew when she would visit again?

'Well, Mother, when we will see you again?' he began manfully.

'Call me Claudia, for Christ's sake. You're far too huge to be any son of mine. The very thought of it makes me shudder. I've been meaning to mention it for years.'

'Oh. Right.' He tried again. 'Did you enjoy your . . .?'

This time she smiled, her thin, beak-like lips almost hiding her small teeth so that she did indeed look very like a chicken. 'I had a wonderful time,' she cheeped.

This surprised Bernard, for whenever he was around she was complaining about something, but then he remembered Mary's match-making and thought perhaps there was something in it. This depressed him even further, because if Carl and Claudia were to marry, she would move into Carl's house, leaving Hugo homeless and so even more eager to pursue Henrietta, who so obviously needed a father for Krissy and was bound to be lonely, especially as Isabel was spending more and more time in Perugia.

Claudia serenely said, 'Without Carl, my visit would have been deadly boring. I am not a country person, as my late husband always said. Luckily, he had fingers in so many pies that we needed to live centrally,' she finished enigmatically.

Bernard nodded unhappily, not even noticing the affront to Mary, the boys, and himself.

'Carl is exceedingly interesting,' Claudia went on, blowing smoke in his face. 'Homosexuals often are. My late husband dabbled in hairdressing establishments so I've met several.'

It took some seconds before, as Mary would say, the penny dropped. Bernard, comprehension slowly dawning, sat up straight and said wonderingly, 'Homosexuals?'

'I don't think we should tell Mary, do you?' she said conspiratorially through a smoke ring. 'She does overreact so. She'd probably want to move the boys back to England, and I couldn't bear that.' She puffed at her cigarette. 'Much as I love them,' she added as an afterthought, and somewhat doubtfully.

Bernard had a very hard time not picking her up underneath her ample bosom and throwing her high into the air with glee. Trying to remain calm, he said casually, 'Er, Hugo?'

'Oh, not nearly so interesting as Carl.'

– 120 –

'I meant, uh, he is also . . . homosexual?'

'Christ, Bernard, don't be so thick!' She looked at him in disdain.

Bernard, euphoric, all rivals for the fair hand of Henrietta having at last been eliminated, expansively ordered more coffee and almond pastries and another pack of foul cigarettes for his mother-in-law. They drank, and ate, and Claudia smoked, in companionable silence for a while, until Bernard suddenly remembered the plane she had to catch in Pisa. Much as he was, for the first time that he could remember, enjoying her company, he certainly didn't want her to miss it. Besides, he wanted to get back to *La Piccola Valle* as fast as possible, his newly discovered knowledge of the true facts sparking inside him like gay (so to speak) little fireworks.

Back at the Little Valley, Carl, adamant for once, was not being taken in by Hugo's wheedling and whining.

'Of course I'm going to sue him, I've already talked to my *avvocato*. That slate could have killed you, dear boy.'

'But that's ridiculous. It didn't. And we're neighbours. Jesus God, Carl, you've been escorting the mother all over the place—'

'That has nothing to do with it. Suing someone is purely a business matter: we can still be friends. The Americans do it all the time. Besides, Claudia was good company. Left me to wander about on my own while she did her own thing. I don't suppose it ever occurs to you that it gets a bit tedious, watching you mooning about, making a fool of yourself?'

'I don't know what you're talking about,' Hugo said sullenly, turning on the television. An American film, dubbed badly in Italian, sprang to life and he stared, mesmerized.

But Carl was just warming up. 'I can't understand you, I didn't know you were quite that insensitive. The man's a philistine and a true blue heterosexual and I think you must have lost your senses.'

Hugo refused to take his eyes off the screen. 'You're obsessing,' he said flatly. 'That old green-eyed monster's at it again and you're imagining things. Like always.'

Carl sighed, suddenly losing heart for the argument, and went into the kitchen. This had happened before and he had weathered it, waiting it out patiently until Hugo's heart started acting normally again. He'd known when he first met Hugo what it would be like; he had accepted it gladly, loving the man wholly and in full knowledge of all his frailties.

Now, however, he was older, it was getting harder and harder, he was losing his sense of perspective. Whatever was he doing, suing that poor uncomprehending farmer next door who hadn't a clue what was going on? Carl looked out of the window at the dull February farmyard, the dog ecstatically greeting the three boys coming home from school, and decided to pull himself together and count his blessings. Bernard wasn't, after all, a threat; he was as straight as the furrow he ploughed, and eventually Hugo would get over him. Reciprocity kept love and passion alive, and when Hugo got none from Bernard, he'd eventually lose interest.

Logic, that was what was needed. Carl prided himself on being a rational man, and the turmoil of emotion throbbing inside him over the past few weeks was alien, uncomfortable, like a small bone accidentally swallowed and lodged persistently in his gullet. He made a conscious effort to remove it, and succeeded. Hugo loved *him*, Carl, and had stuck to him all these years whatever other ephemeral passions happened to have gripped him. There was no reason to suppose anything would ever change.

The next morning Hugo, on his usual walk to the village for bread and a bit of exercise, saw Bernard crossing the farmyard, having finished his morning milking. This time, however, the vision of the farmer, large and looming, across the yard failed to excite him. Carl's words for once had somehow been sieved through his fine lambswool hair into his not unintelligent brain and he feared, alas, he had indeed been making a fool of himself. He was also slightly worried; Carl, usually so placid, so cool, so rational, had acted out of character over all that business with the fallen slate, starting a legal action against Bernard, going off with Claudia in what seemed very like a huff all those times. Hugo, to give him his due, was genuinely fond of Carl, loved him as much as he was capable of loving anyone, and it made him uncomfortable to see the older man distressed.

And so, as he passed Bernard, he gave him only a desultory wave, a vague smile; he would forget the man, turn over a new leaf and all the rest of those homely banalities. He wasn't a fool; he knew when the battle was lost.

Bernard, noticing, was struck with guilt and penitence. He was well aware of his own unfriendliness towards Hugo, and now that the reason for his hostility had disappeared, wanted to make amends. Besides, he was uncomfortably aware that Hugo might have misconstrued his antipathy, taking it for an intolerance of his sexual preferences. Bernard, a simple man, did not number prejudice among his vices, and so instead of his usual curt nod, he waved broadly; instead of his usual determined stare into space, he looked full into Hugo's glittering emerald eyes and smiled.

Hugo, mesmerized, froze on the spot. Carl, watching out of the window, felt unease creeping up his spine like a deadly spider, felt logic rush out of his head like bats from a belfry. Bernard, holy with righteous repentance, said warmly, 'Nice day for February.' And smiled again.

It was the second time in two days he had actually started a conversation, something of a record for Bernard. Hugo, rattled, said, 'Oh, yes. Yes, it is.'

And then Bernard, wonder of wonders, said encouragingly, 'Why don't you and your – um, you and Carl – why don't you two come over tonight for a meal? Henrietta and Isabel are coming. I'm sure Mary will have prepared enough food for an army.'

Hugo, struck dumb with joy, nodded. Bernard smiled yet again with all the warmth he could muster and, waving jauntily, went into the farmhouse, well pleased with his spot of neighbourliness.

Carl, still at the window, threw reason to the wind and vowed he'd sue Bernard for all he was worth.

The dinner party was a disaster. Mary, furious that she had been forced, through her own bumbling, to invite Henrietta, burnt the roast, and her Yorkshire pudding was soggy. The fact that Bernard had invited Hugo and Carl threw her into a complete tizzy; not that she minded them, because she was rather relishing her secret knowledge of their relationship, but because she had rashly, stupidly, confided to Henrietta that she thought Hugo was in love with her, and now felt a total fool in front of them both.

Carl was in a temper, for how could he sue a man with whom he was breaking bread, as it were? He was also uneasy, wondering if perhaps he had been wrong in thinking Bernard inviolable. The scene in the farmyard that morning had distressed him more than he cared to admit.

Isabel, whom one normally could count upon to behave in a civilized English manner, was brooding and unresponsive, toying with her food and looking vacant. Love didn't suit her, Mary thought sourly, it dulled her presence, made jagged her edges. Hugo was feverishly over-excited; the boys were fractious and complaining and were crossly sent off to bed, and Krissy, always quick to catch the prevailing mood, cried and grizzled. This, of course, made Henrietta prickly. So did the overdone meat.

'And how was London?' Carl asked Isabel over the mushy peas.

'Oh, the same,' she replied vaguely, because she had spent

most of the time in Fabrizio's bed in the small hotel where he was staying, emerging only briefly to attend her daughter's marriage ceremony. 'Wet. Cold. Everyone rushing about.'

'I love London!' Mary cried. 'The Chelsea Flower Show, Harrods, the Christmas lights—'

'Oh, for God's sake, Mary, that's not London, that's a fantasy reserved for the country cousins.' Henrietta, having spilt thick gravy over her white silk blouse, was churlish.

'I know what Mary means,' Carl began diligently, remembering he was a guest and had a role to play. 'And I see your point as well, Henrietta. But the fantasy and reality are sometimes mixed, so that it's hard to see what is real and what illusion.' He smiled enigmatically, thinking to himself what a fine diplomat he would have made.

'Oh, Carl, you know you hated London the past few years,' Hugo said. 'It became so dull and tedious. I must say, I'm glad to be out of it.'

'So am I,' Henrietta agreed. 'It's like most cities, dirty and smelly and full of foreigners.'

Mary sniffed, unhappily watching her guests toy with the food on their plates. 'I hate it when the English abroad start bad-mouthing their own country.'

Isabel said, 'I don't think we're exactly doing that.'

'Of course not,' Henrietta said impatiently. 'And even if we were, it's much healthier than romanticizing the soggy island like you do, creating your little bit of England in the middle of Italy and refusing to assimilate.'

At this Mary burst into tears.

'Oh, shit,' Henrietta said. 'I should have known.'

'Henrietta,' Isabel said sternly, 'get a grip. That was bloody rude.'

Bernard, whispering to Mary to pull herself together, said staunchly, 'Henrietta wasn't being rude. Mary is just over-wrought.'

'Oh, for Chrissake!' Carl exclaimed, forgetting diplomacy.

'And no wonder! I'd be overwrought too if I'd been put down like that at my own dinner table.'

'Oh, come now, Carl,' Hugo jumped in. 'We're only having a friendly discussion. Bernard's right, Mary is just overtired. After all, she's been cooking for us all day.'

At this Mary cried harder, thinking of the splendid meal she had planned which had now gone wrong. She prided herself on her culinary skills.

Isabel said soothingly, 'Look, shall I make some coffee?'

'I wouldn't bother,' Carl said. 'I think we should all go home. Then perhaps Bernard will pay some attention to his wife.'

He, bristling, said, 'And what exactly do you mean by that?'

'Sitting there, letting her cry . . .'

'Stop interfering, Carl.'

'Stop taking sides so obviously, Hugo.'

'All this bloody fuss just because that wimp sheds a few tears.'

'Henrietta!'

And then, as one, everyone stood up, mumbled goodbyes or apologies according to their character, and walked out of the house.

And the pudding, apple pie with custard, had yet to be served.

A few days later Alberto the postman, drinking cappuccino in the café with Daniela, said, '*Uffa!* Those English, all tucked away in their little conclave, are they not strange?'

'All English are strange,' she replied philosophically. 'But amusing. What is so particularly strange?'

'Well, they've all moved from England and then they stick together like football hooligans. Most of them haven't learned more than three or four words of Italian.'

'Yes, true,' Daniela mused, 'but if I were living in England, I would want to be surrounded by Italians.'

They both thought about this for a few moments. Living in England was so alien a thought, so improbable, so undesirable, that they abandoned it at once.

'The point is,' Alberto said, draining the last of the coffee from his cup, 'they don't seem to be speaking to each other anymore.'

'*Davvero*? Truly?' Daniela, who spoke to everyone, even her few enemies if only to insult them, was disbelieving. 'You are joking, surely?'

'Yesterday, I was delivering the post, and I see the farmer's wife, the little one like a mouse, and I say, jovially as usual, *buongiorno*! She starts to speak, then sees the blonde one – 'Etta, I call her – and rushes away. Then 'Etta, who is my friend as you know, comes to me for her post and the older homosexual walks up from the village, right past us, and does not say a word!'

'But he seems such a pleasant man.'

'He is, usually. We always exchange a few words in Italian, or sometimes in English now that 'Etta has improved my speech. But this time he is not speaking to anyone, looking extremely surly.'

'*Che peccato*! What a shame,' Daniela clucked. 'This is not like him. He always has pleasant words for us when he comes into the village. Well, and then?' she prodded, loving all this. The English were certainly a rich source of amusement and gossip, just the thing she needed these days now that she was nearing seventy and had just about exhausted the potential of the village.

'*Allora*, you will not believe, but the farmer drove his tractor into the yard, and before he could dismount, everyone walked away without even saying a word, and all scowling furiously. I tell you, there is an atmosphere at *La Piccola Valle* that is not very pleasant these days.'

They tutted and shook their heads thoughtfully, thoroughly enjoying it all. Then the door opened and Henrietta walked in.

Both Daniela and Alberto greeted her affectionately, and spent several minutes chucking Krissy on the chin and bringing her sweet pastries to nibble on. Not knowing English, they both thought Henrietta a sweet, good-natured lady, which, oddly, she was with them, not knowing enough Italian to be abrasive. Her sharp tongue was more a result of habit than forethought; though Henrietta could be wickededly naughty, she was not consciously malicious. Besides, she liked the Italians.

Daniela retreated to serve some customers, and Henrietta settled opposite Alberto across the blue-flowered tablecloth.

''Etta, *cara*, you've not been to the village for days, and yesterday you did not speak to me,' he said with a pout.

'It's not you, it's the others. They piss me off,' Henrietta said sulkily.

There then began a rather involved English lesson as she tried to explain what the English mean by 'pissing off'.

The door opened again and Hugo walked in, nodded curtly to Daniela and Alberto, pointedly ignored Henrietta, bought two *brioche* and walked out again.

'He too has become so unfriendly,' Alberto said. 'What is happening to all you English?'

'He's sulking because he fancies Bernard.'

Albert looked blank. 'Fancies?'

'*L'amore*, Alberto. You ought to know about that, being Italian. Hugo is in love with Bernard.'

'But how can that be? I thought he was happy with the older man?'

'Oh, I'm sure he is, but he's the type who needs other passions, other intrigues. Carl is the faithful sort, but never Hugo.'

'They have told you all this?' Alberto asked wonderingly.

'No, but I was in the fashion world. I've known plenty of men like Hugo. They're as randy as tomcats, just like the straight ones.'

'But Bernard, he is surely not homosexual?'

'Not a bit of it.'

'Ah, I thought not. He is so very married.'

'That does not necessarily preclude gayness, but yes, he is strongly hetero. He is also in love with me.'

'What?'

'That's why Hugo dislikes me, you see. In his heart of hearts, he knows I'm a threat.'

'But . . . you are having the – how you say? – the love sex with the farmer? *L'avventura*?'

'An affair is the word you are looking for, Alberto. Of course I'm not having an affair with that dickhead. And, no, I'm not going to explain to you what that means. I have no time for love *or* sex, and no inclination. The only love of my life is my daughter.'

Daniela, having dispensed with her customers, came over in time to hear the last sentence which Henrietta had managed to say in grammatically atrocious Italian. 'And such a beautiful daughter too,' Daniela cried, picking up the baby and carrying her around the shop.

Henrietta, totally content, listened to the babble of praise for her darling Krishna. Several women came into the shop and all of them talked to Henrietta, cooed over the baby, commented on her thick shiny black hair, her small button nose. Henrietta, swollen like a spring bud with maternal pride and the bit of extra weight she had gained, felt ready to burst with motherhood and maturity. She wondered why she had not had a baby years ago.

'Your baby enjoys the fuss made of her,' Alberto said idly.

'She thrives on it. Love and affection is good for babies.'

'True. But she needs more than friends to do so. She needs family, brothers and sisters. Me, I come from a large family, five of us. It is a good thing. Look how I bloom from all the attention! I am the youngest, you see.'

Daniela, holding the baby high in the air and making her

squeal with delight, agreed. 'I have so many children, and though they are grown now, they are still affectionate with each other. A single child is no good, 'Etta, she will be lonely. You are still young: find a husband, have more babies.'

Alberto, leering, said teasingly, 'There are many Italian men who would be happy to give you a baby, 'Etta. An Italian brother for your little Indian daughter.'

Alberto and Daniela fell about laughing, thinking this a great joke. Henrietta, eyes narrowed, looked at Alberto contemplatively. The postman, with his casual flirtatious words, had watered a seed long since planted in her consciousness; a seed of longing, of desire for her own baby, one conceived and carried in her own body rather than that of another woman far away in a dusty Indian city. Krissy, with her big brown eyes and dark olive skin, her winning ways, had sown that seed. Henrietta, like all lovers, was greedy. She wanted more of a good thing; she wanted, craved, another baby, not just for herself but as a playmate for her daughter whom she adored beyond measure.

She had thought, fleetingly, of adopting again, but it would mean beginning once more the long hauls to India, the weeks of hanging about waiting for an adoption to go through, the legal hassles – the time wasted. She had Krissy now; she had endured it before, patient and stoical, but now she wanted to stay right here in Umbria with her child. Moreover, there was no chance of Isabel's being with her as she had been before; her sister was sinking fast into a quicksand relationship with Fabrizio and certainly was not about to give up her new job, her new man, and go running back to India to help Henrietta adopt another baby.

And so, in this lazy soporific Umbrian village, Henrietta narrows her beautiful eyes and looks calculatingly at Alberto, who is still smirking over his little joke. She takes in first his physique and is pleased to see that, though small, he is neatly made, compact, slim but muscular. Then, the details.

Henrietta carefully studies his face, its bones; she is gratified to see they are good, that his face even in old age will be tolerable.

She notes his nose. It is large and Roman, and she feels this is a good thing; she is aware that hers is far too small and puggish. A perfect nose would be the combination of the two, and this fact she stores away along with the other details of Alberto's appearance. His hair, though prematurely thinning, is dark, almost black: another good point. Henrietta would like a sibling of Krissy's to resemble his or her sister as much as possible.

Alberto stops laughing, noticing Henrietta studying him seriously.

'Is something wrong?' he asks.

'I was just wondering how old you are,' she asks bluntly.

Alberto, a man of the world and used to the funny ways of the English, does not find this question strange.

'*Trentanni.*'

Henrietta makes him repeat it in English, just to make sure. Thirty is a good age; his sperm will still be vigorous.

'You are healthy?'

Alberto rolls his eyes, to show what a ridiculous question this is. He has not been to see a doctor since he was seven and had severe earache.

Henrietta is satisfied. Giving Alberto a slow, sensual come-on smile, which is a bit lopsided because it is so long since she has used it, she invites the unsuspecting postman to dinner at her house in *La Piccola Valle della Tristezza* that very evening.

Chapter Ten

'Isabel! What are you doing home?'

'Henrietta . . . oh my God! Uh, sorry.'

'*Dio mio*! I believe we have intruded.'

'For God's sake, Henrietta, why didn't you warn us?'

'Oh, shut up, Isabel. Why aren't you two in Perugia for the night like you said you would be?'

'*Madonna*! Isabel, perhaps we should leave at once. *Spicciati*, hurry.'

'Oh, do belt up, Fabrizio. It's my home as well as Henrietta's.'

'*Porca puttana! Che situazione imbarazzante!*'

'Oh, stop swearing, Alberto. There's nothing embarrassing about this at all. We're two adults and can do what we like. Now – you know my sister Isabel, and this is Fabrizio. You remember Alberto, don't you, Isabel? Our postman?'

She said yes, of course, and refrained from adding: But not with his trousers down. Fabrizio, trying not to stare, stumbled over a footstool and swore loudly. Henrietta stuffed her capacious breasts back into her lacy bra and buttoned up her silk shirt. Then, completely insouciant, she strolled into the kitchen to make coffee, Isabel following. Alberto, zipping up, was so relieved to find an Italian in the midst of these unpredictable

English that he started babbling non-stop to Fabrizio, who was in total sympathy.

In the kitchen Isabel hissed, 'Why the hell couldn't you have taken him up to your bedroom, instead of fornicating on the sofa like that? What's going on, anyway? I thought you were through with sex.'

Henrietta said crossly, 'I thought you and Fabrizio were staying in Perugia overnight?'

'We were, but his wife is causing trouble again, still trying to get him for adultery even though she's had a lover for years. She's having his house watched, so we worked late, had a leisurely meal, and came back here.'

Henrietta spooned out coffee, pouting. 'Well, your timing was perfect,' she said peevishly. 'A few minutes later and the deed would have been done. Spoilsports!' She turned on the tap furiously, spattering water all over herself and her sister.

Isabel was staring suspiciously at the remains of dinner scattered all over the kitchen surfaces. 'Why, Henrietta, I thought you didn't cook?' she said, noting the remains of a mushroom risotto amongst other succulent goodies.

Henrietta, never able to dissemble in front of her sister, giggled. 'I bought everything ready cooked at the trattoria in the village, picked it up a few minutes before Alberto arrived. He never knew the difference.'

Isabel shook her head, then smiled, then laughed, then took her baby sister into her arms and hugged her.

'Come on,' she said, sitting them both down at the kitchen table, 'let's hear all about it. What exactly have you been up to?

Later, when Fabrizio and Alberto had had their coffee and gone, Isabel said, 'Thank God we came in when we did. Henrietta, that's the most ridiculous scheme I've ever heard, seducing Alberto solely to have a baby.'

'Why?' She was unrepentant. 'If you hadn't come home, I

could be pregnant right now.' The thought filled and mellowed her. 'Never mind,' she said kindly, 'there'll be another time.'

Isabel was horrified. 'But you can't, 'Etta.'

'Why?'

'Why? It's not, it's not – moral, that's why.'

'He wants to fuck me. I'm not forcing him to do anything.'

'I know, but does he know why you're fucking him?'

'He doesn't much care. All he wanted was to get on with it.'

'All right then, what if Alberto gets you pregnant? What then?'

'Nothing.'

'Nothing?'

'He needn't even know, Isabel.'

She groaned. It was late and she was tired. Work had been exhausting lately, with the fine March weather bringing out the spring buyers by the dozens. She was also missing Fabrizio, even though he had only left a few minutes ago. He would have stayed the night but he was working early in the morning, while she had a day off. She was annoyed at herself for missing him, and mourned her lost emotional independence.

Making one last attempt to be the wise older sister, she said, yawning, 'Modena is a small village, 'Etta, not London or Milan or those other cities you used to hang around in going to fashion shows. Everyone will know Alberto is the father. More important, Alberto will know. What if he insists on marrying you, being a proper father? Italians are big on families. Do you think he's going to let you raise his child on your own?'

'Oh, he doesn't want to marry,' Henrietta said smugly. 'He's already told me he's a confirmed bachelor. He was engaged once, years ago, and got cold feet, broke it off. He won't want to know if he fathers my baby.'

Isabel, eyes closing with exhaustion, gave up. She had

fulfilled her self-imposed obligations: she had warned, chastized, given advice. Sod it, her sister was an adult; if she wanted to screw up her life, so be it.

'Right then, Henrietta. I don't for a moment suppose you know what you're doing, but I've said all I have to say. Now all I want is my bed, I'm whacked.'

Henrietta, who knew perfectly well what she was doing, smiled and kissed her demurely on the cheek.

'You're my favourite sister,' she said sweetly, 'if my only one.'

'And you're seriously outrageous,' Isabel responded. They looked at each other affectionately, with total understanding, and then said good-night and went to bed.

The next day Fabrizio, after work, came to collect Isabel, to take her away for the weekend to a little place he knew further up on Lake Tresimeno. On the drive she told him about Henrietta and her plans for Alberto.

'He came by this morning with the post and called in for coffee. He's taking her out tonight to the cinema, would you believe, and Daniela is coming out to baby-sit. Then, I suppose, they'll try to complete what we disrupted last night.'

Fabrizio started to shake; he shook so hard Isabel became frightened and made him pull over. When the car stopped she saw with relief that he was shaking with laughter, and so was able to wait patiently until his hysterics were over.

'Well then, Fabrizio,' she said as he wiped the tears from his eyes. 'What's the joke?'

'Alberto is infertile,' he gasped. 'He had mumps a year or so ago, and the doctors told him it had made him unable to be a father.'

'Poor Alberto,' Isabel said. 'It's cruel of you to laugh at him.'

'No, no, he's relieved; he has no desire to be anything other than a carefree bachelor all his days. He told me all this while you and Henrietta were gossiping for so long in the kitchen. It's your sister that's amusing me so. The surprise she will have!' And he laughed again so hard that he fell out of the car, forgetting he had opened his door to let in the early-March sunlight.

After Isabel had bathed the cuts on his face with some drops of mineral water which she had found in the car, she said, 'I really must phone Henrietta and tell her.'

'No, no, it is such a splendid joke on her, please don't tell her.'

Isabel was tempted, thinking it would be good for her sister's character, make her a little less smug. But she remembered when Henrietta had first adopted the baby, those early weeks in India when her sister had cried tears of anguish because she'd thought she was unworthy of being a mother to such a fine baby as Krissy. Motherhood was no joking manner to Henrietta.

'I have to tell her. She would wonder, as the weeks went by, why she didn't conceive. Become frantic. It would upset her terribly. She really does love being a mother, you know. Besides, she doesn't even fancy Alberto, so what's the point? Let me have your mobile phone, I'll call her at once.'

'Poor Alberto,' Fabrizio sighed. Isabel was inclined to agree.

'Alberto, *grazie*, that was a super film, though I wish I had understood it better. At least in England the Italian films have sub-titles. Oh, hello, Daniela, how was Krissy? Did she wake up at all?'

She said that all was well, but that Isabel had phoned, and wanted Henrietta to phone her on Fabrizio's mobile at once. Henrietta cried, 'I hope nothing's wrong! I'll phone her straight away, Daniela, and then I'll drive you home.'

'It's only a ten-minute walk,' she protested.

'No problem, I'll drive you. Alberto can wait here and keep his ears open in case Krissy wakes up. Then I shall make him a nice drink, to reward him.' She smiled at him in a sultry manner. Alberto preened as she went on, 'But first I must phone Isabel.'

Five minutes later, she was back with Daniela and Alberto. Daniela said, with a jaunty wink at Alberto, '*Allora*, I will go now.'

'Yes, it's getting late, and we all have to be up at fairly early hours. Alberto will drive you on his way home.'

Alberto, astonished, said, 'But . . . but . . . I thought—'

Henrietta yawned widely. 'I'm suddenly so tired, Alberto. I must look in on my baby, and then go off to bed myself. Myself,' she repeated firmly.

At that, as if on cue, Krissy started crying, and in a flurry of goodbyes and thank yous, Henrietta dismissed them and fled upstairs.

'The English, they are crazy,' Alberto said dazedly to Daniela in his car. He felt no anger, no bruise to the ego, for precisely this reason.

'They are certainly strange,' she agreed. She couldn't wait to get home to tell all this to her adult children, several of whom were still living at home and would be up waiting to hear about her evening.

Alberto couldn't wait to get her home either, so that he could drive quickly to Perugia and visit a woman he knew there, one who would be home waiting for him even though his visits to her were sporadic. She might not be as delectable as the beautiful Henrietta, he thought reasonably, but at least she was Italian, and he knew where he stood with her.

Henrietta, consoling her crying baby, felt like crying too, with tears of frustration and a senseless rage against Alberto. She had already been imagining herself pregnant, an embryonic brother or sister for dear Krissy beginning this very night in her rounded white belly. Henrietta, feeling deeply sorry for herself, began sniffling just like her baby.

At last both Krissy and Henrietta stopped whimpering and fell into a deep sleep. Henrietta woke several hours later, cold, miserable, and suddenly lonely. She prowled around the house restlessly, wondering whether she was hungry or horny, whether she craved fucking or feeding, or perhaps getting totally sloshed. She decided, after careful thought, that she wanted none of these things. What she wanted was a baby, her very own birth-baby; she wanted the lot, swollen nipples, stretch marks, a huge tum, varicose veins.

Opening the fridge, rummaging for food, she suddenly felt the need for something substantial, something wholesome and nourishing, as if she were indeed already pregnant, as if the baby she so desperately wanted were already starting to grow inside her.

The fridge was empty except for dried-out prosciutto and a bowl of congealing risotto, the left-overs of the previous night's dinner with Alberto. None of it looked particularly wholesome, so she took a carton of milk and poured herself a glass. It was cold, and tasteless, and she wished she had heated it, wished she had something to put in it, something warming, like chocolate except that was too cloying, something more bland, more soothing . . . something like . . . like Horlicks, she thought suddenly, remembering Mary in the kitchen making endless hot drinks, remembering the great jars of white powder lined up on the open shelves which Bernard had put up, remembering . . . Bernard.

She made herself sit down, made herself take another sip of the cold milk before she thought again: Bernard.

The thought so excited her that it was hours before she finally got up from the kitchen table and went to bed.

'Henrietta, you cannot, you absolutely *cannot*! That is the most preposterous thing I've ever heard of.'

Isabel, home only an hour after an idyllic weekend with Fabrizio, had been listening with growing trepidation to her sister's rhapsodic plans for conceiving the child she was now determined to have.

'It's a disastrous idea,' she went on relentlessly, forgetting that she had decided only a couple of days ago that she wasn't her sister's keeper. 'It would cause total and complete havoc. I absolutely forbid you.'

Henrietta, radiant, took no notice. 'Isabel, it's perfect, perfect. Physically, he's just the sort of man you want for the father of your child. Well-built, well-made, muscular and broad without being fat . . . a bit too tall, I know, but that needn't be a disadvantage. And his features are so even, so straight.'

'Like the man himself,' Isabel said unthinkingly.

'Exactly. Straight, upright, honest.'

'Boring. Oh, sorry, that just came out. Didn't mean it.'

'And he's got the right character traits, too. He's kind, considerate, responsible . . .'

'Boring. Sorry, did it again.'

'Isabel, stop it. You're so cynical.'

'Well, for God's sake, Henrietta, I really don't believe I'm hearing all this. You are proposing, seriously proposing, that Bernard be the father of your child? You must be totally mad.'

Henrietta, billowing like a puffball in her white kaftan, wandered restlessly around the sitting room, looking like a well-fed angel escaped from the top of the Christmas tree. It was late at night and she had been waiting several hours for her sister's return. Luckily, Fabrizio had another early appointment the next day in Perugia so he drove straight home, leaving Isabel alone to face the scheming of her excited sister.

'I was so looking forward to telling you my plan, Bel,' Henrietta was saying reproachfully.

Isabel thought she wouldn't mind so much the confidences she seemed always to be inspiring in people, if they all, without exception, didn't get so ratty when she was unable to share the rapture of their revelations. People not only wanted to confess everything, they wanted the confession to be applauded and approved of, no matter how appalling.

She tried to make an effort. 'Henrietta,' she said more kindly, 'you're a bit obsessive now and hardly in the right frame of mind to make a rational decision. Think for just a minute. Bernard's married, as tied to Mary as the ship is to the anchor.'

'And I wouldn't dream of coming between them!' Henrietta cried, all wounded innocence.

'Calm down, and just think. Our little *villaggio* isn't London. You can't have a quick bonk with someone as casually as you have a cup of coffee.'

'Or Horlicks,' said Henrietta, giggling.

Isabel tried to look stern. 'Be serious.'

'Oh Bel, Bel, listen to me. Bernard fancies me, has done for months – you've noticed it, Fabrizio has noticed it. And it's getting worse, not better. Soon, it'll be affecting his marriage, his relationship with Mary, the boys—'

'His cows,' Isabel said. Then put her hand over her mouth.

'Exactly.' Henrietta smiled. 'Now, if I let him have his wicked way with me, if I let all his fantasies come true, he'll get me out of his system, get over me, and get on with his life again.'

'Fine. Just fine. Except what happens nine months later, when a little Bernard or Bernarda appears on the scene?'

'No one will know it's Bernard's.'

'Oh, no, only him, and how will he feel, seeing the product of his illicit coupling with you every time he walks into the farmyard?'

'Wonderful, probably. Just think how virile he'll feel, his two women and masses of children all around him where he can keep an eye on them. He'll feel macho and Italian. He'll purr, Isabel, believe me.'

'He's too English to purr. But even if he did, what

about Mary?' Isabel said triumphantly, playing her trump card.

'Mary? Why, she's always treated Bernard as one of her boys, to be stuffed with food and protected from the cold and scolded when he doesn't eat his vegetables. So long as he doesn't go off his food she'll never even notice.'

Isabel, seeing the delicate sheen of truth on this bold statement, was surprised into silence. She gave up and went to bed, dreaming of Fabrizio purring in her ear. She awoke in the early hours, frustrated as hell, though she had just spent a gloriously sensual weekend with him. She wondered idly if Italy was good for any of them.

Spring, and the birds are delirious at *La Piccola Valle della Tristezza*, swirling and swooping and making birdsong, as is their nature. The dog is delirious too, running about trying to catch them, but he, like Henrietta, has become full and round with contentment and the slow easy living of this secluded Umbrian *villaggio*.

Bernard, walking around his bottom fields, is too preoccupied to notice the blossoming of the poplars, the tentative green prickling the woodland, indications of the season. He is looking at the land that will never be his, the damp soggy meadows that he will never have the chance to drain, fertilize, and fill with his beloved cows, and his beloved Henrietta too, lying with her in the gentle woodland. Shaking his head mournfully, he decides it is time for his mid-day meal, and his spirits rise considerably when he remembers that Mary, braving the Italian roads at last, has taken the boys all the way to Perugia in the hope that she can find something equivalent to Marks and Spencer's. With relief Bernard realizes that he needn't eat the huge repast she will have prepared for him; he can have a cup of tea and something out of the cupboard and read *Farmers' Weekly* from England while the dog wolfs down the meat pie Mary has left in the warming oven.

Cheered, he walks quickly to the house. Ah, Bernard, innocently contemplating sardines on toast and *Farmers' Weekly*, do you have any inkling what else awaits you on this fecund spring Saturday, what other appetites are about to be assuaged, what other delights may be lurking in your kitchen as you tread steadfastly up the hill? If you did you would quicken your pace, perhaps even break into a run like the dog at your side, whose instinct is much better than yours.

Or maybe not, Bernard, maybe not. Perhaps you would just turn tail and fly away in the opposite direction. There's no way of knowing how a man will react when at last he is about to get what he's always wanted.

'Henrietta!'

'*Ciao*, Bernard. I thought, as Mary was away for the day, I'd be neighbourly and pop in to say hello.'

Henrietta, seated at the kitchen table, narrowed her eyes sensuously at Bernard, at the same time slapping the dog who was jumping up on her thin white flimsy dress. Bernard, grabbing the dog and shoving him back outside, had a wild vision of stark nakedness under all that filmy material, but realized he must be hallucinating. He closed the door firmly on the dog and tried to pull himself together.

'Uh, thanks. Cup of tea?'

'No, thank you.' Henrietta smiled sweetly.

'Coffee?'

'No. Nothing.'

This completely threw Bernard. 'You sure? Sardines? On toast? Or some of this meat pie Mary left in the oven?'

He positively ran to the Aga to get it out, set it triumphantly on the table in front of Henrietta. There it sat, steaming, filling the kitchen with the aroma of wholesomeness and Mary.

'Shit, Bernard,' Henrietta said with some asperity. 'Every time I come here I get stuffed with food.'

'Oh, sorry. It's just that, being dinner time and all, I thought that's what you wanted. To, uh, get stuffed. I mean, uh, have some food. You know.'

Henrietta stopped being seductive for a few moments while she studied him, wondering if she really wanted her baby to have the same brain cells as Bernard's. She eyed him critically as he stood helplessly in front of Mary's meat pie, and decided his body more than made up for the fact that he was a sad, sad simpleton. She would have to trust that her own genes in the brain department would prove to be dominant.

Bernard, wondering if he smelled like sheep shit, stood nervously against the Aga, frightened out of his wits. Henrietta, having made her decision, glowed sex like an illuminated cathedral in his direction, and slowly began walking towards him. Before Bernard could decide whether to flee or fight, or to faint dead away in shock and rapture, the front door opened and Hugo, full of the joys of spring, bounced into the kitchen.

'Bernard! *Ciao*! I couldn't help noticing Mary and the boys drive away, so I thought I'd call and say hello. My dear boy, you look flushed, are you all right?'

He pressed his hand tenderly to Bernard's forehead, letting it linger there, but before he could get a chance to enjoy it Henrietta said, with rather begrudging admiration, 'God, Hugo, I have to hand it to you, you're quick.'

Hugo, after getting over the initial shock (for he did not see Henrietta when he so breezily entered the kitchen), said, 'You too, darling. If I didn't know better, I'd say you had nothing on underneath all that froth.'

They looked at each other with mutual respect, feeling they were opponents worthy of each other. Bernard looked regretfully at *Farmers' Weekly* sitting on the mantelpiece above the Aga and felt unmanned by it all, not that he understood it. The dog, locked outside the house, was howling for food and sympathy; Bernard felt inclined to do the same.

'HENRIETTA, I KNEW YOU'D BE HERE! Oh, you are seriously

wicked!' Isabel, rushing into the kitchen with Krissy in the backpack, looked at her sister in exasperation.

Henrietta pouted. 'I thought you were taking Krissy down to the lake. You said you would on your next day off. I didn't expect you back for hours.'

'I got sidetracked. I stopped at the village and picked up the local paper – look at this. You too, Hugo – Bernard.' She pulled a newspaper out of her jacket pocket and spread it on the kitchen table.

'HUGO, YOU SHIT! I should have known you'd be here,' Carl cried as he stormed into the kitchen. 'How many times have I warned you?'

'Uh, Carl. I thought you were going off looking for antiques today? That place you heard of near Siena.'

Isabel, turning over the pages of the newspaper, said without looking up, 'He was, but we met in Daniela's café and the whole village seemed to be there, talking about *this*.' She pointed triumphantly to the page she had found at last.

They all gathered round, looking at the large photograph at the top of the page, trying to decipher the Italian.

'Why, those are the fields I wanted to buy,' Bernard said.

'The land at the bottom, with the woods,' Henrietta realized.

'Why is it in the paper?' Hugo asked.

'Because it's up for development,' Carl nearly shouted. 'Some bastard has bought it and is trying to get permission to put up a huge complex, a holiday camp for English and Americans. A sports pavilion, golf course – look at all these plans!'

'Look, see the drawings for the proposed buildings, aren't they hideous?' Isabel wailed.

'Bloody Italians!' Hugo exclaimed. 'Those woods are superb, I can't believe they'll be cut down.'

'Surely they won't get permission?' Henrietta said.

Isabel scanned the paper again. 'It says here, everything has just about gone through; they're just waiting for formal notification before the building starts.'

'That could mean anything in Italy. But it doesn't look good.'

Bernard, in a state of total confusion, what with realizing Henrietta did indeed have nothing on under her white dress, and Hugo pressing up against him under pretext of getting closer to the newspaper, and the dog still howling mournfully outside, and a huge holiday complex being built on land he had coveted passionately for his cows and sheep, said dumbly, 'Can't we do anything? We're British, aren't we? We can't let them get away with this.'

There was silence as Hugo, Carl, Henrietta and Isabel straightened up from the table and looked at Bernard, as one would a prophet or an oracle. Then Carl spoke.

'You're right, Bernard, we can't let them get away with this. We'll form a committee, write letters, take this to the top if need be. We'll teach the Italians what we English can do when we are justifiably angry.'

They were all cheering this little speech when the front door flew open yet again and Mary, hair falling out of its band and drooping sadly all over her shoulders, said despairingly, 'Oh, Bernard, you'll never guess what's happened. It's too awful.'

'You've seen the newspaper too, have you?' Isabel said grimly.

'Newspaper? What newspaper?'

'Isn't that why you're back?' Henrietta said. 'You're supposed to be in Perugia.'

'I never got there. That is, I got there but never got out of the car. I just took one look and turned around and came home.'

'Good God,' Carl said. 'Is it in the national press too?'

They all became terribly excited, exclaiming with consternation and indignation that it must be a huge complex indeed to be mentioned in the national papers.

Finally, stamping her foot in just the tiniest bit of what could be called a fit of temper since no one would listen to her, Mary said crossly, 'I've not seen any newspaper – I don't know what you're all on about. It's the boys I'm talking about. They're covered in chicken pox!'

With this, on cue, three little boys trooped miserably into the house, disbanding the party with alacrity.

Poor Bernard. The next few days bring such activity, with Italian doctors and fractious children, with meetings and protests over the proposed building site, with Mary bustling like she has never bustled before – *povero* Bernard is never to know whether he has almost been seduced by Henrietta, or by Hugo, or by neither. Perhaps he too, Bernard thinks, is sickening for some sort of pox; he certainly feels deranged enough to be sickening for *something*.

Bemused, unused to contemplation and temptation and the like, he retreats, and heads back to his sheep, embracing his large woolly flock of security blankets with relief. This respite is, of course, only temporary, but Bernard doesn't know this.

Life's retreat is only momentary. It is still lurking, Bernard. It's best always to remember this.

Chapter Eleven

'*Mi dispiace*, Henrietta. I'm sorry, I don't understand. What's wrong with a holiday estate? Daniela is delighted, all those English coming into the café. She can charge 3000 lire for a cup of tea.'

'Daniela doesn't serve tea here. She says she doesn't understand tea.'

'She will when the English come. And for the Americans, she can charge 4000.'

'She can't have one price for the Americans and one for the English!'

Alberto shrugged his shoulders, watching Daniela at the other side of the shop serving her customers. 'Why not? She has two prices for coffee.'

'Yes, one for a large cup, the other for a small.'

Alberto laughed. 'The English, they always ask for large. The villagers, always for the small.'

'So?'

'So have you not noticed? Daniella only has one size of cup for espresso: both are the same.'

Henrietta, who ordinarily would have got indignant over this, had more important things to talk about. 'I can't believe you really want that beautiful woodland at the bottom of *La*

Piccola Valle all chopped down to make a huge ugly holiday complex.'

Alberto shrugged, and ordered another cappuccino. He would never understand the English. He and Henrietta had resumed their friendship after the abortive attempt to become lovers. That Henrietta had, for about twenty-four hours, wanted madly to go to bed with him, he had no doubt; he also understood perfectly that she had suddenly, inexplicably, changed her mind. He would have been enraged had Henrietta been Italian; because she was English, he chalked it down to a mixture of frigidity and lunacy. Besides, the woman in Perugia, whose arms he had rushed into the night Henrietta had dismissed him, was pleasuring him nightly with renewed passion brought on by his temporary diversion with the Englishwoman.

Alberto, a philosopher at heart, saw no reason why he and Henrietta couldn't carry on with their friendship as before. It was after all to his advantage to be Henrietta's friend rather than lover; he learned more English that way, Italian being the language of love and English that of communication.

The door opened and Hugo and Carl walked into the café.

'Ah, you're back,' Henrietta said, beckoning them to sit down next to her. 'How did you get on in Florence?'

Hugo collapsed on to the bench next to Henrietta, shoving the pushchair with a sleeping Krissy out of the way, much to Henrietta's annoyance. However, before she could say anything, Carl, having ordered coffee from Daniela, joined them and said, 'Useless, totally useless.'

'Weren't they any help at all?' Henrietta cried.

'Not a bit, they didn't seem in the slightest concerned.'

'Bloody Italians,' Henrietta muttered, forgetting she had recently explained to Alberto that 'bloody' was a derogatory term.

'All the way to Florence, for nothing,' Hugo moaned.

'Perhaps Fabrizio can come up with something else,' Carl mused.

It was he who had given them the name of a minor government official who had something to do with conservation in Umbria and Tuscany, and Carl, putting on his best Civil Service suit and manner, had sallied forth, Hugo coming along for moral support, to present the case for *La Piccola Valle della Tristezza*.

'Did you tell him that the woodland is the loveliest for miles around?' Henrietta demanded.

'Plenty of rabbits,' Alberto agreed. 'And pigeons. Good shooting.'

'Of course I told him, and it's all in writing, too, thanks to Fabrizio. In the end I left him our petition and he said he'd see what he could do, but he also said it's we English who are developing the country by moving here, so what right have we to complain about ruining the countryside?'

This brought on a chorus of righteous indignation from the English, with terms like 'Cheeky bugger!' and 'Insolent foreigner!' being thrown about.

Daniela was bringing the coffee when the door opened again and Mary came in. 'Ah, Daniela, *vorrei*, uh, *la*, no, I think I mean *i*. Yes, that's it: *Vorrei i cornetti*. Is that right?' She looked anxiously at the Italians, relieved when they nodded their heads encouragingly. 'Richard, John and David are trying to teach me the language, but I'm afraid I'm such a stupid pupil.' The Italians nodded brightly again.

Mary paid for the *cornetti*, rabbiting on, in English of course, 'I'm in such a state I never got round to baking today. I know these aren't exactly English teacakes but they'll have to do.' She turned and saw the others. 'Carl and Hugo,' she shrieked. 'How did you get on, are you back from Florence already? Wait a minute, let me get Bernard. He's waiting in the car but I know he'd like to hear your news.'

She went out and was back in a minute with Bernard, looking strangely scrubbed and awkward in his city clothes: beige wool trousers and checked country cotton shirt and a tan sports jacket, feet neatly shod in brown lace-up brogues. Everyone shifted and made room for them around the table.

'Oh, Daniela, I wished you served tea!' Mary said. 'She's just being stubborn, you know,' she whispered loudly to Carl. 'Every café in Umbria serves tea. Well, never mind, I'll have a coffee, though goodness knows how I'll sleep tonight.'

'*Grande o piccolo*?' Daniela asked.

'Oh, large, please,' Mary replied in English, forgetting that she was trying to learn Italian. 'I may as well be slaughtered for a sheep as for a lamb.'

Alberto caught Henrietta's eye and winked. He was enjoying all this tremendously even though he didn't for a minute understand this feeling of tenuous alliance blossoming between the little party of English. Only a week or two ago they were none of them speaking to each other and now they were sitting around drinking cappuccino together. And in the afternoon too, Alberto thought with a mixture of amazement and amusement: everyone knew that one drank cappuccino in the morning only, and espresso in the afternoon. He shook his head, marvelling at these foreigners.

After Carl told them about his lack of success in Florence, Mary said, 'We were in Perugia today. Bernard had to go to the dentist.'

'Poor Bernard, do you have toothache?' Henrietta cried sympathetically, smiling angelically at him. She had still not forgotten her plans for him, sidetracked though she had momentarily become by the declaration of war against the new proposed holiday complex.

'You poor thing, Bernard, how dreadful,' Hugo said, determined not to be outdone. 'There's nothing as painful as toothache. You must come to our place for some of Carl's Cognac, it's bliss for medicinal purposes. I'll give you some while he's busy upstairs with his Italian tapes.'

Carl, speechless at this effrontery, would have lost his temper and the whole party would have forgotten that they were allies if Mary hadn't burst in with, 'Bernard *would* have had a toothache if I hadn't insisted he go for his routine check-up. I had to practically drag him away from his cows. One of them isn't too well. He's had two fillings.'

'The cow has two fillings?' Henrietta said.

'No, Bernard.' Mary stopped, confused, suddenly realizing she had been sidetracked. 'Anyway, that's not important. What I started to say was that we went to see our own lawyer in Perugia, and we asked him if there was anything we could do about this awful development.'

'Did you impress upon him how dreadful it will be for the whole village?' Hugo asked.

Alberto, who was just able to follow this, was about to say something to the effect that the ten men, women and children comprising *La Piccola Valle* were not exactly the whole village, but he spent so much time trying to decide whether he should say it in Italian or attempt it in English that he lost his chance.

'Of course we did,' Mary went on. 'I told him the area was on a hillside sloping right down into our valley; I said that you'd be able to see those ugly buildings for miles around; I pointed out that it would totally ruin the village of Modena and especially our little valley of trees.'

No one quite knew what she was on about with the trees (Mary hadn't got as far as *tristezza* in her Italian lessons with her sons) but no one cared enough to pursue this.

'So what did your *avvocato* say?' Carl asked.

'Oh, Bernard, you tell them. It still gets me so upset.'

Bernard, who had as yet not said a word, letting the others talk about him in his presence as if he were one of his own cows, opened his mouth but nothing came out. He was made even more than usually tongue-tied by Henrietta and Hugo sitting opposite him and taking turns narrowing their eyes salaciously at him. Finally he began, 'Well, our solicitor said—'

'He said there was nothing we could do about it,' Mary

cried. 'He said once planning permission has been given, there's nothing to be done.'

There was much consternation about this, with one or two vituperative imprecations against the Italians that, luckily, Alberto didn't quite catch. Daniela, thinking what a jolly lot the English could be when they weren't running about sulking, pulled up a chair and joined them. Krissy, waking, was given a bottle and a taste of some chocolate *baci* from Daniela.

The door opened again and Isabel entered.

'You're early,' Henrietta said as everyone moved around to make room for her sister.

'I was showing someone a property not far from here and decided to call it a day.' Isabel, after chatting a few minutes to Daniela, ordered an espresso. Everyone else then decided to have another round of whatever it was they were drinking. Daniela, busily getting the orders, thought how exciting it all was, and how wonderful that the grand new holiday complex would bring many such English people into her little café and bakery, all drinking cappuccino at all hours of the day and night and of course tea which she made often at home for one of her anglicized daughters but refused out of principle to have in her café. But being a modern woman, she would go with the flow, change with the times: afternoon tea would most definitely be served, in either large or small sizes as requested.

'Did you talk to Fabrizio?' Mary asked Isabel. 'Did he find out who bought the fields and woodland?'

'It would be a help if we knew,' Carl agreed. 'It's easier to know who it is you're fighting.'

'Bloody Italians,' Hugo muttered. Alberto, catching this, reprimanded the Englishman sharply, but no one understood him except Isabel who was too preoccupied to take much notice.

'Did Fabrizio find out?' Bernard pressed her.

Isabel hesitated. 'Well, yes and no.'

Everyone spoke at once.

'Is it someone local?'

'Is it that farmer from the Veneto with pots of money who bought the big farm outside the village?'

'I'll bet it's one of those *avvocato* chaps, someone who knows every lucrative bit of property in Umbria. Crooks, all of them.'

When they'd finally calmed down, and Alberto and Daniela had stopped pestering her for an explanation, for it was all going too fast even for Alberto, Isabel said, 'Fabrizio has found out who bought the property. But he can't tell us who it is.'

There was another outcry. Isabel, exasperated, said defensively, 'Look, I don't like it any better than you do, but it's professional courtesy. Fabrizio happens to know the *avvocato* involved with the property sale, who told him in strictest confidence. The owner apparently wants to remain anonymous.'

'He would, the rotter! If I could get my hands on him—' Mary cried.

'Steady on,' Bernard murmured.

'How odd,' said Carl, 'all this secrecy. I don't understand it.'

'But surely Fabrizio can tell *you*?' Henrietta said. 'I mean, whose side is he on?'

'Henrietta's right. Surely Fabrizio as our friend has a duty to let us know the name of the owner,' Hugo agreed.

Isabel, in the middle of translating the rally of English bouncing around the table, was luckily not able to answer for a moment. She had said this herself to Fabrizio, that very morning in his office.

'What is all this ridiculous secrecy?' she had demanded rather crossly, being in an irritable mood anyway. She and Fabrizio hardly had time alone together these days and it was making her very touchy indeed. His wife was threatening him with ruin again; her lover was proving elusive to Fabrizio's detective work; the house in Perugia was definitely out of bounds to Isabel and the only time they made love, apart from the odd times Fabrizio spent the night at *La Piccola Valle*, was during their infrequent weekends away. Isabel was bothered, and bothered that she was bothered. It was all too reminiscent of the lecturer, which terrified her.

Fabrizio, in no better mood thanks to the machinations of his wife, was not feeling exactly tolerant towards the inhabitants of the *villaggio* and their squabbles. He thought they were going ridiculously over the top about this development business; a tennis player himself, he thought a massive sports complex a good idea, and if he were in their shoes, would be delighted to have new modern courts practically outside his doorstep.

'I don't understand why there is this secrecy, what the big deal is,' Isabel persisted to Fabrizio. 'Why doesn't the new owner come out and face us like a man? He must know that we will fight to the bitter end, that we won't take this lying down. And don't ask me what all those clichés mean, Fabrizio, I'm not myself or I wouldn't be talking in them.'

'There is no, as you say, big deal, Isabel. The owner purchased in secrecy, that was a condition. My friend, another *avvocato* like myself, shouldn't even have told me, but we are old friends and he had had too much *grappa* that night. I wish to God I had not mentioned it to you.'

'And me, Fabrizio? *Us*? I suppose I don't count as an old friend. I suppose old lovers don't count as anything?'

'*Non essere stupida*, Isabel – don't be so silly. All right, if you want, if you insist, I will tell you.' Here Fabrizio paused dramatically for effect, before continuing: 'I will tell you, if you request it of me, but you too must be sworn to secrecy. You must not tell the other English, or anyone else.'

'What's the point of that? You know I'll tell the others – I'll do anything to stop the development.'

'Then I cannot tell you.'

'No, I suppose you can't. Goodbye, Fabrizio, I'm going.'

Fabrizio, hurrying towards her, ran into Francesca, his secretary, who had entered with an armful of papers. He said from the floor, where he was trying to pick up the assorted envelopes and clippings Francesca had been carrying, 'Isabel, what is this goodbye? You are not going to let something as trivial as a holiday estate come between us? Surely our passion can survive a sports complex?'

He was so flustered that he said this in Italian, much to the amusement of Francesca, who giggled. Isabel, replying in English, said coldly, 'I'm off to show someone a house, Fabrizio. I have work to do.'

'Oh,' he said, relieved. 'Will I see you later?' Isabel churlishly said nothing.

Now, in the café in Modena, having finished explaining to Alberto and Daniela exactly what was happening, she said, 'Look, I don't like it any more than you do, but there's nothing more we can do.'

'Something odd is going on here,' Carl said.

'Very strange,' Mary agreed. 'This big conspiracy of silence.'

'Not cricket,' Bernard agreed.

'It certainly is odd of Fabrizio, not telling us,' Henrietta said.

'Almost as if he's hiding something,' Hugo added.

There was a longish silence, giving Bernard time to mull things over and think about whether or not he wanted to speak.

'I wonder,' he said at last, 'whether Fabrizio bought the property himself?'

There was a moment's silence, while everyone digested this, and during which Henrietta thought that maybe she had underestimated Bernard's brain. And then pandemonium broke out as everyone began speaking at once, saying of course it must be Fabrizio, swearing they'd suspected it from the very start. Only Isabel kept quiet; she, and Alberto and Daniela who hadn't understood a word of what was going on.

'He was quite interested in that land on Christmas Day,' Carl said thoughtfully. 'Had a good look at it.'

'And he's a lawyer, he'll have known the land had potential for building.'

'He even said as much.'

'And he found out who was selling it,' Henrietta said. 'I'm sorry, Isabel, but it's true. Don't you remember he said he was finding out for Bernard?'

'He obviously wanted it for himself from the start!'

Isabel, confused and furious all at once, said, 'Don't be so stupid, all of you. Of course it isn't Fabrizio, he wouldn't do a thing like that.'

Henrietta kindly said, 'Are you so sure, Bel?'

'Of course I am. I know him, for God's sake.'

Henrietta graciously kept silent, but smiled at her sister in a particularly pityingly manner, making Isabel crosser and even more confused. She had thought she knew her lecturer too and had been wrong there. Was that what love did, she wondered, obscure reality, tart it up with songs and sex so that one never saw, until it was too late, the bare grimy bones of truth under all the froth?

But she knew Fabrizio, he wouldn't do such a thing.

She'd thought the lecturer would never do such a thing either: drop her in the shit in the middle of her exams.

'I'm going home,' she said, abruptly standing up. 'Do you want a ride, Henrietta, or are you walking back?'

At that everyone stood up and said they had to get home too, and in a few minutes the shop was empty except for Alberto and Daniela.

'*Dio mio*, what a fuss,' he said.

'The English are so excitable,' Daniela agreed. 'Not placid like the Italians.' She smiled to herself in smug anticipation: her youngest daughter was baby-sitting the three English boys who were home with chicken pox while Mary and Bernard went to Perugia for the afternoon; Daniela couldn't wait for her to get home and share the day's gossip.

'I don't understand all this fuss about the woodland,' she murmured to Alberto.

'The English, they care about trees.'

'Oh?'

'Much more than about people,' Alberto said importantly, enjoying displaying his knowledge of the foreigners. 'They care too about animals. They think it disgusting to let dogs sleep outside, even in cowsheds or kennels.'

'*Santo cielo!*'

'Oh, yes,' he went on expansively, 'they are passionate about trees and dogs, yet I don't think they care much about family. Only one mother has come to stay at the *villaggio* in all the time they have been there. It was Mary's mother, and she seemed always most unhappy during that time. And that Isabel, she has three children in England and not once do they come and visit her here.'

'*Santo cielo*,' Daniela repeated disbelievingly. She had seven children and not a day went by that she didn't see at least four of them.

'A strange race, the English,' Alberto said as he had done many times before.

'But so amusing.' They looked at each other and laughed. The past few months, since the English had arrived, had been great fun; they looked forward to many more such diversions to come.

The next day Isabel, wanting to talk to Fabrizio, arrived early at work. The office was empty, which annoyed her; usually he was the first to arrive and she had counted on seeing him before the day began.

She made herself a coffee and tried to settle down, looking through some lists of new properties. It was spring, Easter was just over and the English would be here in hordes looking for rundown farmhouses to be renovated.

Isabel had picked up the intricacies of the job quickly, and Fabrizio had put her in sole charge of the English clients. She was finding it very much to her liking, enjoying the contact with Italian house owners, relishing the beauty of some of the properties on the market. She wasn't so sure about the contact with the English; though many of them were sympathetic, truly in love with Umbria and wanting to live there, there were many also who came over for all the wrong reasons, or so Isabel thought. There were those who came to run away, trying to escape themselves as much as the things they claimed to loathe about their native country: i.e., the weather, the government, their fellow countrymen. They were often bad-tempered because they had already tried house-hunting in Tuscany, and found to their disappointment that they could not afford the high prices of Chianti-shire.

Then there were the idealists, who, to Isabel, were almost worse. They idealized everything Italian, from the climate to the people, which was all very fine except that the first week of wet winter winds combined with the first Umbrian builder or shopkeeper who was less than honest, tended to throw them into paroxysms of bitter despair.

Thinking about these things and slowly sipping her hot black coffee, her thoughts wandered to Fabrizio again and she became annoyed with herself for being distracted when there was such a busy day ahead. Then she got annoyed with Fabrizio for not being there; she had an appointment shortly with an English couple from Kent and would be out with them all day. She wanted to talk to him before she left.

Giving up looking through her papers, Isabel stood up and went to the window, overlooking the Corso Vennucci. The Cathedral Square was filled with giggling Italian teenagers, all looking immaculately beautiful and well pleased with themselves.

Feeling suddenly old and tired, she made herself another coffee. She hadn't slept well last night; she and Henrietta had talked and talked about the property and Fabrizio's involvement in it, and the talking had distressed Isabel, causing her extreme agitation. She had reiterated again and again that she was sure he was not involved; Henrietta, trying uncharacteristically to be gentle with her sister, nevertheless had not agreed.

After a sleepless night during which Isabel questioned all those things people of discernment and sensitivity question during the dark nights of the soul in those black hours before dawn, such as the meaning of love, the existential futility of one human being ever trying to understand another one, and what was the point of even getting out of bed in the mornings anyway, she'd left for work as a limpid sun was rising. She would try to waylay Fabrizio and hear him tell her in Italian, the language of love, that she was his *bellissima*, his *carissima*, and that she mustn't fret because everything was fine and they would live happily ever after.

'Isabel, *buongiorno*, I am late, my wife gave me such problems on the telephone last night and I have a client already in reception. A coffee, please, black. I had a most miserable night lying in my bed in a fury of temper. Quickly with the coffee please, Isabel, the client is a busy man.'

Fabrizio, rushing into the office at high speed, plopped down unceremoniously at his desk and began quickly writing some notes, oblivious to Isabel who hadn't moved since he'd walked in.

'Isabel, the coffee?' he said, not looking up.

'Sod the coffee, Fabrizio.'

'Pardon?'

'I said, sod the coffee. And put down those papers and just look at me for a minute. I too have had a rotten night.'

'Isabel, *mi dispiace*, I forgot to kiss you when I came in, is this the problem? All right, I will kiss you now, then can you get my coffee? The client—'

'Sod your client, Fabrizio. I want to talk to you.'

– 159 –

'Isabel, I am sorry something is wrong, but can we talk later?'

'No, we cannot.'

Fabrizio, seeing at last the agitation of his darling Isabel, at once gave her his full attention. '*Bellissima*, what is it? You look dreadful. So pale, so haggard.'

'That's a contradiction in terms, Fabrizio,' Isabel said acidly. 'I cannot be both your very beautiful one as well as looking haggard.' He tried to apologize with an embrace, but she fended him off. 'You, on the contrary, after a sleepless night, look fine. Your face a trifle craggier perhaps but not much, not much. This is probably the difference in nationality rather than age, Italians being naturally more beautiful in general than the English, but age does tend to create the need for a decent night's sleep.'

She would have gone on in this manner, but Fabrizio said firmly, 'What is all this?'

Isabel, feeling pale and haggard and miserable and furious, forgot all her resolutions to approach the matter tactfully and said accusingly, 'Are you involved in the purchase of the fields and woodland below *La Piccola Valle della Tristezza*, Fabrizio? Have you bought it yourself, perhaps, or gone in with your friend the *avvocato*, who insists on all this secrecy?'

He stared at her, speechless. 'Isabel, I don't believe you are saying these things. All my problems, a client waiting outside, my wife threatening to ruin me, my secretary in reception wanting tomorrow off to visit her mother, the new man I have employed unable to begin work until next week . . . and you plague me with the trivial problems of your little *villaggio*.'

'Trivial? Is that how you see them?'

'Isabel, please, can we talk later? I must go to my client.'

'If you are so uncaring about that land being developed, then perhaps the others are right, perhaps you really are involved in the deal.'

'I don't understand what you are saying.'

'I don't think I even want to know now. I think you and I had better stop seeing each other, Fabrizio. I feel my judgement is impaired, this has all happened far too quickly.'

'Isabel, this is ridiculous! I love you. *Ti amo* . . . Oh, shit! Francesca, what is it?'

Fabrizio's secretary, giggling again, said, 'The client. He is impatient.'

'Yes, yes, tell him I am on the telephone and will be with him in a moment . . . Now, Isabel, what is all this nonsense? We belong together, you and I, how can we not see each other?'

'I didn't want this from the beginning, didn't want to get involved, it's all too painful. And besides, you think I'm haggard.'

'Perhaps that was the wrong word? I meant only that you are tired, you look tired. Isabel, what is all this? This is so unlike you.'

'Please, just leave me alone, I need a break from you, I need to think. It's all got to me: your problems with your wife, this business with *La Piccola Valle*. I don't want to see you until it's all sorted out. Please, Fabrizio . . . No, don't start trying all that kissing and touching stuff, you should have done it when you first came in—'

'Ah, Mrs Norland, there you are!' They were interrupted by an imperious English voice that went on, 'Oh. Is this, perhaps, a bad moment? You *were* expecting us.'

Fabrizio, jumping guiltily away from Isabel, glowered at the couple who had just walked in. They were both in their late-thirties or early-forties and wearing what looked to be identical white Levis, with the type of casual name-brand trainers which cost almost as much as a Versace mini-skirt. The woman had shoulder-length auburn hair and heavy make-up; the man a receding hairline and a thick moustache.

Isabel, smoothing down her skirt, said, professionally, 'Ah, Mr and Mrs Phipps, you're right on time, I see. This is Signor

Fabrizio Manetti. Fabrizio, this is Mr and Mrs Phipps, from Kent.'

Fabrizio said, rather unprofessionally, 'Didn't my secretary ask you to wait in reception?'

'She was deep into a heated discussion with a gentleman waiting there, trying to calm him down. Or so it sounded: we don't understand Italian,' Mr Phipps said with a complacent chuckle.

'My client,' Fabrizio muttered, swearing loudly at the Phipps in Italian but smiling through gritted teeth as he did so, which elicited bright but vacant smiles in return.

'Shouldn't you start learning the language, since you hope to buy a house here?' Isabel said sweetly.

At that point Francesca walked into the room again. 'Fabrizio, your wife would like so much to speak with you on the telephone,' she said in careful English, for the benefit of the clients so that they would feel at home. She had been learning the language from Isabel and was proud of her tenuous linguistic skills.

The Phipps, remembering the groping they had just walked in on, were gratified to see their preconceived notions of philandering Italians verified. They looked at each other knowingly and at Isabel with vague disapproval.

'Should we go, then?' she said breezily. 'I have several properties to show you that you may be interested in.'

Fabrizio, on the telephone and holding his hand over the mouthpiece, hissed at her in Italian, 'We have not resolved our problems. Come back to Perugia later, when you finish with those people, and we will have dinner together.'

'I've told you, I'm not going to see you any more except at work. I can't cope any longer, I need a break from you.'

'Isabel, no, I won't hear of it.'

'*Arrivederci*, Fabrizio. Yes, Mr Phipps, I shall be with you in a moment. No, Fabrizio, don't say anything more. I am sorry, Mrs Phipps, but I am discussing with the *avvocato* which properties would be best to start with. *Ciao*, Fabrizio, and don't look so furious, the Phipps are staring at you suspiciously . . . Well, Mr and Mrs Phipps, shall we go now? I'll drive you in my car, I know these Italian roads.'

'Isabel, *per favore—*'

But she was gone, gone with those two smirking English clients, and not coming back until tomorrow morning when he would be out all day at a meeting.

'Yes, what is it now?' he snapped at his wife, listening impatiently as she listed her latest demands.

Francesca hurried into the office, looking flustered. 'He's gone, Fabrizio. Your client. I tried to stop him but he said he wasn't going to wait a moment longer.'

Fabrizio swore, in Italian and then in English, and hung up on his wife as she was demanding a cheque for the latest vet's bill for the ageing cat.

Grabbing his coat, for the morning drizzle had turned to a steady rain, he ran out into the Corso Vennucci, hoping desperately to catch up not with his client, as his secretary had assumed when he went rushing out of the office, but Isabel.

Fabrizio was, after all, an Italian, and knew how to put things in their proper priority.

Chapter Twelve

The first property that Isabel showed to the Phipps was outside a nearby village. It was a small *palazzo*, moss-covered and exceedingly damp but nonetheless rather charming on a sunny day.

Unfortunately, it was still pouring with rain, and the hi-tech white trainers on the Phipps' feet were soon caked with mud which they trailed around the *palazzo* like snails leaving their slimy marks from room to room. Isabel hadn't been able to find the old stone path leading up to the building; it was, she soon saw, underwater, whether from the rain or an overflowing septic tank, she was not quite sure and did not want to investigate further. So she had brought the Phipps into the house by the back door, through the overgrown vineyard and across the derelict vegetable garden.

'It needs work,' Mr Phipps said solemnly as they all looked up at the kitchen ceiling, watching the rain confidently churning up the plaster.

'I could never live here,' Mrs Phipps cried, looking through some stunning Venetian windows into the murky swamp outside. 'How gloomy it all is!'

Isabel refrained from saying that Kent too could be gloomy in the midst of a downpour. 'It is quite beautiful when the sun is shining. The vineyards need work, but they could be made productive again. Your own wine, pressed from your very own grapes!'

Mr Phipps, stroking his moustache, said, 'Far too much work to be done for the price.'

Mrs Phipps, still looking out of the window, suddenly cried, 'Goodness, that poor Umbrian peasant, all dressed in black and huddled against the rain. Whatever is he doing out there?'

'Good heavens!' Mr Phipps exclaimed. 'He's just standing there, getting soaked.'

'How sinister! Look at him staring at the house. He gives me the creeps.'

Isabel, coming to the window, suddenly threw it open and cried out, 'Fabrizio, *sei pazzo*. You fool, what are you doing out there?'

'Isabel, there you are, where is your car?'

'Around the back. It's too muddy to park in front.'

'I know. My car is stuck by the gate. I went off the lane into the mud and I can't move it.'

'What are you doing here?'

'I came to find you, we must talk.'

Isabel closed the window hurriedly as the rain was thundering in triumphantly, drenching the Phipps' white Levis and the trendy but inefficient waterproofs they had put on before leaving Perugia.

'Who was that?'

'Do you know him?'

'Yes, of course. It's Signor Manetti.'

'Good God, I'd never have recognized him in that black overcoat.'

'No, uh, it's very Italian, that.'

'But why is he here, is something wrong?'

'No, not at all. He's here, well, uh, he's here to help; he knows the properties much better than I do and can answer more fully all your questions.'

The Phipps, hearing this explanation, were gratified; they were after all planning to spend a fair bit of good British sterling on this Umbrian property and thought it right and proper that the boss himself show some interest in their prospective purchase.

After some time, when Fabrizio had dried himself off the best he could, the four of them were in Isabel's car heading for the next property. The Ferrari was left behind in the mud, to be rescued later when the sun came out and when Fabrizio could organize something larger and stronger than a tiny Fiat to pull it out.

'You're crazy,' Isabel said as she pulled into a farmyard full of bedraggled chickens gloomily sheltering under an exposed shed. 'Why aren't you at work?' She took care not to say these things in English.

'How can I concentrate when you are trying to walk out of my life?'

'Here we are, Mr Phipps, Mrs Phipps. Here, let me just open the back door of the car, those handles are a bit stiff.'

'Bloody rain doesn't let up, does it? In Kent it was beautiful when we came away. I thought Italy was supposed to be sunny.'

'It was, Mr Phipps, until today. You must imagine what it looks like in the sunlight.'

'Is that it? It's a ruin.'

They all ran through the rain into an old stone farmhouse, the Phipps' trainers looking more than ever like well-used Wellington boots by the time they got there. Inside, Isabel said, 'Look at that beam, isn't it splendid? And the stonework.'

Mrs Phipps, huddled under the hood of her stylish but dysfunctional would-be waterproof jacket, said, 'But look at all the rubble in that corner. The wall over there is practically coming down. And is that the kitchen? There's nothing there, only that nasty old sink.'

Mr Phipps, trying to fluff up his thinning hair which was

plastered to his head like an unfinished sculpture, said huffily, 'Come now, Mrs Norland, it would cost a fortune to do this up.'

'You exaggerate, Mr Phipps. Builders aren't as expensive here as they are in Kent. Besides, you wanted land, this has twenty hectares.'

'It would need to, that's about all it has to recommend it. It's so dreary.'

Fabrizio, who had been stomping around looking at the ancient beams and old stone fireplace, said politely, 'For the amount of money you want to pay, you won't find a property with a house in immaculate condition as well as land.'

Mr Phipps fingered his soggy moustache knowingly. 'Come now, Mr Manetti, we're not idiots, we've read the papers and know what houses are going for over here. This isn't Tuscany, you know. You can't put anything over on us.'

In the car Fabrizio said to Isabel, 'Let's get rid of them, tell them we have no more houses to look at. I don't need their business.'

'You will if you keep losing clients like the one this morning.'

'Come to my house tonight, Isabel. The hell with my wife.'

'Fabrizio, it's over. I'm sure this is the right thing to do. We need a break from one another. We've rushed into this thing unthinkingly.'

Isabel suddenly slammed on the brakes. The car seized up in front of a run-down farmhouse on the outskirts of a village. 'Sorry,' she said after her passengers had sorted themselves out, 'but it's this rain. I almost drove right past.'

An old couple were living in this house and Fabrizio introduced them to the Phipps, who didn't bother to acknowledge them but began prowling around the house, opening cupboards and poking behind furniture without so much as a by-your-leave, not to mention a please or a thank you.

Isabel, contemplating murder, for the farmer and his wife were looking most distressed, was saved from doing so by Fabrizio. 'They are English and therefore crazy, so we must make allowances. They are also rich and if we humour them a bit, perhaps we can persuade them into buying your property.'

The six of them went through the house, which was large and very nearly bare with only the minimum of furniture.

'What hideous wallpaper,' Mrs Phipps commented in the living room.

'She is admiring your decor,' Fabrizio said to the old woman.

'What a dismal attempt at putting up shelves,' Mr Phipps said in the bedroom. 'They look as if they've been knocked up together by someone with six thumbs.'

'He is admiring your craftsmanship,' Fabrizio said to the old man.

When at last they left and were in the Fiat again, Mr Phipps said, 'Well, it needs total redecoration, of course, but it's solid. The land isn't as much as we wanted, but I suppose we could do with less. What did you say the price was?'

Fabrizio told him, adding another couple of million lire to what Isabel knew was the asking price. Then he said, 'We will go back to Perugia now, to the office. I have no more properties to show you.'

Isabel, knowing this to be untrue, said, 'I am sure you will find no better buy than the house you have just seen.'

'No, no, Isabel, do not rush Mr Phipps,' Fabrizio said in perfect English, nudging her gently on the shoulder. 'He is in no hurry to buy. He must think about things, yes, Mr Phipps? Do you not agree? I am sure you wish to look at what is on offer at the other agencies before you make up your mind.'

'Now hold on a moment, Mr Manetti, are you trying to get rid of me? It couldn't be that you have someone else interested in that property, now could it?'

Mrs Phipps, who did not miss the nudge, said, 'You seem to be reluctant to sell, Signor Manetti. If there is someone else interested, you must be straight with us. It seems just the sort of property we have been looking for. We wanted more land it's true, but it's not really necessary.' She began a whispered conversation with her husband.

Fabrizio, complacent in the front passenger seat, said nothing more in English, but as the Phipps were busy discussing the property in the back, he continued his harassment of Isabel in Italian.

'You are overtired, that is why you say you want to finish our relationship. I know it has not been easy with my wife—'

'It's been horrendous, Fabrizio. I feel like a criminal, skulking around Perugia avoiding your wife and her detectives or whatever they are she's set spying on us.'

'It cannot last much longer.'

'Of course it will, these things take forever. I also think you came to me on the rebound.'

'What?'

'You went straight from one woman to another. You need time to be alone, think about things. Just like I do.'

Fabrizio looked at Isabel coldly, saying, 'So this is what love is to an Englishwoman. Something you need to think about before committing yourself, like you would consider buying a house?'

'Well? And why not?'

'I thought you were more passionate than that.'

'Well, I'm not. Probably because I'm so much more mature than you.'

'Oh, *dio mio*, not that again.'

Isabel, overtaking, skidded a little getting back into her lane. This shook her, which in turn made her angry, so she said irrationally, 'I'm haggard, remember? I need my sleep, I need my time alone, I need peace. Just leave me, Fabrizio, till I can sort out what I want.'

Mr Phipps, rattling around in the back seat, whispered to his wife, 'They're fighting about the property, I'm sure of it. That woman, his assistant, wants to sell it to us, but he is telling her no. There's something odd going on.'

Mrs Phipps agreed. 'I've heard how shady these Italian businessmen are. Perhaps he has a friend he is doing a deal with. Selling it for less, and then his friend will pay *him* a million lire on the sly.'

Mr Phipps said loudly, 'Signor Manetti, my wife and I have made a decision.'

Fabrizio was too distressed to pay any attention to him. 'All right, Isabel,' he said sadly. 'I'm not going to humiliate myself with any more pleading.'

'Sorry? I don't understand Italian, remember? Mrs Norland, could you help out, please? Your boss here doesn't seem to know English that well.'

'I'm sorry, Fabrizio, but I realize how little I really know you. I still don't know if you are keeping something from me over this property deal at *La Piccola Valle*.'

'I said, Mrs Norland, I don't understand Italian. Could you please speak English?'

'*Madonna*! Not that place again, that cursed *villaggio* of yours! Can you not for one minute concentrate on *us*, on *our* problems, rather than the trivial problems of your compatriots?'

'Mrs Norland, could you please tell this bloody Italian to speak English? We want to make an offer for the house we have just seen. Now, obviously the couple will accept less than their asking price—'

'Don't you believe it,' Fabrizio said in perfect English. 'Don't think that for one moment.'

Isabel, coming home from work a few evenings later, said to Henrietta, 'Remember that horrid English couple I told you about, the Phipps? Well, they've bought the property. The old couple are over the moon. They haven't got a bean and

Fabrizio managed to wangle a higher price than they were actually asking.'

Henrietta, curled up in the gold armchair wearing loose white trousers and a white smock slightly soiled with the remains of Krissy's supper, put down the book she had been reading, *Nutrition during Pregnancy*.

'Oh, no, Henrietta,' Isabel said, picking up the book. 'You haven't seduced him, have you?'

'Bernard? Chance would be a fine thing. I can't get near him; if there's not Hugo hanging around, there's Mary.'

Isabel flopped down on the other armchair, kicking off her shoes and curling her feet up under her. 'Perhaps Mary is just worried sick, 'Etta. I wouldn't like it if you were after my husband.'

Henrietta stood up and stretched, her smock flapping around about her, making her look like a dishevelled seagull. 'Be serious, Isabel,' she said, yawning. 'Mary treats Bernard exactly like one of her boys, you know that. She hovers around him like she hovers over John, Richard and David, waiting for them to open their mouths so she can pop food into them; waiting for them to stumble and rip their jumpers so she can rush off and mend them or send to British Home Stores for another one.'

Isabel, conceding this was true, said, 'Well, I'm glad you can't get near him anyway. It was a ridiculous idea and I hope you realize it. Wait until Krissy is older before you think of having another baby. You might find you've changed your mind.'

Henrietta, naturally not listening to a word of this, said sweetly, 'Let's have dinner, shall we? Krissy's sound asleep so why don't we eat here by the fire? I bought this most wonderful prawn and pasta thing from the trattoria in the village. They're so accommodating. I said I don't eat out much because of my baby, and would they pack me a wonderful supper. And look – *voila!*'

'I think you mean *eccola*,' Isabel said absentmindedly. 'We're in Italy, not France, remember? And it looks delicious, but I'm just not hungry. What I'd like is a drink and then an early night.'

Henrietta looked at her sister critically. She looked tired, haggard even, but Henrietta wasn't about to say so – she had mentioned it a few nights ago and Isabel had burst into tears, saying she and Fabrizio were finished and she didn't want to talk about it. Since then Isabel had hardly spoken, hardly eaten, and had taken to having a stiff drink before tumbling exhausted into bed every evening.

'You're losing weight,' Henrietta said. 'It doesn't suit you.'

'I know. I'm becoming haggard,' Isabel said wanly.

'Stop wallowing in self-pity, Isabel. You're an attractive woman but won't be for long if you carry on not eating and exhausting yourself with work and crying every night over Fabrizio.'

'You're eating enough for both of us,' Isabel said cattily. 'The weight I lose, you put on.'

'I *am* putting on weight, aren't I!' Henrietta cried rhapsodically. 'I am so pleased. I feel like a proper Italian mama now that I'm getting plump. Anyway, we new mothers often are a stone or so heavier the first year after the baby is born.'

Before Isabel could answer there was a knocking at the door and the sound of the dog barking outside. Henrietta went to see who it was and to hush the dog so that he wouldn't waken the baby.

'Carl, hello, come in. Go away, dog, and shut up. You can't come in, you shat on the carpet yesterday.'

Carl managed to squeeze into the tiny space Henrietta made with the open door so that the dog wouldn't get in. 'In disgrace, is he?'

'We thought he was house-trained, but he keeps having relapses.'

Carl, seeing Isabel, said, 'I wanted to talk to you about this property thing. I've been nosing about a bit and I've discovered that the lawyer handling the deal is in Perugia.'

'I see. Well, that's nothing surprising. The city's full of lawyers.' They were all quiet for a minute, thinking of the only *avvocato* they knew personally in Perugia. Finally Isabel said, 'Look, I know you're both thinking that it's Fabrizio, but I can assure you I don't know any more than you do.'

'Isabel, I know how you feel about him. It's so hard when personal matters get mixed up with business. But I'm sure we'll all understand if you don't involve yourself on our committee to stop the development.'

'On the contrary, Carl, I want to be involved, whoever it is that's bought the property. As for Fabrizio and myself, we're no longer seeing each other except formally, at work.'

At that moment Henrietta, spotting Bernard crossing the yard going towards his cattle barn, said breezily, 'The rain's stopped, I'm just going outside to get a breath of air.'

When she had gone Isabel brought out a bottle of whisky and she and Carl both had a drink. After a while Isabel asked, 'Where's Hugo?'

Carl, after taking another swallow, said, 'Probably out following Bernard around his cows.'

Isabel, also taking a large gulp, said, 'Like Henrietta.' Then they both looked at each other and laughed.

Later, after Carl had told Isabel all about his problems with Hugo, the first time he had ever done so to anybody; and Isabel had poured out all her doubts about, and love for, Fabrizio, the two discovered they were ravenously hungry and went into the kitchen to find the prawn pasta that Henrietta had bought at the local trattoria.

'Henrietta's a long time, isn't she?' Carl said, rolling his tongue around a succulent scrap of garlic.

'Is Hugo back at the house?' Isabel asked, biting into a prawn with a hunger she hadn't felt for days.

Carl walked to the window, taking his glass of Frascati with him. 'No, the lights aren't on yet, he must still be inside.'

Carl and Isabel both relaxed, thinking of safety in numbers, and carried on eating everything in sight, thus annoying Henrietta immensely when she finally wandered back into the house a little while later.

'Where have you been?' Isabel asked innocently.

'Oh, just talking to Bernard in the cow shed. He was feeding one of his new calves with a bucket of milk. He fusses more than I do about Krissy. Are you *sure* you've eaten all that pasta? And the olive bread as well?'

'Just the two of you?'

'What? In the barn? Well, us and Hugo. He came out a few minutes after me. I can't believe you ate all the Parmesan cheese as well.'

'Are Hugo and Bernard still out there?'

'No, Bernard had to go in. Mary came out to tell him that his supper was getting cold. Steak-and-kidney pie must be eaten piping hot, she trilled in that squeaky little voice of hers.'

'Poor Bernard. Did he go at once?'

'Oh, yes. Mary waited for him until he did.' Henrietta found a crust of olive bread left over and chewed on it crossly. 'I do wish you'd saved me something,' she said peevishly.

Poor Henrietta – hungry for food, hungry for love, or rather for the quick bonk that will bring her motherhood and complete fulfilment at last. She is beginning to despair a little, beginning to feel the slippery sands of time slowly sifting through her fingers. She is, after all, past forty, a bit late at the best of times to become a new mother, and Bernard hasn't even touched her yet, let alone sown his seed in her plump, hopefully fertile, body.

She is also famished. She thinks wistfully of the steaming steak-and-kidney pie he is wolfing down at this very moment and is tempted to join him, tempted to throw herself upon

Mary's mercy and mothering and ask for a slice of the warming, comforting English savoury.

Luckily, she remembers in time the quality of Mary's cooking and pops the rest of the olive bread into her mouth.

Thoughtfully, sensuously, she licks the crumbs from her lips as she thinks of Bernard.

In the farmhouse next door his ears are burning. He thinks, innocently, it is merely the heat from the Aga.

In the next week or so the inhabitants of *La Piccola Valle della Tristezza* arm themselves for the battle ahead, the battle for the preservation of the precious woodland at the bottom of Bernard's fields, and, incidentally, the battle to keep their own view pure and unsullied by the atrocities of Italian builders.

There seems to be a muddle about the planning permission, whether it has actually been given, or is about to be given, or unofficially given, or even merely promised. The village buzzes with conflicting stories and Carl, meeting one Italian official after another, seems to be no wiser. Whether it is his inadequate knowledge of the language that is at fault, or the maddening bureaucracy of the government officials, he finds he is frustrated at every turning.

Isabel could help, and makes a desultory inquiry or two, but her heart isn't in it. She is still wondering if Fabrizio is truly involved; if she has yet again made a horrific mistake about the man she loves. She has stuck to her word about not seeing him except at work, which is so busy these days that she hardly talks to him at all. He is hurt, and shows it by displaying a brusqueness to her that wounds the very core of her fragile soul; she is desolate, and shows it by an icy cold detachment that convinces Fabrizio all the tales told about the English are, deplorably, true.

Mary, full of ire and passion for the first time in years over the proposed demolition of the woodland, does her bit by pestering her lawyer in Perugia every day to see if he can come up with any suggestions. She is, with the help of her sons and the Italian–English dictionary, writing letters to everyone of importance in the village, such as the four shop owners and the doctor who has a surgery in the house behind the trattoria one day a week. The letters are received with much hilarity, Mary's Italian being what it is. The villagers are having the time of their lives, all these goings on.

Bernard does his part by listening to Mary, and making her happy by eating her rich chocolate cake; her fat, oozing savoury pies. He seems to get stronger and broader, his body filling out with good hard muscle that drives Hugo into a frenzy and reminds Henrietta constantly of her final goal.

And what of Hugo? What of Henrietta? What contributions are they making to this strategy of war, this battle plan? They are, it seems, using their artistic skills; Henrietta is making colourful, catchy posters advertising the meeting in the village to discuss the proposed development, and Hugo is using his newly acquired knowledge of Italian (with the help of Carl's dictionary) as well as his poetic skills and is writing a passionate leaflet to be distributed at the gathering.

How dedicated they are, this little group at *La Piccola Valle della Tristezza*, how consecrated to the task of conservation they have set themselves. See how they work together, seriously, amicably; see how they pull together as single-mindedly as Bernard's tractor pulling the plough across the rich Umbrian soil.

We do well to admire them. It can't, after all, last forever.

Chapter Thirteen

The town hall was packed on the night of the protest meeting, with people coming not only from Modena, but from many of the other villages in the vicinity.

Many, it must be said, were there believing it must be some sort of entertainment, so bright were Henrietta's posters, so hyperbolic Hugo's prose. Indeed, there were even those who later confessed they'd thought a small circus was being advertised, so misled were they by Henrietta's abstract drawings of cows wandering in the woodland. However, even these misguided souls were not to be disappointed, the entertainment value proving even greater than a circus.

Daniela was there, dressed brightly in scarlet, her thick grey hair piled festively on top of her head and her feet shod in shiny red patent high heels she hadn't worn for twelve years. Her children were there too, with their assorted children, and this alone nearly filled the village hall. Alberto, foregoing an invitation to dinner with the woman in Perugia, greeted his mates warmly; as a friend of the English, and a special friend of Henrietta's, he was basking in the village spotlight that evening.

Promptly at eight o'clock Francesco and Lucia, who owned the trattoria, shut it, since all the regulars had already left for the town hall, and they weren't about to open it just for tourists and thus miss the evening's fun. Joining their friends and neighbours, they just about managed to squeeze into the hall before the doors shut and the meeting began.

There was a sudden hush as Carl, by common consent the chairman of the committee, stood up. The locals shuffled and twitched on their hard wooden chairs, straining to get a better look at the English who were sitting solemnly around a table in the front.

Carl, wisely, had chosen to speak in English and to let Isabel interpret for him. After a few jocular opening remarks in Italian about the weather, saying the English must have brought the rain along with their teabags, which thoroughly confused the villagers, he reverted to English, much to the relief of everybody.

There was a general air of merriment as the Italians settled down to look and listen. Carl, immaculate in his best civil service suit, a pale grey beautifully cut wool, droned on and on about trees, animals, and the despoiling of Modena and its surrounding countryside by the imminent sports complex and proposed buildings.

Isabel, standing up to translate, immediately became the focus of attention for a while. The Italians admired her long wine-coloured cord skirt, her black leather boots, the fine lambswool jumper pulled down loosely over her hips. They whispered to each other about her modish short hair cut, and those in the front noticed the dangling silver earrings, the careful make-up on the wide eyes. All in all they approved of her, especially as she spoke Italian so beautifully.

After a while, when Carl began to repeat himself, they grew bored with listening and looked at the others, especially at Henrietta, resplendent in her white wool dress that was so tight on her now that the buttons kept popping open all over the place, much to the delight of every red-blooded Italian male in the audience. Her hair, curling with the rain, fell over her shoulders and bosom, which was probably just as well as it managed to hide that which the popping buttons kept exposing.

On Henrietta's lap sat Krissy, exquisitely dressed in a deep turquoise blue playsuit, looking like a precious jewel set finely in white gold. Having just been fed she lay back against her mother's breasts contentedly, bestowing the odd smile or two at the people in the first row and waving her arms merrily at everyone. The Italians were, of course, enchanted, mumuring with pride that the *bambina* was indeed *dolcissima* and could easily pass for an Italian infant.

Next to Henrietta sat Hugo, looking like a film star, straight out of the arty Italian cinema. He was dressed in black jeans, red silk shirt, and a black leather jacket. The Umbrians could hardly believe he was English, until he stood up to speak a few words in Italian.

Mary and Bernard, on the other end of the table, looked definitely English; there was no hubbub of whispered speculation about them. Just what it was exactly that made them stand out, no one was quite sure; it was just there, their Englishness, standing out all over them like the last remains of chicken pox scarring the faces of Richard, John and David who were there because all the potential baby-sitters in the village were at the meeting.

After Carl had finished his speech, and Hugo had attempted his few words in Italian which no one understood but which everyone cheered wildly because he was so handsome and charismatic, and looked so poised in his well-tailored jacket, Henrietta stood up, transferred Krissy to her shoulder, and said a few halting words about the beauty of the countryside. Krissy, struggling to face the audience (for like all babies she was a bit of a show-off), managed to pop Henrietta's buttons open again, much to the wild delight of the Italians and the consternation of the English.

For the next five minutes or so, as Krissy squirmed and

grizzled, Henrietta's full but still beautiful breasts, unclad because she had given up wearing bras since the ones she owned had become too tight and uncomfortable, bounced and jiggled and fell about prettily as Isabel and Carl mimed frantically to try and get her to button up. John, Richard and David, watching, began giggling, then laughing, and then fell about under the table having quiet hysterics while Mary tried to kick them gently, still smiling benignly at the audience. Bernard, staring stoically ahead with only the most surreptitious of glances at Henrietta, grew so red in the face that people tittered amongst themselves, pointing and taking bets whether or not he would pass out then and there, as his blood pressure so visibly rose higher and higher.

The villagers loved it. Henrietta, oblivious, concentrating totally on her speech in this strange language, carried on, blithely unaware that she was half undressed and of the commotion around her. When she finished and sat down, everyone in the hall, except the English of course, cheered; the men, young and old, stood up and stamped their feet and threw their sheets of paper with a projected drawing of the sports complex up in the air; the women, deliciously scandalized and heady with excitement, laughed and chattered away amongst themselves.

The evening was an unqualified success.

'But do you think they'll *do* anything?' Isabel said later, sitting with the others in Carl's luxurious drawing room, drinking from one of the many bottles of special Umbrian red wine presented, ceremoniously, to the English at the conclusion of the meeting.

'They seemed a bit vague when I asked them to write to their MP about the proposed development,' Mary said plaintively.

'Maybe they don't have MPs,' Henrietta said, giving Krissy a bottle that began to drip all over Carl's pale cream carpet.

'Well, they have something equivalent.'

'I loved the speeches,' said Hugo. 'All those wonderful old Umbrian men, standing up and solemnly saying their bit. I must write a poem about it.'

'What were they saying, Isabel? There was a bit of a pandemonium in the hall by then. The Italians seemed so excited – they must truly be committed to stopping the development.'

Isabel, sipping her wine, wondered whether to tell them that the speeches were all about welcoming the English to the village and how happy they were that more of them would soon be arriving when the new holiday complex was completed.

'A lot of it was in the Umbrian dialect,' she said, which was partially true. 'I didn't really understand,' she fabricated. She didn't see the point in agitating everyone all over again. The Italians saw the proposed building scheme in an entirely different way from the English and no amount of speech-making on either side would change that.

'They're obviously in complete agreement with us,' Carl said complacently. 'Look how they shook our hands so warmly at the end, gave us all these wonderful bottles of Tresimeno wine.'

Everyone nodded their heads soporifically, feeling very pleased with themselves, generals on the evening of victory allowing themselves to relax in the aftermath of a battle well fought.

Only Bernard is not relaxing. Bernard, unmanned and unhinged by the sight of Henrietta's full frontal from the waist up, has once again forgotten his cows, forgotten the field he planned to work tomorrow to make ready for the planting of maize. His other fantasies, deeper than the deepest furrow made by his slicing blades, have surfaced.

He wants Henrietta.

★

The rain finally stopped the day Carl and Isabel went to Siena. The sun, watery but intensifying as the day progressed, had enough early-spring warmth to enable them to sit outside drinking late-morning coffee in a tiny courtyard not far from the Campo. The fig tree in the centre of the cobbled yard was not yet in leaf, but had an air of expectancy about it that signified it was about to burst forth at any moment.

'How tranquil it all is,' Isabel said. 'That's what I love about Siena – even though the Campo is always buzzing with tourists, the side streets stay empty.'

The waiter brought their coffee, and they fell into a companionable silence. Though they were no more than a few yards from the heart of the city, there were only the sounds of a warbler sitting in the fig tree. The air was clear, washed after the previous rain. A fuzzy white cat with ginger markings languished in the sun near the fig tree.

'It's so calm, so peaceful,' Isabel went on. 'I can feel myself unwinding.'

'It certainly is restful,' Carl agreed.

The cat yawned and stretched as a huge Alsatian loped into the garden, laying his cavernous jaws on the fresh white tablecloth and trying to reach an abandoned sugar lump with his tongue.

After this was accomplished he barked for another, which Isabel gave him, then carried on barking.

'They're all gone,' Carl said. 'Go away.'

The dog, not believing him, became agitated. Isabel looked around for help but the waiter was nowhere in sight.

The cat, bored with languishing, came over to the table and distracted the dog by hiding under Isabel's chair and swatting the Alsatian on the nose. Both animals, obviously having played the game before, thought this great fun and carried on for quite some time, growling and snarling and hissing and meowing to their hearts' content. Isabel and Carl drank their coffee quickly and decided to look around the city.

They lunched late, in a restaurant on the outskirts of Siena, indulging themselves in wine and good food.

'What a wonderful idea this was,' Isabel exclaimed. 'I've been working non-stop for a fortnight now. Even on Sundays I've been showing clients around.'

'My word, Isabel, what dedication.'

'We had a huge number of English suddenly turn up right after Easter, and of course many of them only have a couple of weeks to find a house.'

'I'm glad you've decided to be sensible and take a day off at last.'

'This is very good for me. I must say it's a strain, working for Fabrizio, feeling the way I still do about him. We're so cold, so formal with each other in the office. I'm glad I'm out most of the time with clients.'

'Poor Isabel. Don't you feel like relenting? It seems pointless, somehow, to torture yourself when you both want to be together.'

Isabel, loosened up by the wine, told Carl a bit about the lecturer, how she had loved so desperately and been hurt so damagingly.

'I jumped into my relationship with Fabrizio in the same way, all hormones and emotion, no reason or even common sense. It's messy too. He's still trying to untangle himself from his wife. And then there's this property business—'

It had been over a week since the meeting in Modena and things were quiet for the moment. The English had done all they could, written copious letters, seen solicitors and public officials, talked to as many people as possible. They assumed that the Italians, stirred by the speeches of last week, were doing the same thing.

Carl, lighting a cigarette, said, 'Is it so important to you that Fabrizio isn't involved in this property deal? Can't you love him and close your eyes to his business ventures?' He, having closed his eyes to Hugo's romantic exploits for years, believed one should be realistic about love.

'I can't, Carl. He knows how I feel about it, how much I truly care about *La Piccola Valle* and that woodland. If he were to be involved in chopping it down I could never forgive him. Especially for the devious way he appears to be going about it.'

They both sighed and thought about love. Since the night they'd first talked in Henrietta's house, Carl and Isabel had spent two or three evenings together, going for gentle walks in the woodland now that the days were getting longer, and one misty dismal night sitting in the trattoria in Modena, causing the owners Francesco and Lucia, as well as the other locals, much confusion as the two English sat alone at an isolated table deep in intense conversation. The villagers had a great deal of trouble sorting out the relationships at *La Piccola Valle*, the way the English carried on, with no one knowing who was angry at whom or who was fancying whom, and who preferred men and who preferred women: it seemed to have no logic whatsoever.

'And Hugo, what's he doing today?' Isabel asked, graciously giving Carl his turn. She was becoming fond of the older man; she enjoyed his company, found him an unthreatening friend. He in turn felt much the same about her; the fact that she was so unconditionally besotted with Fabrizio, despite her protestations of reason and logic, made him feel safe, cosy. He knew she wasn't about to fall madly in love with him, determined to be the one woman in the world who could change his sexual preferences, like others had in the past.

'Hugo? He says he's working on a play. About an old Umbrian farmer who falls tragically in love with a young English poet.'

Isabel smiled. 'You're not worried, then?'

'With Henrietta home and stalking her prey as well? Not a bit.'

When they got back to La Valle, Hugo said sulkily to Carl, 'You've been a long time. I ate dinner all on my own.'

'Play not going well?'

'Play? Oh, no, it's not. Couldn't get into it.'

'A wasted day, then.'

'Yes. Totally wasted.'

Carl smiled, satisfied.

'You're late,' Henrietta said peevishly. 'I thought you'd be home for dinner. Krissy went to sleep early and I've been bored out of my head.'

'Bad day, then?'

'Totally wasted.'

And Isabel, like Carl in the house next door, smiled in satisfaction.

A few evenings later, at the trattoria, Lucia said to Alberto, who was drinking grappa with Daniela after a satisfying dinner, killing time because the woman in Perugia was unable to see him that night, 'Those two, they seem fond of each other.'

They both looked at the corner table where, under the tiny red lamp attached rather crookedly to the wall, Isabel and Carl had linked fingers and were gazing into each other's eyes.

'Ah, they are, they are,' Alberto said knowingly.

Lucia, impressed by the knowledge he had of the English and their ways, said, 'But is he not a homosexual?'

'But of course!'

'And yet they hold hands, they stare passionately at each other, they look as if they are about to make love.'

'But of course,' Alberto repeated enigmatically.

Lucia's husband Francesco sighed admiringly. 'Ah, the English,' he said. 'Such flexibility.'

The four of them stared unashamedly at the corner table.

Isabel and Carl, totally engrossed in talking about Fabrizio and Hugo, failed to notice the attention they were attracting. Isabel was wretched because she had decided she couldn't stand the pain of working with Fabrizio and was seriously thinking of quitting her job.

Carl also was depressed, failing for the first time to let Hugo's little passions run their shallow course without over-reacting. He blamed it on retirement, on the time he had to ponder and reflect; he also thought it extremely tacky of Hugo to sully his own front porch, as it were, by choosing their next-door neighbour as an object of desire.

Isabel, distressed to see her friend suffering so, had taken his hand and was trying to soothe him with words of reason and logic, forgetting they hadn't done her a bit of good in her own relationship with Fabrizio.

'He's making such a fool of himself,' Carl complained, holding on tightly to Isabel's warm comforting hand. 'He's out there tonight helping Bernard muck out the cow shed. Can you imagine?'

They both pondered a vision of beautiful Hugo, with his fine pale hair, holding a pitchfork. An angel besmirched.

'No, I must say I find it hard to imagine,' Isabel said at last. 'Henrietta's out there too. Krissy slept all afternoon so Henrietta has taken her out to the cow shed for fresh air and amusement.'

The two of them were so depressed they couldn't even laugh at this, instead gazing despairingly into each other's eyes.

'I'm feeling wretched, Carl.'

'I'm not feeling too happy myself, Isabel.'

They clung to each other like life lines.

The Italians watched it all with amazement. Perhaps after all the English were not so deficient in passion as was generally believed.

'Krissy. Hush, hush, little darling. Go to sleep, little lovey.' Henrietta, becoming a trifle impatient, bumped the pushchair rather roughly over the straw, causing the baby to yell louder than ever.

'It's no good, Henrietta, you'll have to take her into the house and put her to bed.' Hugo, brandishing his pitchfork, grinned demonically. Bernard, carting cowshit around on his tractor and trailer, couldn't hear and so said nothing.

Henrietta, admitting defeat, picked up Krissy and walked out of the cow shed, thinking she could collect the pushchair some other time, the next day perhaps, when Bernard just possibly might be alone. Desperate as she was to get her new baby going, she was too devoted a mother to put Krissy to bed and then come back outside, not when Isabel was out. Damn her, thought Henrietta crossly, bouncing the baby over the farmyard; she didn't like leaving Bernard alone with that unscrupulous Hugo.

Not very long afterwards the same unscrupulous Hugo, waylaying Bernard and persuading him to stop the tractor and take a break, said, 'I've brought us a flask of real coffee, none of your Nescafé stuff. Let's sit here on these bales for a few minutes.'

Bernard doubtfully said, 'I expect Mary'll be around with a flask of tea soon.'

'She's engrossed in an English film on the telly. I told her not to worry, I'd bring out a flask.' As a matter of fact it was Hugo who had persuaded Mary to watch the film, telling her it was a classic and not to be missed even though it was unfortunately dubbed into Italian. He had also laced the coffee with Carl's best brandy.

Bernard, wanting to keep going, his mind buzzing with all the things he had to do now that it looked as if the weather would stay fine, reluctantly sat next to Hugo, on a bale set slightly below him. The man had after all offered to help him; indeed, Hugo had insisted, and useless though he had turned out to be with the pitchfork, it was still kind of him.

Hugo opened the flask and poured them each a cup. Bernard took several large mouthfuls and tried not to cough; he was too polite to say he didn't like the coffee much. He thought longingly of Nescafé or, better, one of Mary's nice hot flasks of tea.

Hugo refilled the plastic cups and stretched out on the bales above Bernard, his hand resting on the straw nearby, thus enabling him to fool around a bit with Bernard's dark thick hair. Bernard, thinking it was an insect of some sort, put his hand up to investigate and encountered Hugo, or, more precisely, his hand.

Bernard froze as Hugo pounced, squeezing the big brown square fingers in his pale tapering ones. For several minutes they stayed like that, Hugo in complete bliss and Bernard in total terror.

Who knows how long they will stay like that, motionless, Hugo savouring his moment, Bernard unable to extricate himself? He wonders desperately whether he should just ignore that slim but surprisingly strong hand in the hope that, like other unpleasant things, it will eventually go away; or whether he should snatch his hand out of Hugo's grasp, thus creating a scene. Bernard, a true Englishman, hates scenes: see how long he sits, his hand on top of his head in another man's hand, risking not only moral dishevelment but paralysis of his right arm just to avoid making a commotion.

But as they sit there – Hugo, despite the pitchfork, in heaven; Bernard languishing in hell – a car drives into the farmyard. It is the Jaguar, with Carl and Isabel inside returning from the village. From their vantage point on the bales the two men can see the car and its occupants but cannot themselves be seen: it is, of course, quite dark by now.

Watching like one hypnotized, Bernard sees Isabel and Carl get out of the car, lean against it, not talking but not making a move to go inside either. Like a man in a dream he wants to shout, scream, bellow for help, but is paralyzed, no sound comes. He simply hasn't a clue what to do.

Hugo, still sensuously fondling Bernard's rough worker's hand, is also watching Carl and Isabel. He sees them lean back against the car as if they are loath to end the evening; he sees them lean towards each other; he sees – good God! He sees them kissing, for fuck's sake!

'Bloody hell, Carl, you shit. What are you up to?'

'Hugo, what in Christ's name are you doing, leaping out at us like that? You scared the life out of me.'

'Uh ... perhaps I'd better go in. Henrietta will be wondering what's happened to me.'

'No, don't rush off, Isabel.'

'Why are you trying to stop her? What's going on? Christ, you were all over her, Carl!'

'And where were you – spying on us? I'm ashamed of you, Hugo.'

'I think I'd better be going in now. Henrietta will be wondering—'

'*You're* ashamed of *me*? You were practically eating each other right in the middle of the farmyard and you say you're ashamed of *me*?'

'Good night, Carl, it was a lovely evening, thank you. Good night, Hugo.'

Isabel walked serenely across the yard and into her house.

Carl, trying to get Hugo back into theirs, steered him forcibly up the path.

Bernard, slinking past the cow shed, waved timorously, having decided he would pretend nothing at all untoward had happened.

Hugo never even noticed, struck by a sudden terror that Carl might leave him. The thought had never, ever occurred to him before.

Chapter Fourteen

Even though the pitchfork was abandoned, Hugo stayed in hell for the next few days. Carl, refusing to talk about things that night, went to bed at once, saying he had a piercing headache.

'I thought you didn't like women?' Hugo shouted up the stairs as Carl went into the bedroom.

'I bet you've been deceiving me for years,' he hollered, following him into the bathroom as he brushed his teeth.

'All those secretaries,' he went on truculently, sitting on the edge of their king-sized bed as Carl turned over and went to sleep. 'I bet you've been screwing them for years – despite all this bullshit you've been giving me about not liking women.'

Finally, when Carl started gently snoring, Hugo gave up and went downstairs. For several hours he thought about his relationship with Carl, something he had not done for years, if at all. He thought, with discomfiture, of his own role in that relationship; thought, in some despair, of Carl's never-ending patience that now, suddenly, seemed to be thinning and crackling around the edges.

The next day, at eight-thirty, Hugo was dressed and standing in the bedroom doorway with a breakfast tray. There was even a bright red poppy on it, plucked surreptitiously from Mary's garden.

'You poor darling!' he cried expansively. 'How is your head this morning? Look, I've bought fresh cakes to go with your coffee. I went all the way down to the village while you were asleep.'

Carl, sitting up in bed and leaning back on several pillows, thanked him politely but distantly. Hugo, panicking, opened the deep blue brocade curtains and waffled, 'Look at the sun! Spring seems finally to have arrived after all that rain and cold. At least we know it will carry on warm and sunny – not like England – ha, ha.'

Carl said something suitable and concentrated on his almond cake.

'I was down at Daniela's shop at eight for those,' Hugo said proudly.

'Oh? Kind of you,' Carl said vaguely, not sounding at all grateful.

Hugo, babbling, went over to the window. 'Listen, not a breath of wind, just the doves cooing to each other.'

His words were drowned by the sound of the tractor roaring underneath their window.

'Hmm,' Carl said mildly, picking up an old copy of *Private Eye* from his bedside table. 'Bernard will be busy today, the sun shining at last. I'm sure he'll be needing your help to finish mucking out the cow shed.'

Hugo, looking wan, emerald eyes dulled to an ordinary green by unhappiness and lack of sleep, said he didn't want to help Bernard any more, that farming was not his scene, that it bored him, that Bernard bored him, and that perhaps he and Carl could go somewhere together for the day.

'I'm sorry, dear thing, but it's Isabel's day off again and I promised her another day out. We thought we'd have a look at Assissi before all the tourists get there.'

'That sounds fun, I'll come with you.'

'Oh, I'm so sorry, but I thought you'd be helping Bernard today. I told Isabel I was free. I really think it's best we go alone. She's been working so hard lately,' he added enigmatically.

Later, walking between a row of lime trees in Assissi, drinking in the sunshine, Isabel said, 'I'm sorry Hugo was so upset last night. Has he calmed down yet?'

'He's tiptoeing around me like a man barefoot on glass. I've never seen him this way before.'

'He's afraid of losing you.'

'That's preposterous! He knows I've never even considered another person since I met him.'

'Especially a woman?'

'Especially a woman,' Carl agreed, smiling.

Isabel, enjoying the sun, stretched out her legs, bare for the first time this year. She watched a pigeon shit unconcernedly on a couple of Americans taking photographs of each other.

'It might not be a bad thing,' she said, ducking as the pigeon flew over them. 'Hugo has been taking you for granted for years.'

'I know. I'm keeping very quiet, letting him stew for a time.'

'Good.'

'Isabel, you don't mind, do you?'

'Mind what?'

'Hugo. Thinking that you and I are, or might perhaps be, lovers.'

'Of course not, Carl. You're a very attractive man and I'm quite honoured to have the delectable Hugo jealous of me.'

They looked at each other and grinned. The kiss last night had been unpremeditated, and something of a surprise to both of them. They had been drinking first wine at the trattoria, then the strong and tangy *limoncello*, and the drink had worked like yeast on the doughy emotions of sadness and despair, causing their shared misery to rise simultaneously and bring them closer. They had clung to each other last night as one human being clings to another who may, wonder of wonders, understand him or her; the clinging, in their alcoholic haze, seemed to lead naturally to embracing, the embracing to kissing – and who knows to what else if Hugo hadn't suddenly arrived in such an abrupt manner.

There was also, it must be said, a hint of experimentation there for both of them. For Carl, who had not kissed a woman in about forty years, it was to see if he had, perhaps, been missing something; something he wouldn't have been aware of at twenty. Isabel had hoped to exorcize the memory of Fabrizio by this indulgence. For neither the experiment worked, nor had they truly expected it to, nor did they feel anything other than relief that it hadn't.

But Hugo, poor Hugo, at home now and in a terrible fret, is not to know all this and Carl isn't about to tell him. Even the sight of Bernard walking back and forth across the farmyard is no longer soothing, no longer the wonderful distraction it once was: he wants Carl, and Carl is out dallying with a woman. Hugo thinks about Isabel and despairs: is Carl, after all, bisexual? He wouldn't have believed it even a few days ago, but now, that kiss, that embrace – Hugo groans out loud and thinks he must leave the house or he will go mad with imaginings. He decides to go the trattoria, shunning Daniela's sunnier café, and sit there in the gloom on this glorious spring day, drinking grappa and writing poems on the futility of human relationships.

On the way he passes Bernard, whose teeth show for a stilted moment in a stiff and terrified smile, muttering something about a nice day and turning beetroot red as he does so. Hugo, so preoccupied he hardly notices the sturdy farmer, acknowledges him distractedly but without much interest as he carries on towards the village.

Bernard, wild with relief, breaks into a run, going the

opposite direction from Hugo down into the field where his cows are frolicking. He walks amongst them happily, a man at peace with himself, a man at one with his own soul.

And wonders when he will next see Henrietta.

He sees her in about five minutes; she is walking along the edge of the woodland at the bottom of his field. She is wearing something loose and flowing and looks like an advert for a gentle English shampoo with the pale green sheen of the new spring leaves on the trees behind her, and all that cascading golden hair. He likes that word, cascading: he didn't even know he knew it, but he can see instantly that it applies to Henrietta and her magnificent thick hair.

He walks towards her, away from his cows, without giving them so much as a backward glance. His long stride grows quicker as he sees she is waiting for him, sees she is facing him placidly with Madonna-like stillness. The Madonna bit nearly throws him for a few seconds until he realizes her long white cotton shirt is unbuttoned in the front, revealing to him and to the cows what all Modena saw not that many nights ago. The sight unhinges him; he breaks into a run and in a few moments he is holding her, the Henrietta of his fantasies, now, *here*, out of the darkness of dreams and into the sunlight of reality.

Deep in the woods the birdsong becomes background music, the trees a love-hut, the wild poppies and wood anemones a bed for the breathless lovers. Neither of them speaks for what need is there of words? Except for Henrietta rather sharply asking Bernard if he has had mumps since his sons were born.

Bernard, too demented to wonder about this, says no and carries on kissing her overblown bosom while she does incredible things to his trousers, such as unzipping them and trying to get them off. But then, just as things start to get terribly out of hand, he remembers he is English and therefore responsible. He whispers, in a voice thick and coated with lust about to be gratified, 'Are you, uh, protected?'

And here Henrietta makes her one tactical error. 'It doesn't matter,' she murmurs, 'just don't stop, whatever you do.'

Bernard – honest, upright (if also slightly uptight), English Bernard – is smitten, touched to the heart by those careless words, pierced by an arrow of tenderness every bit as salient as the one of lust lodged permanently in his groin. He must at all costs protect Henrietta; he must be responsible, for look how she loves him, urging him on when obviously nothing has been done to prevent conception. It is all so overwhelming and glorious, both his lust and his responsibility, that he squirts his seed in a burst of uncontrolled gratification all over the woodland; or, more precisely, all over Henrietta and the poppies and the wild white wood anenomes.

'Fucking hell!' Henrietta swears, when she realizes what has happened.

'What a fucking waste,' she mutters dangerously, rolling over on her side to investigate for herself the flaccid Bernard.

Bernard, in bliss, angels and the odd insect singing in his ear, doesn't hear. He doesn't speak either, until he feels Henrietta's wondrous fingers roughly prodding his detumescent manhood.

'Henrietta . . . ow! That hurts, dearest.'

'Bernard, you shit, you – oh, my God! Oh, no. Oh, Christ.'

'Henrietta, what is it?'

'I don't know. It's my back, I think . . . ow, I seem to have twisted it. I think I'm in a rabbit hole or something. I slipped as I tried to prop myself up. Look, can you help me stand – oh, bloody hell! Stop, I can't bear it.'

About ten minutes later she says, plaintively, 'It's no use, I just can't walk, it hurts. You'll have to get help.'

'I'll carry you.'

'Don't be silly, you can't, it's too painful for me to move. Just get help, quickly.'

She closes her eyes and lies back against the wood anemones. Her face is pale and a thin sheen of perspiration covers her upper lip. Her white shirt is wide open and her large full nipples stare accusingly up at Bernard. Her hair, cascading over her shoulders, is snarled and tangled with twigs and the odd sperm or two. She looks absolutely gorgeous and Bernard is torn between ravishing her again (if that first abortive time counted), and asking her please to cover herself up and make herself presentable before help arrives.

He ends up doing neither. Throwing his fate to the gods he decides that what will be, will be, which is very philosophical for Bernard. Taking a last look at Henrietta lying prostrate in the wild flowers, he sprints quickly up the hill to find help, and to face stoically whatever awaits him.

Lucky Bernard, the gods were good to him that sunny spring day. The first person he met as he ran into the farmyard was Daniela, with Krissy in the pushchair. Daniela had come up to do some gardening for Henrietta who had suddenly decided her baby would need fresh organic vegetables in the summer. Not having a clue how to go about starting a kitchen garden, she'd offered Daniela a hefty sum to do it for her, with a bit of baby-sitting thrown in. Daniela, pleased to be out of the café on occasion, and leaving the running of it in one of her daughters' capable hands, enjoyed the amusement value of her new employment even more than she did her inflated wages.

Now, the garden finished for the day, she was just about to take the newly awakened Krissy for a stroll in the warm spring air when Bernard came panting into the yard. There was some difficulty in communication at first, but with the help of mime and some shouting, he was able to make Daniela vaguely grasp what had happened.

She immediately took over. She telephoned the doctor, handed Krissy to Mary, who had come out to see what all the commotion was, and ordered Bernard to take her to

Henrietta. When she got to the woodland, she took one look at the state of the Englishwoman and ordered Bernard back up the field to await the doctor and prevent Mary from rushing down into the woodland. It would take some doing to get Henrietta in order.

When Bernard appeared again, this time with not only the doctor in tow but also Mary carrying Krissy, and Hugo who had met them on his way back from the village, Henrietta was propped up chastely on Daniela's full lap, looking like a Madonna once again, shirt buttoned to the neck, hair smoothed and pristine, white espadrilles neatly back on her feet. Even her lacy knickers, abandoned sometime during the previous fray, were back in place, Henrietta's back pain having eased enough to allow Daniela to wriggle them on. Bernard's heart leaped with love and relief as Daniela winked broadly at him. She was panting to get home to tell all this to her children.

Mary, at her best in an emergency, fussed around Henrietta, clucking motherly advice: 'You know you shouldn't go for walks in those skimpy shoes, the woods are too full of holes and brambles and broken branches.' At this Henrietta started giggling, which everyone attributed to the slight hysteria brought on by pain. The doctor then gave her some kind of an injection which eventually enabled her to move enough to be carried by Bernard and Daniela out of the woods and into the house. The doctor, a small, elderly, emaciated man, carried his bag, and Mary held Krissy.

After they had got back to the house and put Henrietta to bed, the doctor, who luckily spoke English, gave her a full examination. He was closeted with her for over half an hour and when he finished, spoke solemnly to the gathering who were waiting expectantly for his diagnosis.

They stared at him in disbelief. Then, with one accord, they all got up and trooped silently into Henrietta's room.

That evening when Isabel and Carl returned late from their day in Assissi they were surprised to find every light blazing in Isabel's house while the rest of the hamlet was dark and uninviting.

They got out of the car quickly and went into the brightly lit house together. For a moment or two they didn't see Henrietta for all the people milling about, all the adults and children of *La Piccola Valle della Tristezza*, including the dog, whose sins had obviously been forgiven him, and several familiar faces from the village: Daniela and two of her daughters, Alberto, Francesco and Lucia. Everyone was drinking what looked like champagne except for Krissy, of course, and Richard, John, and David who were tearing around the house in a most excitable manner.

Carl and Henrietta spotted, finally, on the coffee-coloured sofa, propped up with downy white pillows and demurely wearing her Victorian nightie and dressing gown, Henrietta, glowing like a beacon in the heaving sea of people.

'Isabel, you're back at last!' she cried, throwing her arms wide and then wincing a bit at the pain.

'Henrietta, whatever is going on? Are you ill? But why is there a party?'

Henrietta, radiant, clapped her hands together like a child. 'I asked everyone to come, I couldn't bear not to share it.'

'What are you talking about? Share what?'

'I'm pregnant, Isabel. Pregnant, pregnant, pregnant!'

Henrietta, beside herself, smiled hugely, pulled Isabel down for a sisterly embrace (wincing as her back twinged with effort), and accepted another glass of milk from Mary who had been hovering nearby.

Isabel, bewildered, offered congratulations as best she could before being swamped by people and offered champagne and congratulations, as the proud sister of the mother-to-be, in both English and Italian.

She decided now was not the moment to ask who the father was.

It was quite late when all the guests left and Isabel was able to begin her interrogation.

'It must be Bernard. All these months you've been screwing him behind my back.'

'Isabel, how can you think that?' Isabel said, outraged. She had already totally forgotten this afternoon in the woodland. 'And besides, it couldn't be Bernard, not unless we bonked on the first day we arrived at *La Piccola Valle*.' She giggled. 'Even I'm not that fast a worker.'

'Well, I must say, I'm totally lost. Can you please explain to me, from the beginning, what exactly you have been up to?'

'Well, the doctor says I'm probably five months pregnant.'

'Five months!'

'That's why I've been gaining weight, I suppose. Why my jeans got too tight, and I had to abandon bras. My breasts are huge now,' she said with milky maternal pride. 'I'm sure I'll be able to breastfeed the baby. It's so much better than bottle feeding. What did *you* do?'

'Oh, for God's sake, Henrietta, stop getting side-tracked. So you're five months pregnant. How the hell could you not know?'

'Well, I was gaining all this weight, which I attributed to Italian food and motherhood, feeling placid and contented and all that – did you feel like that, Bel?'

'*Concentrate*, Henrietta. We're trying to figure out how you could not know you were pregnant. What about your periods? Surely when they stopped you must have known?'

Here Henrietta looked rather sheepish. 'I've never really kept track of my periods. They've always been so irregular anyway I never bothered. I was so wrapped up in Krissy I didn't really notice I hadn't had one for a while. When the thought did occur to me, I supposed it was the first sign of menopause. That's another reason why I suddenly decided I hadn't much time to waste.'

'You idiot. You're far too young for the menopause.'

'That's what the doctor said. I just thought I was starting early. Some women do.'

Henrietta, propped up on huge soft pillows on her bed where she had been carried with loving ceremony by Hugo and Alberto, Bernard being in too much of a state of shock to be much help, yawned contentedly, a plump white cat sitting in a frothy bowl of cream.

'I'm so happy, Isabel,' she murmured, closing her eyes and preparing to drift off to sleep.

Isabel, rather crossly, shook her. 'You haven't told me who the father is,' she said with some asperity.

'The father? Oh, him. It must have been that dishy Indian student. You know, the one that used to visit me in Calcutta when I was adopting Krissy? My little daughter will have a real honest-to-goodness Indian brother or sister.'

With that, Henrietta fell promptly asleep.

Isabel, going slowly downstairs and making herself another pot of tea, knowing sleep would be hard to come by that night, thought about Vikram, handsome son of the solicitor in Calcutta through whom Henrietta was adopting Krissy. The young man had spent a great deal of time at the small house the two sisters had rented while waiting for the adoption to be completed, saying he was interested in the law and especially as it pertained to foreign adoptions. Neither Isabel nor Henrietta was fooled; Vikram's infatuation with Henrietta was blatant to the point of idiocy. The two had spent days together, those hot, dusty, windy Calcutta days, while she, Isabel, was out exploring the city.

'I really believed you,' Isabel said, having gone back upstairs to wake up her sister crossly. 'When you said you and Vikram spent hours talking about the intricacies of Indian law. And all the time you were bonking like crazy!'

Henrietta, about to be peevish about being woken up so rudely, had the decency to look sheepish instead. 'You had just split up with your lecturer, Bel, and I didn't want to upset you by flaunting a lover. Anyway, it was just a fling for both of us. We both used each other, I suppose: he wanted my body, and I wanted to assimilate something of India, so that I would be a better mother to Krissy.'

'That's the most ridiculous thing I have ever heard,' Isabel said, aware that she had spoken these words to her sister more times than she cared to remember. 'Didn't pregnancy ever occur to you? You didn't want your own birth child at that time, remember? You'd plenty of chances all over Europe, for God's sake, with all your other lovers. But you always scrupulously avoided pregnancy.'

This time Henrietta definitely did look embarrassed. 'Actually, no, it never did occur to me that I'd get pregnant with Vikram. I was totally bewitched and obsessed by Krissy, and because of her with India, and everything sort of became muddled. I mean, we did use contraception, but I suppose we didn't concentrate on it as we should have. Perhaps we lapsed.'

'Obviously,' Isabel said drily. 'Are you going to write to Vikram? Tell him about your coming bundle of joy?'

Henrietta was shocked. 'Of course not! He was engaged to be married, remember? To someone chosen by his family, and quite acceptable to him. Vikram was merely sowing some of his wild oats with me.'

'He did a good job then,' Isabel muttered.

Much later, as she left Henrietta and fell into her own bed, Isabel let herself be grateful for eager, lustful Vikram, sowing his seed in Henrietta's willing womb. At least Bernard had been saved from having a little Bernardo or Bernarda following him around the farmyard and jeopardizing his marriage and his peace of mind in the process.

*

'Poor Henrietta! What a blow, having a nerve trapped in her back like that while innocently out walking – and then suddenly learning she's five months pregnant.'

Mary, unable to sleep either, was sitting at the kitchen table with Bernard. The events of the day had brought colour to her cheeks and body to her normally limp hair which was standing out all around her head like a dandelion. Bernard, by contrast, looked pale and tragic; Hugo would have approved.

'She's taking it so bravely,' Mary went on, not minding that she had been reiterating this conversation all evening. 'And I must say I admire her for not being bitter against the father. He's an Indian – imagine!'

Bernard, imagining, groaned slightly.

'What's the matter? Not indigestion again. You've been off-colour all day. Do you want a Rennie? Or is it your irritable bowel again?'

Bernard shook his head.

'You do look rather peaky. I hope you're not getting chicken pox, though your mother wrote that you've had it already.'

Bernard grunted.

'You do look dreadful, Bernie. It's probably just the shock, finding Henrietta like that in the woods. It's a good thing you happened to be wandering around looking for your cows or she might still be there, poor thing.'

Mary and Bernard stared into space for a few moments, both contemplating, in slightly different ways, of course, Henrietta lying in the woodland.

'I must admit I misjudged her,' Mary said finally. 'She's really very sweet and shy and that's why she's sometimes so abrupt. This afternoon after the doctor left she was asking me all about my pregnancies: what I ate and how I felt, what the boys' births were like. I told her I'd go over there every day and teach her the antenatal breathing and relaxation exercises.

And when her back is better we'll do some of the more strenuous preparations.'

Bernard, unable to contemplate these things, slumped down in his chair, numbed.

'Bernard, you'll have to help too.'

'What?'

'Because there's no man in Henrietta's life, she might need a hand sometimes. Especially if she has a little boy,' his wife added, mysteriously vague.

Bernard straightened a fraction.

'You'll have to be a kind of uncle to her children,' Mary warbled on. 'A father figure.'

Bernard sat erect.

'Henrietta will have me, of course, but it will be nice for her to have a man to rely on too.'

Bernard, triumphant, raised his chin and squared his shoulders, rousing himself at last from the confusion and torpor he had been in since late-morning. All the responsibility for his beloved he had felt in the woods came back to him; all the lust he put aside forever, like a man packing up his youth and stoically stashing it in the back seat of life's rather bumpy jalopy.

Mary was right, he had a role to play in Henrietta's life after all, a noble role, an honest one: a true English part in this scenario of Italians and Indians and other such foreigners. He would be her guide and her mentor, her protector and her comforter; he would, chastely, love her from afar but cherish her always.

And all with the complete approval of his wife!

Bernard stands, stretches, and follows Mary manfully to the double bed upstairs. His future is secure and happy; he has found his place, the role he must play; he feels calmer than he has for months.

Magnanimously pecking Mary on the cheek as she tries, timorously, to hint that she would like to make love, Bernard falls asleep a happy man, knowing exactly, for the first time in months, where he stands and what his future will be.

But do you, Bernard? Do you really?

For at this moment Henrietta also sleeps, dreaming tranquilly of babies and oozing nipples and umbilical cords tying her to her children; the one born, the other only just realized. Will it be enough for her, these two babies, or will motherhood, having gone to her head and heart, fill her with more insatiable longings so that she will want still another sibling for her two precious infants?

Unlikely perhaps, but still. Still . . .

Henrietta in her dream smiles seductively at Bernard. It never hurts to have something in reserve, she thinks as she wakes, her wide white smile glowing luminously in the dark Umbrian night, lingering like the Cheshire Cat's until she turns over carefully and goes back to sleep.

Chapter Fifteen

When things had calmed down somewhat after Henrietta's extraordinary surprise, ECCA held a meeting around Carl's shiny waxed mahogany dining table. ECCA was, of course, the committee composed of all the residents of the *villaggio*, the full title being: the English Conservation Committee Abroad.

They were all there: Henrietta in the place of honour in the throne-like chair at the head by virtue of her back, which though better was still not quite right, and her pregnancy, which no one was quite allowed to forget. This last fact might have niggled everyone but for the fact that she was so obviously radiant, so joyous, that her neighbours could not help being drawn into her excitement.

'Nothing seems to be happening,' Carl said as the meeting started. 'I've been making a few discreet inquiries in the village and not one person, it appears, has written a letter, talked to his *avvocato*, done anything at all to stop that land below us from being developed.'

Everyone muttered about how ghastly the Italians really were, despite their superficial friendliness.

'There isn't much else we can do,' Hugo said, replenishing Carl's glass with mineral water and apple juice, squeezing his shoulder fondly as he did so.

'It's so frustrating that we can't seem to find out what is happening,' Isabel said. 'Everyone Carl talks to says it's some other department involved.'

'Typically Italian, that is,' said Mary, and everyone nodded their heads. 'Lazy, dishonest Italian officials. Bribe-taking, hypocritical civil servants. Just like the government itself.'

They all nodded again, forgetting how many times they had said the same thing about the English government. Carl looked slightly uncomfortable, with all this talk about crooked civil servants.

Bernard, sitting opposite Henrietta where he could keep a chaste but firm eye on her, thought he ought to say something, since people would expect it of him. 'Odd that there's not been anything in the newspaper since that one big story,' he said finally.

'Probably some huge cover-up,' Hugo scowled, then brightened up again when he saw Carl looking fondly at him. Hugo had been a paragon of love and devotion the past week and thought he might soon be reaping some rewards: Carl certainly was not seeing quite so much of Isabel as before, and was beginning to show a little more of his old affection towards Hugo. Satisfied, he patted Carl's arm, rather relishing his strange new role of pursuer, placator, wooer. He had even written one rather good poem about it.

'A cover-up wouldn't surprise me,' Carl was saying. 'In fact, I wonder if something exceedingly fishy hasn't been going on.'

'The Italians are terribly corrupt,' said Henrietta placidly, not really caring whether they were or not, and knowing most people were basically corrupt anyway, whatever nationality. Her one darling baby was sleeping on Carl's black leather sofa and the other was growing daily inside her.

'What should we do now, then?' Isabel asked, as the others started on about the horrid Italians again.

Everyone seemed to have an idea for they all began talking

at once. Henrietta favoured a sit-in in front of the town hall, Hugo recommended writing aggressive letters to every newspaper in the country, Mary suggested picketing the council offices in Perugia and the conservation sector of the government in Florence. Finally someone said, 'Why doesn't Isabel ask Fabrizio what's happening? If he's involved in the purchase of the property, he should know whether planning permission has been granted or not. I can't see the need for secrecy now.'

Isabel, weakly, agreed to talk to him. 'It'll have to be next week, I'm afraid, he left today for a long weekend off.'

As everyone assured her that this would be fine, that ECCA could wait a few more days before intensifying their campaign against the Italian bureaucrats, Isabel found that her heart was doing all sorts of odd lurching things at the thought of speaking to Fabrizio again. Of course she spoke to him every day, about clients and properties, but rarely alone, and always at the office. Fabrizio, after that terrible stormy day with the Phipps when Isabel had told him to leave her alone, had done just that. Not once since then had he tried to get her to change her mind; not once had he broached the subject of love. Isabel, grieving, told herself she was right: he hadn't really loved her, their affair was transient as all these things were, and Fabrizio had only used her as a plaster for his wounded marriage. About his involvement in property development, she no longer cared; it seemed unimportant, as did everything else in her life these days.

But she would speak to him. She would show him that she could be as cool, as detached, as professional as he was.

She vowed she'd get a good night's sleep the night before so she didn't look haggard.

But then, the next day, Claudia returned.

Mary and Henrietta were sitting on lawn chairs in the back garden, the new blossom from the flowering poplar trees falling like snow around them, knitting and chatting cosily. Their topics were those things dear to a mother's heart such as how long the second stage of labour lasts and how to care for cracked nipples, during which part Bernard, deliberately closing his ears to the nipples bit, interrupted them to say, 'That was your mother on the phone, Mary. It was ringing when I went inside to change my boots.'

'Mother? Is she all right?'

'Well, not exactly. She's in Pisa, at the airport, and furious that no one is there to collect her.'

'Pisa?'

'It seems she sent a card telling us the exact time of her arrival.'

'Naughty Alberto,' Henrietta said placidly. 'He's spending far too many nights in Perugia. I'm sure he's not doing his job properly.'

In a flurry of hysterics Mary ran inside to air the guest bedroom while Bernard was sent to fetch his mother-in-law. Mary privately thought it most odd that her mother should come to visit again, having only just been here two months ago.

Many hours later Claudia, feathers ruffled, strutted angrily into the kitchen and complained about the flight, the sun which was far too hot for the season, and the gross inadequacies of the Italian postal system.

'If only your late father were around,' she said darkly, 'heads would roll. He had some influence on the continent.'

'But what are you doing here, Mother?' Mary asked, when Claudia took a breath to light a cigarette. 'Not that we aren't happy to see you, of course.'

Her mother took a long drag and stared at the walls of the living room, noting again how hideous Mary's colour scheme was.

'Is anything the matter, uh, Claudia?' Bernard said, when his mother-in-law didn't speak for a few minutes. Claudia, inhaling deeply, coughed and spluttered for a few seconds, worrying Mary to death until she realized her mother was wild with fury and not ill with some dreadful lung disease.

'Is anything the matter?' Claudia mimicked, her chicken-like head bobbing up and down as she shook with anger. 'Of course something's the matter. Do you think I'd be here if nothing was the matter?'

'What is it, Mother? Do calm down, you're going frightfully red. What's happened!'

'They've refused me planning permission, that's what's happened.'

'What?'

'I was promised, absolutely promised, else I never would have dreamed of buying that property . . .'

'Mother, what are you talking about?'

'A friend of your father's, it was, from the days he dabbled in the frozen pasta market. Totally disastrous, frozen pasta, but one meets influential people in the catering business, he used to tell me.'

'Mother, could you please explain what you're talking about?'

'Not influential enough, that was the problem. Though he said he was – the bastard!'

Claudia inhaled again in such a fury that she turned terribly pink and coughed a great deal before she could go on. 'I shall have to get rid of it, of course, it's no use to me. That's why I'm here.'

'Get rid of what, Mother? I still don't understand.'

'The property, naturally. Don't you listen to anything I say?'

'What property?'

'The one at the bottom of your fields, Bernard. The one with the woodland.'

In the silence that followed she was able to smoke half a cigarette without interruption. Finally Mary said, in a flat dull voice, 'You never told us you bought that land, Mother.'

'Didn't I? Probably not, now I come to think of it. You know how I like to keep my little business ventures secret.'

'So it wasn't the Italians after all,' Carl exclaimed.

'It was one of us.'

'An Englishman.'

'Woman.'

'And someone we knew.'

'But not Fabrizio.'

The English Conservation Committee Abroad were gathered together at Henrietta's house that night, having been summoned there for an emergency meeting, despite the lateness of the hour, while Claudia peacefully slept away the effects of a bumpy flight and her unprofitable business venture.

Mary, having cried on Henrietta's shoulder for a full twenty minutes before the meeting, was pale and subdued.

'It's all right, Mary,' Isabel said kindly. 'How were you to know? We're all so relieved that no planning permission has been given, nor ever will be.'

'The Italians are much more sensible than we gave them credit for,' Carl said.

'I'm sure all our petitioning and letter writing must have helped,' Hugo mused.

Isabel, listening to this, rather thought not; she suspected Claudia's husband's influential friend had merely tried to pull a fast one somewhere along the line and that it hadn't worked. She doubted if the English Conservation Committee Abroad had anything to do with anything, but she didn't think she'd say so. Everyone was feeling too happy and jolly about the way things had turned out and the part they thought they had played in it. Even Mary, after her initial shock and embarrassment over Claudia's role in the whole messy business, began to cheer up, feeling something very like relief that she didn't have to pretend to like her mother anymore.

'What's Claudia going to do with the land?' Henrietta asked.

'Sell it,' Bernard told her.

'That's why she's here.'

'I think you ought to buy it, Bernard,' Henrietta said, giving him a delectable smile, reward for his new status as platonic friend and surrogate uncle to her born and unborn babies.

'Bernard would give anything to own that land!' Mary cried passionately just as he was beginning to open his mouth. 'But we can't afford it.'

'It would be handy if you could buy it,' Carl mused. 'Keep it in the family, so to speak.'

'Claudia would want at least what she paid for it,' Isabel warned.

'She might have to take a bit of a loss. When she bought the property no one knew planning permission would definitely not be given. Whereas everyone now knows that the land will have to be used strictly for agriculture.'

The next day Carl spoke to Claudia. He spoke long and persuasively, and she, recognizing the truth of what he said, listened and calculated.

'Bernard wants that property,' Carl finished. 'You'll save yourself agent's fees as well as a good deal of time if you lower your price and sell to him.'

The thought of concluding the deal quickly, and leaving Italy as soon as possible, was almost as appealing to Claudia as saving as much money as she could out of the whole sordid affair. She was not, in spite of this fiasco, an inexperienced businesswoman; she knew she had paid through the nose for the property and would never get her money back on the venture. She would, as her husband used to say, cut her losses and run.

Leaving Claudia at the kitchen table glued to a World Service financial programme on the radio, Carl left the house and joined Mary and Henrietta who were once again knitting under the poplars, this time with Hugo sitting at their feet writing a poem on enduring love.

'Any luck?' Mary cried.

'What did she say?'

'She'll come down a bit in price,' he said, quoting the figure Claudia had settled on.

Bernard, coming in for morning coffee, by-passed his kitchen with Claudia in it and joined the others reclining in the warm sunshine.

'That's still too much,' he said. 'I can't afford that much.'

'She won't come down any more, I'm afraid, not even for you, Bernard. It was hard enough persuading her to come down that far.'

They all stared towards the woodland in dismay. From the garden you could see the pale green sheen of the trees beginning to come into leaf, the colours shimmering with their newness and the morning heat.

'How much more would she have to come down, Bernard?' Henrietta said thoughtfully.

He considered, and named the price he could afford to pay.

Henrietta looked at the woodland again and said casually, 'I'll make up the difference. I'll give you the money.'

They all looked at her. Bernard was speechless, but Mary said, 'Oh, how kind! But we couldn't . . . we couldn't possibly.'

'You're so predictable,' Henrietta said to her, but with a smile, definitely mellowed by the baby inside her. 'Don't be so correct all the time. Why couldn't you possibly? I have the money, Bernard wants the land: I'm sure we could arrange something. If you prefer, you can have it as an interest-free loan and pay me back when you can afford it. Or I can be part owner of the woodland . . . whatever. I'm sure we can get Fabrizio to help work out the details.'

Mary went over to her and hugged her, much to Henrietta's

annoyance as the sudden gesture jarred her back again and she still had to be careful with it.

'Steady on,' she said, frowning a little.

Bernard, overcome, was almost incoherent as he tried to thank his beloved Henrietta.

'Don't mention it.' She smiled at him when he finally trailed to an embarrassed halt. 'I have a deep fondness for that bit of woodland.'

Bernard, ecstatic, blushed deeply while the others all laughed, thinking Henrietta was referring to her nasty fall and the subsequent doctor's examination which had led to the discovery that she was pregnant.

And perhaps she was, perhaps she was.

Bernard, in heaven, thinks of the woodland, of the land adjoining it that at last will be his, will be drained and grassed and thronged with his cows, his beloved herd that he can now expand, another dream which will now come true.

He thinks about Henrietta too, a different fantasy this time – she in her billowing white frock walking in the woodland with her two children, picking wild poppies, the three of them waving to him as he mounts his tractor in the field beyond and roars mightily off towards his cows.

It's a good fantasy, a safe fantasy, one that he can even share with his wife for she will probably be there too, making Marmite sandwiches for all of them, spreading plaid blankets over the wood anenomes and pouring good strong PG Tips from her ample flask.

Bernard sighs contentedly, enjoying his dreams. He tries not to notice that Henrietta, in his vision, still has no underclothes beneath that flimsy billowing white frock.

There is still Fabrizio to contend with, still Fabrizio to be reinstated and apologized to. Isabel, knowing she must do this and not wishing to do so in the office with Francesca popping in every other minute and clients impatiently waiting in reception, telephoned the house in Perugia when Fabrizio returned from his weekend away and asked him to come to *La Piccola Valle* in the evening.

'It's a business matter,' she told him on the telephone. 'But I don't want to talk about it in the office.'

He arrived the next evening, the dog joyously trying to leap up at him in welcome, crumpling his casual but elegant linen jacket and putting him in a bad mood before he even walked through the door. Isabel, on the phone, had sounded as cold and as distant as ever, so he had no illusions that this evening would be anything other than polite and impersonal.

Inside the house he was pounced on by Henrietta who told him all about her pregnancy. Then he had to admire Krissy, who cooed and smiled and pretended she remembered him, and only then was he offered a drink which he felt he deserved, seeing Isabel so cool and so beautiful in loose black trousers, a pale creamy T-shirt, her hair newly cut and almost spiky, adding emphasis to her eyes which already took up a great deal of her face.

'Looking haggard, am I?' she said coldly, seeing him staring at her.

This was so unfair that Fabrizio did the only thing he could, being an Italian. He took Isabel in his arms and began kissing her.

It saved all that time, saved having to make all those explanations. Between kisses she tried to apologize about not trusting him over the property venture, and Fabrizio tried to explain that he had been leaving her alone until he could sort things out with his wife. Then they both tried to tell each other all those banal and tedious things, like how miserable they had been without each other and how they would never let each other go again, at which point Henrietta, being a mother and above all that, left the room in disgust.

It was some time later that they joined her outside in the garden. She was watching the sun setting over the woodland, lighting up the few fluffy clouds with brilliant reds and oranges. Isabel and Fabrizio, arms around each other, watched silently with her for some time.

'I shall be quite happy here alone, with my two babies,' Henrietta said peacefully, eyes still on the darkening woods. 'I have Carl and Hugo and Mary and Bernard around me, and Alberto and Daniela in the village, and all Daniela's daughters who claim they want to baby-sit.

'Not that I'm rushing you,' she went on, smiling at her sister and Fabrizio, 'but I know it would be much handier for you to live in Perugia.'

Fabrizio pulled Isabel down on the blanket spread on the grass, where Krissy had been playing earlier. 'Your sister and I have just been talking about this. I want to sell the house in Perugia so that I can afford another, one where Isabel and I can begin life together. But my wife . . . she still causes such trouble that I cannot sell.'

'She's still trying to pin adultery on Fabrizio.'

'I thought she had a lover herself?'

'She does, I've known this for ages,' he groaned. 'But he is so elusive. I cannot find out anything about him. Only his Christian name, nothing else.'

'I didn't know you even knew his first name,' Isabel said. 'How did you find that out?'

Fabrizio said tersely, 'She called me by her lover's name one night, just before we split up. We argued, of course, and in the heat of the moment she admitted he was her lover. Now, to the lawyers, she denies she even has one.'

'Poor Fabrizio.'

'So all I know is that his name is Alberto. Such a common name – there must be hundreds of them around Perugia.'

They were all quiet for a few minutes, watching the sky

throb with colour, inhaling the scent of blossom and fresh growing things.

Then Henrietta said languidly, 'That's odd. Alberto, our postman from Modena, has been seeing a woman in Perugia for ages. He's told me all about her. She used to be married and now she's left her husband. What's your wife's name, Fabrizio?'

'Maria Teresa.'

'Well, well, well. That just so happens to be the name of Alberto's woman.'

They had a bottle of champagne to celebrate, Henrietta finding one in the back of the fridge left over from her pregnancy party. She went around to all the neighbours and invited them too, except for Claudia who didn't in the slightest mind or even notice, so busy was she trying to book a flight home now that she had sold her property to her son-in-law.

Because the night was still and perfect and not too cold, though it was only early springtime, everyone decided to stay outside, spreading themselves on blankets and lawn chairs and indolently lying about, staring up at the Umbrian sky which was now pierced with bright glittering stars.

'Oh, look,' cried Henrietta suddenly. 'Oh, look, look, look!'

They all, as one, turned their heads and looked at the sky, expecting to see a shooting star, a comet, a meteorite at the very least.

But Henrietta, lying back in a lawn chair, was gazing rapturously at her own stomach.

'It moved,' she said softly. 'My baby moved.'

Moving to the Country
Anna Cheska

A new home – and a fresh start?

All Jess wants is her husband Felix, a chance at a new career and a taste of her sister Louisa's bohemian lifestyle. All Louisa wants is a place to call home. Nobody is sure what Felix wants, let alone Felix himself. But Jess is hoping that their move to the small village of Brocklemouth in Dorset will revitalise Felix's business, their marriage and Jess herself.

Only as their daughter moves out, Louisa moves in, and their lives become entangled with their new neighbours. And now that Jess has time on her hands to develop her own interests, she also has time to entertain doubts about her errant husband. Has she been papering over the cracks in their marriage for too long? She's married to a man she still loves but hasn't trusted for years. A house can be transformed, but is it too late to hope that Felix will ever change?

'A warm, witty, intelligent novel about love, marriage and village life.'   *Newcastle Evening Chronicle*

The very best of Piatkus fiction is now available in paperback as well as hardcover. Piatkus paperbacks, where *every* book is special.

☐ 0 7499 3166 3	Moving to the Country	Anna Cheska	£6.99
☐ 0 7499 3190 6	Big Fibs Little Fibs	Joanne Simms	£6.99
☐ 0 7499 3188 4	Mother Love	Martine Oborne	£5.99
☐ 0 7499 3193 0	Moving On	Emma Lee-Potter	£5.99
☐ 0 7499 3182 5	Good Husband Material	Trisha Ashley	£5.99
☐ 0 7499 3143 4	Big Girls Don't Cry	Francesca Clementis	£5.99

The prices shown above were correct at the time of going to press. However, Piatkus Books reserve the right to show new retail prices on covers which may differ from those previously advertised in the text or elsewhere.

Piatkus Books will be available from your bookshop or newsagent, or can be ordered from the following address:
Piatkus Paperbacks, PO Box 11, Falmouth, TR10 9EN
Alternatively you can fax your order to this address on 01326 374 888 or e-mail us at books@barni.avel.co.uk

Payments can be made as follows: Sterling cheque, Eurocheque, postal order (payable to Piatkus Books) or by credit card, Visa/Mastercard. Do not send cash or currency. UK and B.F.P.O. customers should allow £1.00 postage and packing for the first book, 50p for the second and 30p for each additional book ordered to a maximum of £3.00 (7 books plus).

Overseas customers, including Eire, allow £2.00 for postage and packing for the first book, plus £1.00 for the second and 50p for each subsequent title ordered.

NAME (block letters) _____

ADDRESS _____

_____

I enclose my remittance for £ _____

I wish to pay by Visa/Mastercard   Expiry Date:_____
